FREAKY DEAKY TIKI

A MOONSTONE BAY COZY MYSTERY BOOK THREE

AMANDA M. LEE

WINCHESTERSHAW PUBLICATIONS

❀ Created with Vellum

1

ONE

"You're doing it wrong."

"Excuse me? I'm not doing it wrong. You're doing it wrong."

"I most certainly am not doing it wrong. You only think that because you're a man."

"Yes, my gender has taken over the world and the end is truly near. You get the ark, I'll get the animals."

Outside of the lighthouse I live in, I managed to stifle my laughter ... just barely. The day was hot, the sun beating down on my bare shoulders thanks to the fashionable tube top I picked up at a Moonstone Bay shop the previous day, and the noise coming from the building I, Hadley Hunter, now called home was deafening.

"Do you think they'll ever stop?"

Galen Blackwood, my boyfriend (we'd never technically defined our relationship, so that term might be something of a stretch), merely smirked as he glanced up from the spark plug he was cleaning and tilted his head while listening to the argument inside. "You were the one who couldn't understand why May and Wesley divorced," he said finally, referring to the grandparents I'd never known until a few weeks ago. "This is exactly why they got divorced and cut their visits down to once a week ... twice if it was hot and they were cranky."

I rolled my eyes. "I never knew two people could scream and yell this much," I admitted. "I didn't know it was possible. Shouldn't their vocal cords be swollen by now? Shouldn't they need to take a break?"

Galen merely shrugged as he lifted the spark plug so he could study it under better light. "What do you want me to say? May is a ghost. I don't think she technically has vocal cords any longer. As for Wesley ... he's just now getting his full wind. He could carry on for hours if history is any indication."

That wasn't what I wanted to hear. "Well, awesome."

I grew up an only child. My mother died in childbirth and my father raised me to be a "normal" girl. That probably wasn't the word he would've used, but it was the most apt. My father was determined to make sure I had all the right clothes, went to the best schools, joined the cheerleading squad, had a serviceable car to get me to and from school, and never once did anything that was considered odd or out of the ordinary.

By the way, if you believe I dislike him for that, think again. I don't dislike him … or blame him for how things turned out. He thought he was doing right by me, protecting me from the stories my mother told him before her death. There was no way he could understand what her hometown of Moonstone Bay really was, so he made things worse in his mind. That was probably only one of the reasons he fought so hard when I said I was moving to the island my mother called home for most of her life. The other reason was that he was a control freak, but that was hardly important now.

"They'll calm down." Galen gave me a sympathetic shoulder squeeze as he reached for another spark plug. "They've been separated for months. The animosity they usually blow off after a week's time has built up. They need to get it out of their system."

I didn't like the sound of that. "I'm afraid they're going to blow the top off the house in the process."

Galen pursed his lips and shrugged, his blue eyes traveling to the top of the lighthouse. "I don't think their anger can reach that high. At best, they'll blow the top off the mudroom."

"Ha, ha." The look I shot him was withering. "Do you think that's funny?"

He grinned, clearly enjoying himself. "Maybe a little."

"Well, I don't!" I leaned closer so only he could hear me, even though there was no one outside close enough to overhear us. In my short time since moving to Moonstone Bay, I'd learned that not all people were visible all the time. No, really. I'll explain later.

"I think it's going to make our lives extremely difficult if we don't nip this in the bud," I told him, deathly serious. "Wesley has been here five of the last seven days. Now, I like him a great deal and want to get to know my grandfather, but that's five of seven days." I repeated the number in case he hadn't heard me the first time. "At five hours a day — and that's a bare minimum — he's taken up twenty-five hours of my life. Do you think he's spent any of that time with me? No. He spends all of it screaming at May."

"I don't know what you want me to tell you." He adopted a pragmatic tone. "You're the one who suggested Wesley stop by whenever he missed May because she seems to be anchored to the lighthouse."

"That's because I thought he missed her."

"He did miss her."

"All they've done is scream at each other since being reunited," I shot back. "That doesn't seem like deep emotional stuff. In fact, it's the stuff of nightmares."

I lowered my voice to a conspiratorial whisper. "My father had this girlfriend when I was about fourteen or so. They used to argue all the time. I had no idea what to make of it because the other women he dated were quiet and demure. This woman, she used to push every single one of his buttons, and she made it so steam would practically blow out of his ears. No, seriously, he looked like a cartoon character. This reminds me of that."

Galen chuckled, amusement rolling off him in waves. "That's kind of funny."

“Yes, it was hilarious,” I drawled. “She once threw a frying pan at his head because he said her eggs yolks were too hard.”

“You never have to worry about me complaining about hard egg yolks. I like all types of egg yolks. You know what I don’t like? When there’s all that runny white stuff on undercooked over-easy eggs. Now that I’ll complain about.”

He was handsome, ridiculously so. He had dark hair that fell over his forehead in silky waves, cheekbones cut from granite and a square jawbone that made him look like a recently sculpted statue of a Greek god. That didn’t mean I was above fighting with him.

“Are you even listening to me?” My temper threatened to come out to play. “We have a real problem here.”

“And what is that?” Galen was blasé as he returned the spark plug to the engine of my golf cart. Oh, yeah, I have a golf cart. Wesley bought it for me two weeks ago. Cars aren’t allowed on the island except under special circumstances, so the only way to get around is a golf cart. Wesley lives miles from town, so he thought the golf cart would be a nice gift.

As someone who was getting tired of walking in the stifling heat and humidity, I couldn’t help but agree. I was in love with the thing, which is why Galen agreed to look it over and give it a tune-up.

“Well, I’m sure you haven’t noticed because you haven’t been around evenings the past week, but Wesley tends to stay late, and then May is worked up after he leaves,” I replied, choosing my words carefully. “When she’s worked up, she wants to have a conversation. She’s a ghost, so she can talk and talk and talk without ever getting tired.”

“So ... basically you’re saying you want her to get tired.”

“I’m saying that ... at night ... if she’s around ... it makes certain things difficult.” I struggled to find the right words to convey what I felt.

“What things?” Galen asked, clearly oblivious to my issues. “Just tell her you need some sleep and she’ll go away. Do you want me to talk to her for you?”

That was the last thing I wanted. “No. I’m not just talking about sleep.”

"What are you talking about?"

He was frustrating me. "Never mind." I averted my gaze and huffed out a sigh while reaching for my bottle of water. "It obviously doesn't matter."

"Now, wait a second." He held up his hand, furrowing his brow as he regarded my agitated profile. "I can't help but feel as if I've missed something. Why don't we take it from the beginning and we'll see if I can actually pick up on whatever is irritating you this time."

A particularly loud and indignant screech assailed my ears from inside. "Really? You can't pick up on what's irritating me?"

"I get this isn't your cup of tea, but they'll settle down," Galen offered. "I mean ... they went months without seeing each other. May is dead. Wesley was broken-hearted even though they divorced years ago. They've always had a unique way of interacting."

"I understand that." I honestly did. "And if I thought this was a momentary blip and they would quiet down in a few days I'd do my best to ignore it."

"But you don't feel that way," Galen surmised. "Okay ... have you considered asking them to head out to Wesley's house? May is a ghost, and even though it appears she's anchored to the lighthouse, that's probably not true. If she puts her mind to it, she should be able to visit Wesley whenever she wants."

"Now that's what I'm looking for." I brightened considerably. "How can I ensure she does that without hurting her feelings?"

"I don't know. Maybe just tell her that you need some time to yourself."

"I wasn't thinking about time to myself," I muttered under my breath, dark thoughts taking over. "I was thinking about when I have overnight guests."

Galen had to crane his neck to hear what I was saying, and when he made it out his expression lightened. That, in turn, made his already handsome face even more breathtaking (if that was even possible). "Ah. Is that what you're worried about?"

I felt like a dolt. Galen and I had been dating only a few weeks. Heck, I'd been a resident of Moonstone Bay for only a few weeks.

Galen was one of the first people I'd met, and we'd immediately clicked.

That's not to say our relationship was without issues. He was a shifter — wolf, to be exact — and I was a witch. I didn't realize I was a witch while growing up. My father insisted I was normal, as I previously said, and I never knew my mother, so I had no idea about her colorful lineage. Once I hit the island, though, things started happening and the truth spilled out.

I was almost used to being a witch now, and I'd been experimenting with the powers I didn't know I had. I wasn't quite to the level I wanted to be, but I had time to explore and grow into my new reality. What I didn't have time for was the crimp that Wesley and May's constant arguing was putting in my love life.

"What do you think I'm worried about?" I asked, conveniently averting my gaze. "I have no idea what you're talking about."

"Right." Galen was the sort of guy who said whatever came to his mind and didn't wait for an invitation to tackle difficult topics. "You want to know why I haven't spent the night in the past week."

My cheeks burned as I fought to maintain control of my emotions. I wasn't envisioning this conversation taking the turn it did. "I don't care. What makes you think I care? It's not as if I want you to spend the night. I don't, by the way."

I'm a blatherer of the first order. I can't seem to stop myself.

"Uh-huh." Galen scratched the side of his nose as he regarded me. "Listen, if you want me to spend the night, I'm all for it. I just thought that I would probably hold off spending the night until you were ready for ... you know. Sleeping in the same bed and pretending to be a gentleman is an exercise in high blood pressure."

I definitely knew what he was referring to and that made my cheeks burn doubly hot. We'd yet to take things to the next level, opting to stop at kissing and groping after our dates. He didn't seem determined to push me for more, and I was happy with the status quo. Of course, I was also happy when I woke up next to him. That happened a few times, even though we hadn't yet made it to the big show. Sure, those instances usually happened when I was in some form of danger, but I'd come to enjoy them all the same.

Admitting I missed his overnight visits was absolutely mortifying.

"I don't care about that." I refused to meet his steady gaze, which I felt on my cheek. "You can stay ... or don't stay, I honestly don't care. I can't even remember why this conversation popped up. I'm going to grab a bottle of water from inside. Do you want one?"

I hadn't even finished the bottle of water I was drinking, which wasn't lost on Galen. He grabbed my wrist before I could get to my feet and tugged me to the ground, keeping me close on the picnic blanket I'd laid out so we could enjoy an afternoon snack away from the yelling.

"I'm sorry." Galen was earnest as he forced me to stare into his eyes. "I wasn't trying to ignore you. It was the exact opposite. I wanted us to have time to get to know one another without any pressure. I didn't realize that upset you."

I balked. "I'm not upset. Why would I possibly get upset about something like that? In fact, I prefer it when you're not in my bed. You snore and take up too much room."

He chuckled, his eyes lighting with mirth. "I've got news for you, you snore, too."

"I do not."

"You do."

"I do not!"

"You do!"

I narrowed my eyes and stared for a long beat, finally shaking my head as I lifted my face to the sky and absorbed the pounding rays. "Now we sound like May and Wesley. That's not how I want to be."

"Me either."

"I don't care about you spending the night. Mostly." I adjusted my tone so I didn't sound so shrill. "It's just ... we've had fun the last two weeks, went on a few dates and everything, but we've barely had any time alone together unless we left the lighthouse. And our destinations are limited because of outside factors. I guess it doesn't matter."

"No, it matters." He grabbed my hand and gave me a tug, pulling me into his lap as he rested his back against the golf cart and running his hands up and down my arms. "I didn't realize we weren't spending enough quality time together. I thought I was being respectful."

"Maybe I don't like you respectful. Have you ever considered that?"

He chuckled. "I will take that under advisement." He tilted his head, catching my gaze as I shifted to look into his eyes. "How about we compromise for the rest of the night? We'll walk to town, get some ice cream and then I know a private beach that's not too far from here. It's closed to tourists. How does that sound?"

"Good, but it still doesn't change my overall problem."

Wesley picked that moment to bellow about crazy women giving him ulcers from inside the house.

"No, it doesn't solve your problem," he agreed. "We'll talk about that and come up with a plan while we spend some private time together."

"I have news for you, buddy, I'm not going to want to talk during our private time."

He laughed, his chest shaking as he turned my body to give me a long kiss. "We'll figure it out while we're getting our ice cream. I promise we'll manage to do both."

"Well, as long as you promise."

We sank into a long kiss, both of us ignoring the raised voices from inside the house. I was so lost in the moment it took me a long beat to realize that my rear end was vibrating. "What is that?"

"My phone." Galen made a disgusted sound as he shifted me and searched his pocket, coming back with his cell. "I'm sorry." His eyes were apologetic. "You have no idea how sorry I am."

He served as Moonstone Bay's sheriff, so I understood he had a job to do. I didn't begrudge his work. My very alive grandfather and very dead grandmother were a different story.

"Blackwood," he growled as he answered the phone, his hand warm as it ran up and down my back. I couldn't hear what the person on the other end of the call had to say, but he didn't look happy when he started shaking his head. "No, don't do anything. I'll be there in a few minutes. Just ... don't touch anything."

He disconnected and gave me a rueful smile. "I'm sorry. There's a body at the docks. I have to go."

"It's okay." I meant it. "Maybe next time?"

"Yeah, well … ." Galen didn't look as if he was in a hurry to end our evening despite the call. "I don't suppose you would want to go to the docks with me? There's always the chance that it's natural causes and we can get ice cream after."

"Sure." I had nothing better to do, especially with my grandparents screaming at each other. "I didn't know we had docks."

"Where do you think the boats land?"

"I … didn't really think about it."

"It's not just passengers either," Galen noted as he got to his feet, pulling me with him. "This is an island. Our resources are limited. We get incoming shipments at least three times a week."

"I honestly never thought about it."

"Well, now you know."

"And we're going to the docks." I grabbed the picnic blanket and folded it, leaving it on the table to retrieve when I returned later. "Do you think there are weird things going on at the docks? Like drug deals and prostitution rings. Ooh, maybe there's some human trafficking for us to take on."

Galen scowled as he shook his head. "You watch way too much television."

"Believe it or not, you're not the first person to tell me that."

"I definitely believe it."

2

TWO

When I came to Moonstone Bay, it was via plane. That made visiting the docks an adventure of sorts, something Galen didn't particularly understand.

"Why are you gaping like that?"

I snapped my mouth shut and shrugged, trying to tear my eyes from the fantastic vista. "It's just very pretty. Look at the way the sun is setting over the water. It makes it look like the ocean is on fire."

Galen cocked an eyebrow, clearly amused. "You're a mystery wrapped in a pretty package. Has anyone ever told you that?"

"You're the only one."

"Well, let's keep it that way." He poked my side before picking up his pace and walking toward the crowd that had gathered on the east side of the docks. "What do we have here?"

While I was interested in seeing the body — I have a morbid streak, sue me — I took another moment to study the layout of the area. I'd pretty much stuck to the main drag of Moonstone Bay and Wesley's farm since arriving, so I was always in the mood to investigate a new locale. The docks seemed to be an interesting place, with a variety of gift kiosks and drink carts littering the wooden facade. I made a mental note to return when I could waste time looking around. For now, though, I followed Galen.

From the moment the body popped into view, I wished I had the foresight to remain focused on the kiosks.

The man looked to be in his early thirties if I had to guess, with sandy blond hair streaked with what appeared to be blood. His body was displayed in ritual fashion, his arms and legs spread. I couldn't tell much about his face because a garish mask was placed over it. His green eyes were open, something I could see through the mask holes, and his blank eyes stared at the sky. Even though I couldn't see his features, I imagined them being twisted into a grotesque reenactment of his last few minutes of life, which probably meant he was frozen in a silent scream.

"What the ...?"

Galen spared a glance for me, the serious nature of the situation causing him to frown. "Don't touch anything, Hadley."

I had no intention of touching anything. "What's the deal with the mask?"

"I have no idea."

"It's a tiki mask," one of the men kneeling next to the body offered. He was dressed in a blue polo shirt and khaki shorts, essentially the uniform doctors and nurses wear at the tiny clinic that serves as the island's hospital. He was going over the body with a pair of micro goggles. "They're available at a variety of shops on the island."

"A tiki mask?" I pursed my lips as I pictured the tiki bar my friend Lilac owned. Now that the guy mentioned it, I had seen similar masks on the walls there. Lilac used them as decorations. "Oh. What's it mean?"

"I have no idea."

I turned to Galen. "Do you know what it means?"

"Huh." He looked lost in thought when he shifted his eyes to me. "I'm not exactly up on tiki culture, other than the glasses everyone has at the various bars. I haven't given it much thought."

"It can't be that hard to look up, can it?" I pulled my phone from my pocket and started searching, frowning when I realized the search window continued spinning instead of returning information. "What's up with the service out here? My phone has zero bars."

"It's the location." Galen absently ran his hand over my back before slipping in front of me. "The island only has two cell towers, and this is kind of a dead zone."

That was interesting ... and somewhat annoying. "Okay, well ... ." I cast another look at the body and internally cringed. "I'm going to move over to the bench and stay out of your way."

"Okay." Galen managed a smile, but it didn't make it all the way to his eyes. "I'm sorry I brought you here. I thought for sure it would be some form of accident. I don't foresee ice cream in our future this evening. If you want, I can try to call Booker to get you a ride back to the lighthouse."

Booker, in addition to being a cupid — something I was still wrapping my head around — was one of the few shuttle drivers on the island. I knew him relatively well, was comfortable with him, and had hundreds of questions about his nature I still wanted to ask him because he'd been avoiding my eager queries the past two weeks. That didn't mean I was in a hurry to leave the docks.

"I'm fine." I meant it. "I'm going to get a bottle of water and sit on the bench. It looks to me that a ship is about to dock." I pointed toward the end of the wood structure, to where a huge ship was closing in. "I'll just people watch. I'm perfectly capable of entertaining myself."

"Okay. Let me know if you decide to wander anywhere." Galen's gaze was measured. "In fact ... don't wander anywhere. While I doubt whoever did this stuck around to see how we would react to his handiwork, you never know. I prefer knowing you're safe."

"Yes, sir." I kicked my feet together and offered him a saucy salute. "I'll follow your orders with a giggle and a smile, sir."

"Very funny." He poked my side before turning his attention to the body. "Let's get photos and then remove the mask. We need to know who we're dealing with here."

. . .

TWO HOURS AND THREE BOTTLES of water later, Galen joined me on the bench. He looked wiped. He'd spent the better part of those two hours blocking the body so the incoming tourists wouldn't see it, I couldn't exactly blame him for the fatigue that seemed to seep from his pores.

"Why's it taking the ship so long to dock?" I asked. "It seems to be circling."

"That's because it is. We've been in contact with the captain. We told him what happened. We needed time to process the scene before all those tourists roil up the atmosphere. It's easier to keep them on the ship."

"Ah." That actually made sense. "Are you done now?"

"Pretty much, but the medical examiner has a few things to finish before we can load up the body. They're letting passengers off the ship anyway. We've pretty much got it blocked off."

He'd rearranged kiosks to serve as a buffer, so I found that declaration mildly entertaining. Any tourist looking hard enough would notice the body. There was no hiding that. Still, he had enough resting on his strong shoulders. He didn't need the obvious pointed out to him.

"Do you know him?"

"Yeah. Jacob Dorsey. He's a local, never given me much trouble. I've had to warn him about being drunk in public a time or two, but he's hardly the first. He works construction. In fact, I think he's been working on the new hotel that's being built down the beach."

"There's a new hotel?" That was news to me. "Where?"

He pointed. "Do you see the way the trees jut out a bit there, the way the inlet flares out?" I nodded. "Right there. Construction has just begun, so you can't see anything yet. It's supposed to be a state-of-the-art facility. It was first proposed five years ago, but it's taken the developers a long time to get all their ducks in a row and start construction."

"Oh." I pursed my lips. "I'll be able to see that from the lighthouse."

"You will, but your parcel is elevated enough that it won't obstruct your view. That was one of the reasons some of the residents fought the construction. They didn't want a hotel marring the vista. Even they couldn't deny it would bring more tourists and money to the island, though, so they eventually backed down."

I cast him a sidelong look, intrigued. "You know a lot about everything, don't you?"

Galen's lips twitched. "I'm a genius. Are you kidding me?"

"I'm serious. You're a smart guy."

"You act surprised."

"I won't lie. I was initially attracted to you because of your looks. It makes me feel better knowing that you're smart, too. That means we'll be able to sustain when your looks start to fade."

He barked out a laugh. "You're a funny girl."

"That's what will sustain me when my looks start to fade."

"You have more going for you than that." He gave me a quick kiss and then stood. "It shouldn't be much longer. If you play your cards right I'll swing by the ice cream place and get you a treat after all."

"I guess that means I have to behave myself."

He winked. "I didn't say that."

I ALLOWED MY MIND TO drift as Galen worked. It was easier than focusing on the body. Eventually, they removed the mask and I was right about the look on the man's face. He looked as if he'd seen something absolutely terrible, something horrible enough to steal the oxygen from his lungs. Given the fact that he had a knife wound in the center of his chest, though, I had a feeling that's what ultimately killed him.

For lack of anything better to do, I turned my full attention to the passengers departing the ship. They looked happy, seemingly unaware of the upheaval happening around them, and they greeted the kiosks and food offerings with the same awe I felt upon initial viewing.

"Look at this." A woman, her long black hair flowing well past her shoulders, stopped next to a lei kiosk and pointed toward a ring of purple flowers. "Have you ever seen flowers like this?"

The man with her, who wore a simple T-shirt and shorts, merely smiled as he regarded the flowers. "They match your eyes." He dug in his pocket for his wallet and caught the salesclerk's attention. "How much?"

He bought the lei, draped it over the woman's shoulders, and leaned forward to give her a long kiss. He whispered something that caused her to laugh, and for some reason a quick image of a wedding filled my head. That's when I realized that they were on their honeymoon. I had no way of knowing that, but I did.

"You have a filthy mind, Griffin Taylor," the woman announced, her tone bossy. "I guess it's good that I happen to like your filthy mind."

"You have as filthy a mind as I do," he said, linking his fingers with hers. "In fact, you're way filthier than I am when it comes to stuff like this."

"That is a lie."

"No, baby. That's the truth."

They noticed me watching as they started moving again and I did my best to shrug away my embarrassment. I hated being caught, but there was nothing I could do now that it had already happened, so I smiled. "Welcome to Moonstone Bay."

"Thank you." The man tugged the woman's hand and dragged her closer to the bench where I sat. "Are you with the tourism board?"

The question threw me for a loop. "No. I ... are you expecting someone from the tourism board?" I glanced over my shoulder, hoping for a familiar face. I didn't see anyone I recognized. "Are you looking for a specific hotel?"

"We're staying at the Bay Breeze," the woman replied, fanning her face. "Do you know where that is?"

Thankfully, I did. "Yup." I slowly got to my feet and pointed toward the island's main drag. "Do you see that big building with the pink walls and white trim? That's the Bay Breeze."

"Oh, see, that's not tacky at all," the woman drawled, smirking when her husband gave her a dark look. "I was expecting something with a beach theme."

"It has a beach theme," I offered. "Everything here has a beach theme."

"She knows," the man said, shaking his head. "Don't worry about it. I'm Griffin, by the way." He extended his hand. "This is my wife, Aisling."

I shook her hand in turn. "Mr. and Mrs. Taylor, it's great to have you on the island. I'm sure you'll enjoy your stay." I wasn't part of the welcoming committee, but it seemed being friendly was the thing to do.

"Grimlock," the woman interjected.

I arched a brow. "Excuse me?"

"Grimlock," she repeated. "I kept my last name."

"Oh, of course." I barely missed a beat. "I think a lot of people do that these days."

"Why did you have to tell her that?" Griffin complained. "I've been a good sport about you keeping your name. Why couldn't you just be Mrs. Taylor for the honeymoon?"

Aisling made a face. "Because that would be a lie and I have no intention of living an inauthentic life."

"Whatever." He rolled his eyes. "Do we have to walk to the hotel or are there shuttles? It's extremely hot and my wife doesn't take heat well."

"Oh, you're getting a charge out of saying 'my wife' like that, aren't you?" Aisling complained. It wasn't exactly a whine as much as a loud grievance. "I'm not property."

For his part, Griffin was laid back and calm. It was almost as if he expected his new wife to melt down at every turn. "Of course you're not my property. I would never suggest otherwise. Do you think I'm some sort of terrible rogue or something?"

"Ugh. You're in far too good a mood." Aisling fanned her face with what looked to be a map of the island. "Seriously, though, I don't have to walk to the hotel, do I?"

Her attitude made me want to laugh. "There are golf carts at the end of the dock," I supplied. "The drivers will get you there."

"Oh, well, great." She smiled, which lightened her features. Up close, her eyes really were the oddest color purple I'd ever seen. They were almost mesmerizing.

"I hope you enjoy your time on the island," I said finally. "There's a lot to do, and if you're in the vicinity of the lighthouse go ahead and stop by. That's where I live." I didn't know the offer was going to escape my lips before it was already too late.

"Well, thanks for that." Griffin wrapped his arm around his wife's waist and smiled. "We're here on our honeymoon. The only thing I plan to do is plant myself on the beach and eat my weight in seafood."

"I think that's what we're both going to do," Aisling agreed. "Thanks for the offer, though. Hopefully we'll see you around."

"Probably. It's a small island."

I watched them go with a mixture of amusement and pity as they immediately started bantering. Aisling complained about the heat and Griffin promised to give her a long massage as soon as they were comfortable in their room. At a certain point, they slowed their pace.

At first, I thought they were looking at another kiosk. Then I realized that would be an odd place for one to be located. When I finally focused, I found they were staring at a man ... and there was something oddly familiar about him.

"What are you doing?" Galen asked, appearing at my side.

"Why does that guy look familiar?" I asked.

He followed my gaze. "The guy with the hot woman with the white streaks in her hair? I have no idea. Maybe you know him from home or something. I've never seen him before."

I scorched him with a dark look. "Not them. That's Griffin and Aisling. We had a nice chat while you were dealing with your body. They're on their honeymoon ... and she is not that hot."

"She's pretty hot," Galen argued, snickering when I playfully smacked his arm. "She's a married woman, though. I like my women unmarried." He graced me with a placating smile. "You and she kind of look alike, but she's much paler and has those streaks in her hair. They make her stand out."

"She also has purple eyes. They're weird, but really cool. I wish I had purple eyes."

"Your eyes are beautiful." He gave me a soft kiss. "If you weren't talking about the guy with her, who were you talking about?"

"The guy standing next to those crates," I replied, pointing. "See. He's right there. He has blond hair and green eyes."

Galen's lips twisted. "Um ... I don't see anyone there."

"You have to see him. He's standing right there." I automatically shifted to the side when the medical examiner's team began wheeling the gurney toward me. It was only when the body was directly in front of me that I realized I was looking at the same face. "Oh. Um ... oh, my!"

"What's wrong?" Galen read the change in my demeanor and was instantly alert. "What is it?"

"That's the same guy." I pointed at Jacob on the gurney. "That's the guy standing down by the crates."

"Oh." Realization dawned on Galen. "You're seeing his ghost. I guess we should've been prepared for that."

I pressed the heel of my hand to my forehead. "I guess."

"Well, come on." He grabbed my hand, refusing to let me wallow. "Let's talk to him. Maybe he knows who killed him and we'll be able to put this one to bed before ... well, we go to bed."

"Okay, but ... ." I trailed off when I glanced back at the spot where I'd seen the spirit only seconds before. "He's gone."

"Are you sure?"

I searched the area for good measure. "He's definitely gone."

"Well, we can try again tomorrow." Galen sounded perfectly rational. "My understanding is that ghosts can't easily control their environment when they first pass. It's not the end of the world."

"Okay. I'll come back tomorrow." That sounded fair, especially because I wanted to investigate the docks further. Something occurred to me and I pulled up short. "Hey!"

"What?"

"I understand why I could see the ghost — that's my new thing, after all — but why could Aisling see the ghost?"

"That's your new friend?"

"I wouldn't call her a 'friend,' but yeah."

"I don't know." Galen was legitimately bemused. "Maybe she sees ghosts, too. She could be a witch. She has the hair for it."

"Let's not start talking about how hot she was again, okay?"

"I only want to talk about how hot you are." He slipped his arm around my waist. "Right now I need to talk to my guys and make sure they have everything under control. Then I'm taking you to dinner. After that, if you're good, I'll get you ice cream. There's not much else we can do here, but I'll check just to be on the safe side."

I blew out a dramatic sigh. "I guess I can live with that."

"Somehow I knew that."

3

THREE

I may be the witch, but Galen was much more comfortable with the paranormal community. He grew up on Moonstone Bay, after all, and was a shifter. I didn't know that when we'd first met. In fact, I didn't realize his true nature until he found me on the highway between Wesley's ranch and town. I was being stalked at the time, although I had no idea by what, and he shifted to protect me.

I still wasn't used to it, and I hadn't seen him shift since. I'd decided to hold off on asking him to see it again. Some things I could wait for.

"Are you sure they saw him?" Galen asked as he paced in front of me.

I was back sitting on the bench because one of his deputies stopped him from leaving before we could depart for dinner, and the oppressive heat forced me to start another bottle of water.

"She looked right at him," I replied, searching my memory. "I don't see what else she could've been looking at."

He pursed his lips. "You were talking to them. Did you notice anything odd about her?"

Was he kidding? "I talked to them for, like, five minutes. They seemed like any normal married couple ... but she was kind of persnickety. He seemed used to it and was fine."

"What about him? Was there anything odd about him?"

"No. He was just a normal smoking hot dude."

Galen glowered. "Is that my payback for saying she was hot? If so, I take it back. She was ugly ... like, totally homely. And you're the prettiest woman on the island."

Even though it was a serious situation I couldn't stop myself from laughing. "You're way more attractive. Does that make you feel better?"

"A little."

"He didn't seem odd to me or anything," I volunteered. "In fact, he seemed to be all about her. They're on their honeymoon."

"What makes you say that?"

"She said she didn't take his last name."

"How did that come up?"

"They introduced themselves and they had different names. He said he was fine with her keeping her own name but didn't see why she couldn't be 'Mrs. Taylor' for the week they're here together. I think it's a running joke between them. Er, at least that's the vibe I got.

"I don't know," I continued, rubbing my forehead. "I didn't pay that close attention. I don't see why you're so worked up about this. They clearly didn't kill the guy."

"How do you know that?"

"Because they were on the ship and it didn't dock until after the body was discovered."

"Yes, but that could've been a ruse. Maybe they were here the whole time, hiding, and pretended to join the disembarking passengers. In fact ... that makes sense to me. They didn't have any luggage."

Hmm. Now that he mentioned it, I realized that was true. "Maybe the ship is transporting their luggage for them."

"Everyone else leaving that ship had their own luggage."

He was getting awful huffy for a guy I was convinced was barking up the wrong suspect. "I don't think they're viable suspects, but if you do, go nuts. I'm betting that woman will be nothing but pleasant if you interrupt the first night of their vacation to ask if they're murderers."

"I'm not an idiot." He offered me a withering look. "I'm not going to question them until I get a cause of death."

"I'm pretty sure that huge knife sticking out of his chest was the cause of death. I mean ... I'm not a medical examiner or anything, but that would be my first guess."

"I'm done talking to you." He held up a hand and dug into his pocket. "We need to take a five-minute break from the conversation."

"Knock yourself out." I slowly got to my feet, taking time to stretch my muscles.

"Where are you going?"

"You just said you weren't talking to me."

"Yes, but I want to know where you're going." He was firm. "It's my job, as your boyfriend, to make sure you're safe."

Now he was using the B-word. That was promising. Of course, given his attitude, I wanted to use another B-word when referring to him at the moment. For the record, that word was butthead.

"I'm going to wander around and see if I can see the ghost again," I explained. Technically, I didn't think I should be forced to tell him anything, but it was easier than getting into an argument. "Are you okay with that?"

"Yes, it's absolutely fabulous," he drawled. "Don't fall in the water when you're looking for your ghost."

"I'll try to refrain."

"I'll be right here."

"Great."

"We're still getting dinner … and probably ice cream. I just have to look something up first and make sure my deputies have the scene under control before we can leave."

I didn't want to smile — that would only encourage him, after all — but I couldn't stop myself. "I'm getting sprinkles on mine. Ice cream, I mean. I'll probably refrain from getting them on my dinner."

"I think that's a great idea. I happen to like you even more when you're hopped up on sugar."

"You're only saying that because I want to kiss you when I'm sugared up."

"You want to kiss me regardless. I'm just that good-looking."

I made a face. "Now I'm done talking to you for the next five minutes."

"Well look at that, a meeting of the minds."

GALEN WAS STILL BUSY ON his phone when I returned ten minutes later. He looked more curious than conflicted.

"Did you find what you were looking for?"

He held out his hand so I would take it as I sat. "Yeah. I think you were right about the couple. I ran their names, and I doubt they're murderers. They were definitely on the ship."

I knit my eyebrows. "How do you know their names? I didn't tell you their names."

"I heard them introduce themselves to you."

"From across the dock?"

"I have good hearing."

"That must be that wolf thing you've got going. Is that like a super power or something?"

His smile was flirty. "I have many super powers."

"Oh, well ... ." My cheeks burned. "Um ... what were we talking about again?"

He turned serious. "Griffin Taylor and Aisling Grimlock. He's a detective in Detroit, with a solid work record and several commendations. He seems to be exactly what you'd expect – a guy on his honeymoon."

I didn't miss the fact that he'd mentioned only Griffin. "And her?"

"She's a reaper."

For a moment, I thought I'd heard him wrong. "I'm sorry, but a reaper? Like a grim reaper?"

"That's exactly what she is." He nodded. "She's the only girl in a family full of reapers. Cormack Grimlock, her father, is the head of the region. He's high in the Michigan reaper council."

I craned to look at the phone in his hand. "Did you manage to Google that information? I must be using the wrong search engine."

He chuckled. "There's a paranormal database that certain law enforcement representatives can access. I happen to be one of those representatives. Griffin Taylor and Aisling Grimlock were married several days ago."

"And she's a reaper?" I couldn't wrap my head around it. "Does that mean she goes around killing people?" I thought about the dead man on the docks. Wait ... that didn't make any sense. If she killed people for a living, she probably didn't leave masks around when she did it. That would become expensive over the long haul.

"Reapers don't kill people," Galen explained. "They don't interfere. They simply absorb the souls of the dead after they expire. The reason she could see the ghost is because that's part of the job."

"Oh." I was mildly placated by the information. "That actually makes me feel better. I was worried she was another witch, and since my meeting with the last one didn't go well I didn't want to risk another potential near-death experience."

He wasn't exactly over the last two times I almost died — more like five times, if I was actually keeping count — so Galen didn't find the statement funny. "Let's not dwell on that."

"Of course." I held up my hands in mock surrender. "I'm being good. I told you I wouldn't find trouble for at least two weeks and I'm holding up my end of the bargain."

"That's good." He turned his attention back to his phone screen. "There's a lot of information about her. The guy is essentially completely clean, although she shows up in his files a few times."

"Maybe they met on the job."

"I'm guessing that's true. The first mention of her in his files — and, yes, I ran a search — is almost two years ago. He found her at a crime scene with her brother and thought it was weird that she was there."

"He obviously didn't know she was a reaper."

"No, and she probably didn't tell him right away."

"Do you think he knows now?"

Galen shrugged. "I don't think you can have a true relationship if you don't know the important things, so I'm guessing yes. Besides, she pops up in his files a few more times. He was rather vague on all those cases, which makes me believe he was protecting her."

"That's kind of romantic."

He rolled his eyes. "I think she sounds like a real pain in the behind. His record was easy to track down because there's very little there. Her record is all over the place. And she has multiple arrests on file."

That didn't sound out of the ordinary. "She's probably been caught at several crime scenes because she was there to do her job."

"No. Most of the things she's been arrested for are auto theft, drunken disorderly and bar fights. And apparently there's some woman named Angelina Davenport she threatens with great bodily harm on a weekly basis."

"Maybe this Angelina woman deserves it."

"Or maybe your new friend is a whack job."

"She's hardly my friend."

"Well, that's good," Galen said. "I don't think they have anything to do with our case. The only reason the woman stopped is because she saw the soul. At least I can mark her off my list."

"But you haven't solved the case of their missing luggage yet," I teased.

"Yes, I have. Her father is loaded. He arranged for them to have a stateroom on the ship. That's the best room available, and the ship is delivering their luggage. I checked."

I pressed my lips together to keep from crowing. Galen didn't look at me, but I imagined he understood it took everything I had to keep from laughing at him.

"Keep it up," he warned. "I'll see you don't get sprinkles on that ice cream if you're not careful."

"I didn't say a word."

"Yeah, well … ." He finally dragged his eyes from the phone, but he didn't plant them on me. Instead he focused on the end of the dock, frowning when a blonde with a huge belly came into view. "Oh, man."

"Who is that?" I was obviously curious. The woman's pregnant stomach gave me pause. "She's not, like, your ex-girlfriend or anything, is she?"

He spared me a dark glare. "Really? Do you think I would keep something like that from you?"

I held my hands palms out and shrugged. "I don't know you that well, especially with you playing it cool and not putting the moves on me. I was just wondering. There's no reason to get your tail in a wad."

"I'm going to put the moves on you," he muttered as he got to his feet. "I'm going to spank you until you cry for mercy."

"Who told you I'm into that?"

For once, instead of my cheeks turning crimson, his did. "You need to control yourself. That's Casey Dorsey. She's Jacob's wife."

I felt like a real jerk. "Oh. Well, then strike that comment about her being your ex-girlfriend. It was mean ... and completely inappropriate."

"Half the things that come out of your mouth are inappropriate. That's why I like you." He gave me a small wink before focusing his full attention on Casey. She was trying to hurry, but she could barely manage a waddle as she closed the distance.

"Where is he?" Her face was so red I worried she would topple over from heat exhaustion. "Someone said Jacob was here. I want to see him right now!"

Galen hooked his thumbs into his utility belt, clearly bracing himself for the emotional onslaught to come. Me? I tried to make myself small because I felt like something of a heel for my earlier comments.

"You need to sit down, Casey," Galen instructed, gesturing toward the bench.

I hopped up to make sure she had room. "You should definitely sit down," I agreed.

Casey barely managed a cursory glance for me before glaring at Galen. "I don't want to sit down. I'm looking for my husband. I know he's down here. Someone at Lilac's tiki bar said I should come here when I stopped there looking for him."

Galen dragged a hand through his onyx hair as he fought to control himself. "Here's the thing, Casey: He was here. He's gone now."

"Where is he? Do you know he didn't come home last night? I mean ... can you believe that? I'm, like, days away from giving birth to his baby and he didn't bother to come home. Do you think he was out running around on me? Oh, wait ... did you catch him with a woman?" Her eyes went to narrow green slits. "If you did, I'll rip his penis off and feed it to him. That will teach him to cheat on me."

I couldn't help agreeing with the sentiment. If someone cheated on me, that's the first thing I'd do. In fact, I needed to find a sly way to work that into a conversation so Galen wouldn't think I was overtly threatening him.

"He wasn't cheating on you, Casey." Galen's voice was gentle. "Well, I guess I can't be certain if he was. That wasn't what he was doing last night, though."

"Oh." She straightened, which only made her stomach look bigger. Seriously, it almost looked as if she was smuggling a beach ball under her shirt. "If he wasn't cheating, that means he was drinking. He promised to clean up his act.

"Let me guess," she continued, working up a full head of steam. "The guys on the construction team talked him into going to the bar and he got so drunk he passed out on the dock. That's just like him. He did that once when we were in high school."

Galen licked his lips and I could see the resignation settling on his shoulders. His job was hard. I didn't envy him what was to come.

"Casey, I'm sorry to have to tell you this, but Jacob is dead."

He said it just like that, as if ripping off a bandage. I knew he couldn't say it any other way, but I still felt for her.

The shock of the words rippled across her face. The first emotion that was clear was disbelief, then unmitigated fury. There was no sadness there. Instead, she exploded.

"What kind of joke is that? Do you think that's funny? That's not even remotely funny. If he put you up to that, I'll rip his balls off and feed them to him!"

She clearly had a fascination with ripping appendages off and feeding them to people.

"It's not a joke." Galen reached out to her, but she jerked away. "He was found here a few hours ago, right before the ship came in. We delayed the arrival until we could get a handle on the scene."

"The scene?" Casey's skin went blotchy. "I don't understand. Are you saying that he was murdered?" She seemed disconnected, as if she was about to travel outside of her body. In fact, that's exactly the feeling I was getting, and I jumped forward at the right moment so I could catch her as she began to list.

Galen stepped closer to help, swinging her up into his arms as if she weighed nothing as her eyes rolled back in her head and she lost consciousness.

"Wow," I muttered, dumbfounded. "She fainted."

He cast me a sidelong look. "Do you blame her?"

I shook my head. "I don't think I've ever seen anyone faint. It was ... ." I remembered where I was and what we were dealing with and shook the unimportant thoughts out of my head. "What should we do?"

"We're taking her to the clinic and calling her parents so they can take care of her. Then we're going to dinner."

"You want to eat after this?"

"We need to, and I can't do anything until I have more information. Casey clearly isn't up to answering questions, so that will probably have to wait until tomorrow. I'm not sure when I'm going to get the medical examiner's report."

"So ... dinner." It seemed as good an option as any. "Can we still get ice cream later?"

"I don't see why not."

"Okay." I fell into step with him as he carried the unconscious woman. "Your job sucks, by the way. You did your best to tell her without traumatizing her."

His lips split into a crooked smile. "My job doesn't always suck. This aspect, this definitely sucks."

"I'm sorry I made the joke about you knocking her up."

"That's okay. I'm sorry I said the reaper was hot."

"That's okay."

We lapsed into an uncomfortable silence, something I couldn't take. "So ... where do you want to eat?"

"I'm open to suggestions."

4

FOUR

Galen was with Casey behind the clinic's security doors for a long time. In fact, he was gone so long I was about to write him a note to tell him I'd gone back to the lighthouse when he re-emerged.

"I didn't know if you were coming back," I admitted.

"I'm sorry." He absently ran his hand up and down my arm. "I wanted to make sure she was comfortable before I left."

"Did she wake up?"

He nodded. "She's very upset. Thinks I'm lying to her, and has convinced herself this is some sort of elaborate joke."

"She doesn't really believe that. She simply can't accept the alternative, that all the plans she made, the dreams they had together for that baby, are gone. Instead of her and Jacob working together to raise their child, now she's a single mother who has to bury her husband right before what's supposed to be the happiest time of her life. Anyone would be overwhelmed by that."

He tilted his head to the side. "That was fairly profound. I think you nailed what's going on. Her family is on the way. The doctor gave her a sedative that's safe for the baby. He wants to monitor her blood pressure overnight because he's afraid she's so upset she could go into labor. That wouldn't be good right now because the baby isn't in position, whatever that means."

"It means the baby's head hasn't moved to the down position," I said knowingly. "If that doesn't happen you can have a breech birth, and those are more dangerous ... and totally painful."

"Good to know."

Something occurred to me. "I don't know from personal experience or anything. I watch a lot of television."

He snickered as he rested his hand on the small of my back. "I wasn't worried. Come on. I believe I owe you dinner."

"And ice cream."

"I definitely owe you ice cream."

WE PICKED ONE OF THE smaller restaurants, because Galen was too tired to answer questions. By now, word had spread about what had happened to Jacob and the entire island buzzed with gossip. He hated the gossip, and in this particular instance, I couldn't blame him.

"What's good here?" I kept my smile in place as I glanced at the menu of Rita's Surfside Bar, even though I was worried about eating anything that came from what looked to be a rundown establishment.

As if reading my mind, Galen leaned back in his booth seat and shot me an amused look. "Don't worry. The health inspector comes by once a month. Everything is on the up-and-up. The food here is amazing."

I would have to take his word for it. "Why don't they don't clean the place up? You know, give it a good spiff? Wouldn't that bring in more tourists?"

"I don't know that Rita wants more tourists. The locals hang here more than the tourists, although some tourists do manage to find their way here. In fact ... ." He trailed off, inclining his chin toward the front door.

When I swiveled, I found Griffin and Aisling walking through the door. They seemed relaxed as they chatted with one another and headed toward our section of the restaurant. They saw us at the last minute, pulled up short, and I found myself mired in an awkward situation.

"Hey," I offered lamely.

"Hello." Griffin nodded. "Um ... we're just getting dinner before taking a walk on the beach. We plan to take it easy tonight and hit the touristy stuff tomorrow."

"That sounds like a good plan." I felt like an idiot. "Um ... would you like to join us?"

"Oh, I ... ."

"Sure," Aisling answered for him, a bright smile washing over her face as she waited for me to get up and scoot to the other side of the booth with Galen. My newly-minted boyfriend — if he was going to use the word there was nothing holding me back — seemed fine with the idea of sharing a meal with a reaper.

"So, what can you tell us about this island?" Aisling asked, grabbing the menu I'd left behind and flipping it over. "I mean ... what is there to do here?"

"What do you like to do at home?" I asked. "You're from Detroit, right? I'm from Michigan, too. Although ... not the city."

Aisling's eyes were glittery purple slits when she lowered her menu. "How do you know where we're from?"

Uh-oh. "Oh, well ... ." I looked to Galen for help and found him laughing. "It's not funny."

"It's totally funny," he argued, lightly squeezing the back of my neck. "I ran you," he offered, extending his hand to Griffin. "Galen Blackwood. I'm Moonstone Bay's sheriff."

"Ah." Griffin shook his hand. He didn't seem offended by Galen's announcement. "It's nice to meet you."

Aisling, on the other hand, was nowhere near ready to accept Galen's response without further information. "Why would you run us?"

I was trying to think of a believable lie when Galen answered for me.

"Because we know you saw the soul on the dock," he answered

without hesitation. "You were looking right at him. We were out there investigating his murder, which I managed to hide thanks to the bevy of kiosks on the docks before you got off the ship. It was obvious you saw him when we were leaving.

"No offense, but seeing ghosts isn't a common gift here, and I was curious," he continued. "That's why I ran you. You're a reaper, which explains a lot, but you have a rather colorful past. Exactly how many times have you been arrested?"

Instead of being offended, Aisling merely shrugged. "Enough times to know that I'm not sorry for any of them."

"I would say she's exaggerating because she likes to act tough, but she's really not sorry about being arrested," Griffin interjected. "Her father bailed her out each time, so it's not as if she suffered."

"He likes bailing me out."

"If that's what you need to tell yourself."

I found them amusing, and that was a relief. After Galen told me she was a reaper I wasn't sure what to expect. She seemed perfectly normal. Er, well, for the most part. For someone who sucked souls for a living.

The waitress picked that moment to gather our drink orders, and I was thankful to have something to do while my nerves settled.

"I'll have a rum runner," I said.

"That sounds good." Galen's hand was busy on my back. "Make it two." He flicked his eyes to Aisling and Griffin. "That's basically the drink of choice on the island. They're really good here."

"Oh, well ... ." Griffin shifted on his seat. "I think we'll just go for something light tonight, like iced tea or lemonade."

Aisling made a face. "You can have a drink."

"It's no fun drinking alone."

"You won't be alone. You have these two."

"Yes, well, I don't want to drink in front of you." Griffin was clearly uncomfortable as he steadfastly avoided his wife's pointed stare. "I'll have some lemonade."

Aisling had clearly perfected her eye roll over time, because she snagged the menu from him in one motion as she shifted to get the server's attention. "He'll have a rum runner and I'll have an iced coconut water. Thanks."

Griffin didn't protest until the waitress left. "I'm not spending the whole week getting drunk while you're miserable ... and on the wagon."

"I don't see where we have much choice."

I was confused. "Are you an alcoholic?" I asked, hoping the question didn't come off as invasive.

"I wish." Aisling wrinkled her nose. "I'm pregnant."

"And she's really happy about it," Griffin enthused, flashing a sarcastic thumbs-up toward his wife. "Baby, if you keep announcing it like that people will think you're not thrilled about our incoming bundle of joy."

"Did you have to get married?" Galen asked, the question causing me to squirm. "I mean ... is that why you got married?"

Griffin's smile slipped. "We got married because we love each other. We were engaged long before we found out she was pregnant. In fact, we didn't find out she was pregnant until the day of the wedding."

"My father is still screaming," Aisling muttered.

"He'll get over it." Griffin didn't look particularly worried about Aisling's father. "By the time we get back, he'll probably have a baby room already put together in that castle he calls a house."

"Then he'll be way ahead of us."

"Yeah, well, we'll figure it out."

I took a moment to study them. The baby news was obviously still fresh and they were getting used to the idea. Their foundation was solid — a baby wouldn't shake that — but expecting this turn of events and wrapping their heads around it wasn't an easy task.

"You'll be good parents," I announced, taking everyone — including myself — by surprise with my fortitude. "Don't worry about that. I know this is a surprise, but you'll settle and things will be fine."

Galen slid me a sidelong look. "Are you suddenly a therapist?"

The question caught me off guard. "No. I ... simply feel it. When I feel things, they tend to escape through my mouth. I didn't really think about it."

"Don't worry." Aisling waved off my concern. "I don't think before I speak either."

"She's not lying," Griffin intoned.

"As for the baby, we're ... taking some time to absorb it before making plans," she continued. "We were both surprised."

"It'll be fine." Griffin's tone was soothing. "We'll be better at this than you think."

"And if we're terrible, my father will hire someone to take care of the baby for us." Aisling's eyes momentarily darkened. "That is if he ever forgives us."

"He's not angry," Griffin countered. "He was simply surprised ... like us."

"He tried to chase you around the church."

"It's good exercise for his heart."

"He said he was going to cut your hands off," Aisling added. "He said that's what he should've done the second I brought you home."

Griffin's lips quirked as he caught my eye. "He really likes me. He's just overprotective. Aisling is his only daughter and he's spoiled her to the point she's a monster. Thankfully she's an adorable monster."

"Oh, just wait." Aisling adopted a far-off expression. "If you think I'm bad, just imagine how he's going to spoil his first grandchild."

"That won't happen."

"Puh-leez." She made a face that told me she was officially enjoying herself. "You're going to let him spoil the baby because it will get him off your back. You know it, and I know it."

Griffin didn't immediately respond, because the waitress arrived with our drinks. We placed our orders. I opted for crab legs, Galen calamari and Griffin went with fish tacos. Only Aisling didn't know what she wanted.

"Would I like grits?" she asked Griffin with a straight face.

He immediately started shaking his head. "They taste like bad oatmeal, and I've seen you on the rare mornings when your father makes you eat oatmeal. You won't like them."

"No." She furrowed her brow. "Can I eat seafood? I never even checked on that. I know I can't have sushi — which is fine, because sushi is gross — and I'm supposed to stay away from any locally caught fish when we're in Michigan, but can I have seafood?"

Panic licked Griffin's handsome face at the question. "I don't know. I ... um ... ." He looked to me for help.

"How am I supposed to know?" I shot back, frustrated.

"Hold on." Galen pulled out his phone and started typing. "As long as it's cooked, you're fine. What do you like? The lobster tails are really good here. So are the scallops."

Aisling didn't look convinced. "Maybe I should just have a salad or something."

"No." Griffin vehemently shook his head. "You love seafood. We'll make sure it's cooked. You don't need to deprive yourself. I already feel guilty you can't drink on your own honeymoon."

"You should feel guilty about that," Aisling muttered. "I wanted banana daiquiris. Lots of them ... with pretty little umbrellas. Now it'll be months before I can have anything to take the edge off."

"I'm sorry." Griffin looked legitimately contrite. "I know this isn't the way we thought things would happen, but we have to deal with it. I won't drink while we're here. I'll be sober in solidarity with you."

He looked so earnest my heart went out to him.

"No, I'm not punishing you that way," Aisling countered. "Besides, I'll be so whiny when I get big that you'll need a drink to survive. We both know it. Don't play the martyr now."

"Fine. I'll drink the whole pregnancy, if that will make you happy."

"It will. You can drink through the pregnancy and I'll drink through the birth." Her shoulders slouched as she sipped her coconut water. "The horrible, horrible birth, where the kid rips my insides to the point I'm never the same again."

"And on that happy note." Galen squeezed my knee under the table as he shifted to get comfortable. "Do you guys mind if I ask a few questions about reaping?"

"I don't mind, but I don't know that much about it, to be honest,"

Griffin replied. "Depending on how sorry Aisling is feeling for herself, she might be able to clear up a few things."

"I'm not feeling sorry for myself." Aisling screwed up her face as she made a visible effort to return to the conversation. "What do you want to know?"

"Well, for starters, how does it work? I mean ... do ghosts occur when you miss a soul?"

"My grandmother is a ghost," I explained. "She kind of likes it. She hangs around my lighthouse and argues with her ex-husband while spying on Galen and me."

"She's a ghost by choice?" Aisling asked, confused. "What's the deal with your reaper? He's not supposed to allow that. Souls get crazy if they're left to their own devices for too long. They can turn murderous and sit around watching the Kardashians all day rotting their brains. It isn't pretty."

I smirked. "My grandmother seems fine. She said she purposely stayed."

"Her grandmother was a witch," Galen volunteered. "My understanding is that makes a difference."

"I've heard it does, but I've never seen that up close and personal," Aisling said. "Witches aren't a big thing in Detroit, at least not that I've heard of. We've seen a few, but not enough to test any theories."

"I wasn't really thinking about May when I asked the question," Galen admitted. "I was thinking about Jacob. Shouldn't his soul have been absorbed shortly after he died?"

"Jacob is the soul I saw on the dock?" Aisling asked.

"Yeah."

"I would think he would be absorbed right away. How many reapers do you have?"

"To my knowledge, one. Adam Grimport. Have you ever heard of him?"

Aisling shook her head. "No, but I don't pay much attention to other reapers. I can barely stand the ones in my own family."

"She's exaggerating," Griffin supplied. "She's completely co-dependent on her brothers and father. She pays way too much attention to them."

"Ignore him." Aisling waved her hand in Griffin's face to shut him up. "There could be any number of reasons your reaper was late. If he's the only one, maybe someone else was dying at the same time. Seriously, though, I can't believe you only have one reaper."

"It's a small island," Galen pointed out. "We have, like, one death a week, sometimes only one a month. Our reaper doesn't have much to do."

"That sounds like the perfect gig."

"Maybe we should move here," Griffin suggested. "That might keep you from tripping over a life-threatening situation for a full three weeks."

"I doubt it. I find trouble wherever it is."

"You do." He slung an arm around her shoulders and pressed a kiss to her temple. It was an effort to soothe Aisling, who seemed happy for the contact. The pregnancy news was definitely new, and they were thrown for a loop, but they were dealing. Soon they would have everything under control.

At least I hoped that was true.

"Tell me about your wedding," I suggested, opting for a happier topic. "Was it beautiful? Tell me about your dress."

"Well, two days before the soul of my dead mother showed up to help me kill her body, and then my father found out I was pregnant three minutes before the ceremony, so I can safely say that the wedding was extremely loud," Aisling started, causing me to gape and Griffin to chuckle. "What part do you want to hear about first?"

"The part where your mother's soul came back," Galen answered.

"The part where your father found out you were pregnant," I countered. "Did he yell?"

"Oh, you have no idea. Griffin is lucky to be alive."

5

FIVE

Galen was thoughtful as he walked me to my doorstep later that evening. He'd been polite throughout dinner, asking the appropriate questions and laughing at some of Aisling's hilarious stories about her family. He'd been distracted, though.

"Are you okay?"

"What?" His eyes drifted to me. "Did you say something?"

"I asked if you're okay."

"Why wouldn't I be?"

That was the question. "I don't know. You seem distracted. In fact, if you weren't my ride I think there's every chance you would've drifted away from the table during dinner and never come back. Do you not like Aisling and Griffin?"

"I like them fine. In fact, I like him a great deal. I think she's going to run him ragged over the course of this pregnancy. She is ... something else."

I narrowed my eyes. "You still think she's hot, don't you?"

His chuckle was warm and dry. "She's an attractive woman. I won't pretend I don't see that." He tapped the tip of my nose and leaned forward. "I only have eyes for you, though."

His admission made me feel warm and gooey, which was ridiculous. I hated being such a girl, but he brought it out in me. "I don't think it's bad that she's going to be demanding. She is the one who has to carry the baby. Besides, she's not being demanding to be demanding. She's terrified of giving birth."

He cocked an eyebrow. "How do you know that?"

"I could feel it. Couldn't you feel it?"

"No." His head shake was long and slow. "What do you mean you could feel it?"

"I could feel it." I wasn't sure how else to describe what I sensed at the dinner table. "Whenever talk turned to the baby, if they wanted a boy or a girl, if they were going to get a new house, all that other stuff ... when the conversation shifted, I felt this overwhelming wave of panic. It wasn't coming from me. It had to be coming from her."

Galen was officially intrigued. "You felt her panic?"

It was only then that I realized that might not be normal. "Or maybe I imagined it. I don't know." I averted my eyes. "So ... thanks for dinner. We never did get our ice cream, but maybe next time." If he wanted there to be a next time after I admitted I could occasionally see inside Aisling's head.

"I'm sorry about the ice cream." As if reading my mind and recognizing I was about to bolt, Galen wrapped his arms around me so I had no choice but to remain. "I promise to get you ice cream as soon as we have time. Our dinner with Aisling and Griffin went a lot longer than I expected."

"She's chatty."

He snickered. "You're chatty, too." He kissed my forehead, washing away some of the worry that was starting to build. "I'm glad you like her. As for feeling her fear, I'm guessing that's because you're growing in your powers. Before you know it, you'll be the most powerful being on the island."

If he thought that was going to make me feel better, he was wrong. "I didn't even realize it was weird that I could feel what she was feeling until I mentioned it to you. Doesn't that suggest there's something wrong with me?"

"No. You're perfect ... even that out-of-control mouth of yours." He rocked back and forth as he moved his hands over my back. "Don't let this get to you. I understand you're new at all this, you don't grasp how everything works yet, and you're feeling uneasy because your footing doesn't appear solid.

"It's fine," he continued. "You'll get your bearings. The island is amplifying your powers, making things happen faster than they would anywhere else. You're handling it incredibly well."

Wait ... what did he say? "The island is amplifying my powers? How?"

"It's a magical island, Hadley. You're a magical person who was denied knowledge of your powers for twenty-seven years. The island wants you to get control of things. It's trying to help."

I pulled back, more confused than before. "You're making the island sound like a living entity ... like on *Lost*. If this is going to turn into *Lost*, I'll have to leave. I can't deal with polar bears ... and ghosts ... and all those unanswered questions."

He chuckled. "I'm just saying that magical beings come here to make their homes for a reason. This is your home now. You can relax and be who you were meant to be. Because you can, things are starting to happen. There's nothing to fear, because you inherently know what you can and can't handle."

He sounded so reasonable. "That actually makes me feel better. Thank you for that."

"I aim to please." He cupped my chin and gave me another kiss, this one softer and more sensual. Before I knew it, the breeze picked up and we were twined around one another, all groping hands and wayward tongues.

We were so wrapped up in each other we didn't notice the front door open until we heard a very distinctive throat-clearing.

I jerked my head toward the door and found my grandfather watching us with cool-eyed contemplation. "Hello, Wesley," I choked out.

"I've decided you can call me 'Grandpa' if you want," he said by way of greeting. "It seems weird for you to be calling me Wesley."

"Oh, well … ." I didn't know him that well. Sure, he'd killed a man to save my life, but even though he was spending a great deal of time at the lighthouse, very little of it was shared with me. He was much more interested in May and her ghostly antics.

"She might not be comfortable with that yet, Wesley," Galen interjected. "You guys need to get to know each other better."

"What's to get to know?" Wesley made a face. "I'm her grandfather. She should call me 'Grandpa.' It's not rocket science."

"I get that, but … ." He trailed off, collecting himself. "You know what? That's between the two of you. If you want to argue about what she should call you, have at it."

"We can't argue if you have your tongue down her throat."

Galen's cheek felt warm against mine. It was dark enough I couldn't tell if he was blushing, but I had the distinct impression that he was wishing for a hole to open up in the ground beneath him so he could escape the conversation.

"Give him a break, Gramp-sley." I corrected myself halfway through, eliciting a chuckle from my grandfather.

"That's an interesting thought. Maybe we'll go with Grampsley, huh?" He patted my shoulder before fixing Galen with a pointed look. "It's getting late. Thank you for making sure Hadley got home safely. I'll take it from here."

I pressed my lips together to keep from laughing.

"I'm not done saying goodnight yet," Galen argued. "My tongue feels lonely."

Wesley scowled. "It's not right for you to be making out in public like this, where anyone can see."

Galen glanced over his shoulder. "Who's watching? The lighthouse is set back from the road. Besides, there's nothing wrong with making out. In fact, I kind of like it, so … ." He gave Wesley a small nudge with his hip. "Go away. Our date isn't over."

"You go away," Wesley shot back. "I want to spend time with my granddaughter and it's almost her bedtime."

My eyebrows shot up my forehead. "Okay, wait just a second … ."

Wesley ignored my warning tone and grabbed my arm. "Say your good nights, Hadley."

"Goodnight, Galen." I flashed a wan smile. "Do you remember what we were talking about on the picnic blanket earlier? You said it wasn't a concern. Do you still feel that way?"

He shook his head, rueful. "No. We definitely need to come up with a plan."

"At least you're finally seeing reason."

"Yeah, yeah." He used his muscles to keep Wesley from shutting the door in his face and gave me another quick kiss. "I'll be in touch tomorrow. I'll make sure you get that ice cream I promised you."

He didn't get a chance to say anything else because Wesley finally managed to slam the door and then turn his frustration on me.

"Was that a euphemism for something? The ice cream thing? Do I need to have a man-to-man talk with him?"

I decided to ignore the question. "I'm going to bed. Try to keep it down to a dull roar if you and May start arguing again."

"No promises."

I WOKE WITH THE BEGINNINGS of a bad headache the next morning. I showered, ran a comb through my hair and then headed for the kitchen to hunt down some aspirin. Thankfully, Wesley had left sometime during the night. May, however, hovered near the sink when I made my entrance.

"Good morning, Sunshine."

I mumbled something unintelligible in return.

"You're always such a grumpy goose in the morning," May chided. "I don't see why when you live on this fabulous island. You should be happy all the time."

Her tone grated. "May, while I'm thrilled that you seem to be a morning person — upbeat and perky despite the fact that you can't imbibe caffeine — I'll never be that way. Can you just, I don't know, take it down a notch?" I rubbed my forehead as I regarded her.

If she was bothered by the suggestion, she didn't show it. "Do you have a headache?" She made a clucking sound. "You really should take some aspirin."

"That's what I'm working on." I found the bottle of aspirin in the cupboard. "It must be extra humid today. I always get headaches when the humidity skyrockets."

"You're simply not used to it," May said. "In a few months you won't even notice."

I hoped she was right. "Yeah, well ... did you hear about Jacob Dorsey? He was found dead yesterday on the docks. Someone stabbed him ... and put a weird tiki mask over his face."

"Jacob Dorsey?" It was strange to see a ghost wrinkle her nose, but May managed to pull it off without looking completely nutty. "I know him. He was a local boy, married that girl ... um ... what was her name?"

"Casey?"

"Yes, but her maiden name."

"That I don't know. I met her briefly last night. She's extremely pregnant and she fainted when Galen told her the news. We had to take her to the clinic and leave her there for the doctors overnight. I'm sure Galen will be heading back there today."

"Galen is good at his job. You don't have to worry about that." May managed to pour me a cup of tea, seemingly proud of herself as she slid the cup in my direction. "There are fresh lemons in the refrigerator."

"This is fine." I dunked my teabag and watched her. I wanted to ask if she could find a way to cut down on Wesley's visits — or perhaps spend time with him at the ranch — but I was desperate to do it in a way that didn't offend her. I didn't get the chance because she decided to take the conversation in another direction.

"Why haven't I been seeing as much of Galen the last two weeks?" she asked rather pointedly. "You two aren't running into trouble, are you?"

"No trouble." That was mostly true. "Wesley pretty much kicked him out last night. We didn't even get a chance to say a proper goodbye."

"Oh, Wesley." She made a dismissive hand gesture that caused me to grin. "Don't worry about him. He was the same way with your mother when she started to date. He can't stop himself from being an overprotective prude."

"Yeah, well, I don't know that he needs to be overprotective." I chose my words carefully. "I am an adult. I mean ... if I want to have an overnight guest, I should be allowed."

"Who says you can't have an overnight guest? It's your lighthouse. You can have whoever you want over."

That wasn't exactly true with Wesley and May taking over my private space. "I don't think Galen feels comfortable spending the night with Wesley watching his every move."

"I don't see why that would be an issue. It's not as if you and Galen are doing the clamshell shuffle or anything. At least not yet."

It took me a moment to realize what she was saying ... and I was scandalized. "May!" My cheeks felt as if they were on fire as I tried to rein in my rampant embarrassment. "I can't believe you just said that."

"Don't be such a prude. You get that from your grandfather, by the way. It's not an attractive trait. You just finished telling me you were an adult and didn't need to be watched over, and now you're acting like a school girl and refusing to make eye contact.

"This may come as a surprise to you, my dear granddaughter, but I'm well acquainted with sex," she continued, pinning me with a dark look. "I'm not so old that I don't know how it works in a new relationship. It's not my fault that Galen isn't spending the night."

I didn't like what she was insinuating. "Are you saying it's my fault?"

"I'm saying that you need to put it out there if you want him to take it."

I was growing increasingly uncomfortable with the conversation. "I happen to believe that things will occur naturally if we ever have time to ourselves," I countered. "It's impossible for that to happen if Wesley is kicking Galen out of my house."

"Then you need to tell Wesley how you feel. I'm not his keeper."

"You both need keepers," I muttered under my breath. "By the way, after seeing you two in action the last two weeks I can see why you divorced. All that yelling is another reason I have a headache."

"I think you have a headache because you want Galen to alleviate all that stress you've been carrying since you found out you were a witch," May countered. "That will never happen if you don't open the door and let in the horses."

Her euphemisms were getting more and more difficult to swallow. "I don't even know what to say to that."

"Then don't say anything. Just get it done. Like tonight, for example, when Galen comes to pick you up, answer the door wearing nothing but plastic wrap. I saw that in a movie and it was very sexy."

Now it was my turn to make a face. "What movie?"

"I don't know. That young man from television was in it, the one who was on the show about the family of funeral directors."

I searched my memory. "Michael C. Hall?"

"I have no idea."

"Are you sure it was a movie? Could it have been a television show? And were the people wrapped in plastic wrap perhaps on tables instead of answering doors?"

"I don't know. I just remember the plastic wrap."

"Yeah. That was a television show and he was a serial killer in it. He wasn't having sex with his victims, just killing them. I don't think I want to go that route with Galen."

"Definitely not," May agreed. "Are you sure he was a serial killer? He was very funny and went after bad guys."

"That's the whole point of the show. He can only kill bad guys." I held up my hand and sucked in a calming breath. "You know what? It doesn't really matter. I don't think I'm going to pull a *Dexter* on Galen. That's not a turn-on for anybody. Besides that, I can't do anything with Wesley acting as my great protector. He needs to knock that off."

"You need to discuss your issues with your grandfather. I can't get involved."

"Why not? You fight about everything else."

"Those are our disagreements. You need to handle your own."

"Maybe I will."

"I think you should." May leaned closer. "Drink that tea. I didn't make it for nothing."

"Whatever." I did as she asked, but only because I was in no mood to kick off another argument. Once I was finished, I slowly got to my feet. "I need to shower. Then I need to figure out what the mask that was placed over Jacob Dorsey's face represented. Tiki masks represent different things, right?"

"Absolutely." May bobbed her head, solemn. "The tiki culture is rich and goes back a long way on this island. Why are you so interested in Jacob's death?"

"Because it looked ritual."

"Ritual? As in pagan?"

"Yeah. I definitely don't think it was a straight death. Plus, his soul was running around after the fact. I met a reaper last night, so I know that's not supposed to happen. Speaking of that ... why are you still around? If reapers are supposed to absorb souls, shouldn't you be on the other side?"

"I am not bound by the same rules as others, my dear. I may do whatever I want."

That wasn't really an answer – at least a definitive one – but I decided to let it go. "I'm showering and then heading out. If you and Wesley can get your arguments done before the end of the day that would be great."

"Because you want to use my plastic wrap idea on Galen?"

"Because I would like a quiet evening around this place for a change."

"No promises, but I'll do my best."

"That's all I ask."

6

SIX

I left before Wesley showed up. Actually, I had no idea if he planned to visit — he had work to tend to at his own farm — but I didn't want to risk a run-in. May was ridiculously chatty when it came to my love life, and the last thing I wanted was to continue that particular conversation in front of the grandfather I'd just met.

I wasn't sure where to start looking for information on the tiki mask. May had a multitude of books in the upstairs library, which happened to be one of my favorite rooms, but I didn't remember seeing anything having to do with tiki masks. I figured Moonstone Bay had a library, but I had no idea where it was located. I didn't want to bother Galen with something so trivial, so I decided to hit up another source.

Lilac Meadows – that's her real name, no joke – was one of the first people I'd met when I moved to the island, and she'd essentially adopted me as a sidekick of sorts shortly thereafter. She owned a tiki bar downtown, and I figured if anyone knew where I could find information on tiki masks, it would be her.

"Hey, Hadley." She offered me a half wave when I entered her bar, drinks balanced on a tray as she delivered them to a table in the corner.

I greeted her with a smile and headed to the bar. She was back by the time I situated myself on a stool and she spoke before I had a chance to get a single question out.

"So, what's the deal with Jacob Dorsey? I heard he was found on the docks yesterday, his head ripped off and stuffed on a pike and his innards taken for some sort of ritual."

My mouth dropped open. "Who told you that?"

"It's going around town."

"Well, that's not what happened." I told her about the body, glossing over some of the grosser details. Moonstone Bay was a small community, so gossip spread like a communicable disease in close quarters. It was only after I told her the truth that I realized it was potentially a mistake. There was every chance Galen might not want his crime scene details spread about. "You might not want to share that information."

"Why not?"

"Galen will probably be angry that I told you."

"Don't worry about Galen." She offered up a haphazard wave to tell me exactly how she felt about the subject. She clearly wasn't worried in the least. "You can't keep anything secret on this island. Don't worry about that."

I wanted to take her words to heart, but worry remained. "I was actually hoping you might be able to help me."

"Help you do what? Do you want me to help you change the locks? I've seen Wesley there practically every day the past two weeks. That must be cutting into your private time with Galen."

"Galen and I aren't having private time. At least not yet."

Again, my mouth opened before I thought better of it. Again, I felt like a complete and total dolt after uttering words that I wished I could choke myself with.

Lilac's mouth was a huge "O" as she stared at me. "You can't be serious."

"I ... um ... ." I wanted so badly to learn how to control time so I could go back five minutes and think before I spoke.

"You haven't boned the big kahuna yet? What is wrong with you?" She leaned closer and lowered her voice. This was after she'd yelled the previous statement, of course, so people were staring. "You're not a virgin, are you? If so, honey, let it go. I guarantee Galen will make you wonder why you waited so long. He has quite the reputation."

I scorched her with the darkest look in my repertoire. "I'm not a virgin, and can you not yell my private business all over the bar? As for the other, we're simply not there yet. We don't know each other all that well."

"You walk around holding hands and staring at each other as if you're in a romantic comedy. You know each other well enough." She sucked in a bracing breath and smoothed her frizzy blond hair. "Here's what you do. Call him over, tell him there's a bat in your attic, greet him in nothing but a see-through robe and let nature take its course. Trust me, he'll know what to do the second he sees that you're dressed to party."

I wanted to crawl under my stool and hide. "I'm done talking about this." I kept my voice even and firm. "It's none of your business. I have everything well in hand where that's concerned. You have no reason to worry."

"Oh, I'm worried. You have no idea the sort of vipers we've got running around this island. Galen is considered a big catch, a mackerel, if you will. As in 'Holy mackerel, I've died and gone to Heaven because he's naked.' If those women find out you're not letting him surf your ocean, they'll start sniffing around again, and you don't want that."

I slapped my hand to my forehead, hoping if I hit myself hard enough I would either lose consciousness or she would stop talking. "I've got it, Lilac. I'll get right on that tonight. Satisfied?"

"If you need help, call me."

"Yeah, I don't think I'll need help." I gulped down half the iced tea she pushed in front of me and collected my thoughts. I was almost at the point I couldn't remember why I'd entered the bar in the first place. "So, um, I came in for a reason."

"Just a second." Lilac moved away from me and toward the door, causing me to swivel so I could see who was entering. To my surprise, it was Aisling, and she was alone.

"Hey."

She widened her eyes when she saw me. "Hey." She headed in my direction, giving Lilac a curious smile as the woman returned to her spot behind the bar. She grunted as she climbed onto the stool and slapped her hands on the bar.

"What will it be?" Lilac asked, amused at Aisling's show.

"I would like the world's biggest rum runner."

"I can oblige you there."

"I'll just have a virgin piña colada, though," Aisling said. "I can't drink."

"Oh, on the wagon?"

"Pregnant," Aisling replied, her features twisting. "It's the only reason I would willingly go on the wagon."

Aisling slid her eyes to me. "What are you doing here in the middle of the day? Don't you have a case to solve?"

"I'm not with the police department," I reminded her. "And, technically, I don't have a job. At least not yet. I haven't decided what I want to do yet. I'm not sure I'm qualified for anything on this island."

"Hey, if you can get by without working, I say go for it." Aisling plopped her purse on the bar and smiled as Lilac delivered her drink. "My father said I didn't have to work, but to get him to pay my bills I had to stay under his roof. So, of course, I got a job and moved out. It was a great motivator. Now I kind of want to move back in so he can take care of this baby."

Her terror over the baby both amused and confused me. She seemed almost lost at times. "Not that I want to fan the flames of your discontent, but where is Griffin?" I expected the man to follow Aisling through the door any second. They were on their honeymoon, which meant it was supposed to be all about romance and each other.

"He's riding some sailboat around the island. They're going to swim with sharks."

"He's riding a sailboat without you?" That made absolutely no sense to me. "Why?"

"Because my father booked a few adventures for us when he set up the honeymoon — it was his gift to us and I think he wanted to make sure Griffin and I actually left the hotel at least a few times — and he didn't know I was pregnant when he did it.

"I didn't think a sailboat ride would be that big of a deal," she continued. "But when we got to the landing, I was informed I couldn't go if I was pregnant. Griffin offered to stay behind, but that didn't seem fair. I told him I was going back to the hotel to put my feet up. He said he would come with me, but I want him to have at least a little bit of fun."

"He's on an island," Lilac noted. "There is tons of fun to have."

"Not with me. I have a weak stomach and I'm grouchy. This isn't exactly the honeymoon I envisioned. It's definitely not the honeymoon he envisioned, especially since I spent the whole morning puking."

I felt sorry for her. "That sucks."

"Yeah, well ... what are you going to do?" She sipped her piña colada and smiled. "This is really good. I almost don't miss the alcohol."

"It's not that good." Lilac sympathetically patted her hand before focusing on me. "You were going to ask me something?"

"Right." I remembered my purpose and pointed at the tiki masks on the walls. "Where did you get those? Jacob had one placed over his face, although it looked more authentic than what you have on the walls. I'm trying to figure out if there was a specific meaning behind the mask."

Lilac's face was blank. "Where did I get the masks?"

I nodded.

"Pier One ... and I think a few of them might have come from Cost Plus World Market. None of them are real, but I'm sure there is some legitimate tiki action on the island. Somewhere. Maybe in the boonies. Downtown, it's just for looks."

Darn. That's not what I wanted to hear. "Huh." I rubbed my cheek. "You don't know anyone who could help?"

"Not off hand. Why are you so certain the tiki mask has anything to do with it? Maybe it was just convenient and the killer placed it over his face because he wanted people to think Jacob was passed out or something."

"I guess that's possible." I said the words, but I wasn't sure I believed them. "Still, I think the mask had to be symbolic of something. What can you tell me about Jacob?"

"Not a heckuva lot," Lilac admitted. "He was older than me by quite a bit. He hung out with my older brother. He was quiet, kept to himself. I don't remember him being a troublemaker."

I waited for her to continue. When she didn't, I cocked an eyebrow. "That's it? Two days ago you told me about some old woman who got mad at her neighbor and tossed a bunch of tampons on her front yard to get back at her for being a 'bloody mess' as you termed it. I had to listen to that story, but you can't tell me anything more about Jacob?"

Lilac let loose a long-suffering sigh. "That tampon story was funny."

"I didn't find it very funny."

"That's because you're not getting any and you're crabby."

I frowned. "We're done talking about that," I hissed. "You promised."

"I didn't promise anything." She shook her head. "I'm not letting up until you let Galen torpedo your battleship. I'm just warning you that it won't go away, so you best get to it. As for Jacob, he really was a quiet guy.

"He'd been working construction for a bit," she continued. "I believe he was working on the big hotel that's finally going up."

"Galen mentioned the hotel," I confirmed. "He said it was a big deal because the locals initially didn't want it but changed their minds because of the money it will bring to the island."

"Then he glossed things over," Lilac said. "The locals out in that area are essentially a tribe."

"Native Americans?"

"Kind of." Lilac didn't elaborate, so I didn't push. "They believe the land is magical and a hotel shouldn't be built on it. The DDA overruled them."

"The DDA?" Aisling wrinkled her nose. "Like the Downtown Development Authority?"

Lilac lowered her voice. "They're much more than that."

"I've heard horror stories about them but have yet to see them in action," I offered. "Frankly, I think it'll be a letdown when I finally do get to meet them."

"Okay. Continue." Aisling sipped her drink and grinned as Lilac slipped back into her story.

"There was a big fight, but I don't know all the ins and outs of it," Lilac explained. "The DDA stepped in and overruled the people fighting the development. That's it. End of story."

"What about Jacob?" I pressed. "Do you think any of the locals would've been angry enough about the development to attack the construction crew?"

"Oh, I didn't really think about that." The bubbly blonde tapped her bottom lip as she considered the question. "I can't see anyone doing that, but I'm not all that familiar with the players ... so maybe.

"As for Jacob, he really was a cool guy," she continued. "He and Casey dated all through high school. They were kind of the golden couple, were voted prom king and queen and rode on a float. Neither left after graduation, and they got engaged pretty quickly. They were married about two years after high school and started trying for a family right away."

Something about the way she phrased the sentence caught my attention. "They tried for a family?" I pictured Casey's huge stomach. "I'd say they succeeded."

"Not at first." Lilac almost looked sad as she rested her slim frame on her elbows. "They both wanted a big family, but rumor is there was something wrong with Casey and she couldn't get pregnant. She was devastated and assumed Jacob would leave her, but to his credit he didn't. They got through it."

"I saw Casey yesterday," I argued. "She's pregnant. I mean ... she's about to pop she's so pregnant."

"Their miracle baby." Lilac turned whimsical. "Like I said, Casey had issues and they tried everything to correct them. I believe there were a ton of fertility treatments. Her parents took out a loan to help them because the treatments were so expensive.

"They tried in vitro fertilization and other things that I don't know how to explain," she continued. "Then, finally, when they both hit thirty they decided to give up. I heard they were sick of the heartbreak and wanted to enjoy each other without the pressure.

"That's exactly what they did for, like, two and a half years," she said. "Then, one day, Casey woke up and puked. She did it again the next day ... and the next ... and finally Jacob insisted she go to the doctor because he was worried. It turned out that after they quit trying, somehow they found a miracle."

It was a beautiful story, and it made me feel sick to my stomach. "I can't believe they went through all that only for him to die the way he did, so close to the baby's birth."

"Yeah. It's awful," Lilac agreed. "She has her parents and they're incredibly close, but it's not something she'll ever get over. At least she'll have a little piece of Jacob to hold onto going forward."

I risked a glance at Aisling and found her frowning. She didn't look nearly as moved by the story as I felt.

"What are you thinking?" I asked finally. "Are you feeling less freaked about your baby now that things have been put into perspective?"

Aisling immediately started shaking her dark head. "No. That story is sad and I'm glad she's getting her baby. This baby is still a downer. It's making me sick ... and I can't drink on my own honeymoon. It has terrible timing. I bet it's a girl."

"Why do you say that?"

"Because my father claims I was such an awful kid that I have a huge case of karma coming my way. That means it will be a girl."

Even though I felt sad after hearing the heartbreaking story of Jacob and Casey, I couldn't stop myself from laughing. "How are you feeling now?"

"Hydrated and refreshed."

"That's good. Do you want to go on an adventure?"

She tilted her head to the side, intrigued. "What do you have in mind? And I'm not walking anywhere. I don't handle humidity well."

"That's okay. I don't either. I have a golf cart."

She brightened considerably. "You should have led with that. Let's go."

7

SEVEN

"Okay, this is the best thing ever."

Aisling took one look at my purple golf cart and fell in love. She slid into the passenger seat, ignored the provided seatbelt, and waited for me to start the engine.

"I think you should fasten your seatbelt." I wasn't keen to be a mother hen, but she was pregnant.

The scowl she shot in my direction told me exactly what she thought about the suggestion.

"I haven't had this thing very long," I explained. "Galen complains that sometimes I take turns too quickly. I don't want you falling out with your ... ." I gestured toward her stomach, making the scowl deepen.

"Whatever." She fastened her seatbelt, her smile turning into sulk. "This is how it's going to be for the next eight months. I'm no longer going to be a person. I'm simply going to be the incubator that needs to be kept safe."

"Is that what you really think?" I paid attention even though traffic in Moonstone Bay was almost nonexistent. Only certain shuttles and business vehicles were allowed on the island, and none were in sight right now.

"It's how I feel," Aisling replied, her gaze focused on the scenery as we zipped down the road. "Where are we going?"

"I thought we might head back to the docks for starters. You can see Jacob if he's there, right? Talk to him?"

She cast me a sidelong look. "If you see him I'll bet you can talk to him, too. By the way, why can you see him?"

I shrugged, unsure how to answer. "I guess it's because I'm a witch."

"Have you always been able to see souls?"

"I don't think so. I didn't even know I was a witch until I arrived here last month. I was raised by my father, and he kept all of this stuff to himself."

"What happened to your mother?"

"She died giving birth to me." I felt vaguely embarrassed at the revelation, although I had no idea why.

"That's too bad." Aisling was thoughtful. "My mother is dead, too. Technically she died twice."

"How does that work?"

"It's a long story. Suffice to say, she died when I was a teenager and came back about a year and a half ago. I guess she was back before then, but she never bothered seeking us out. Her body survived what happened to her the first go-around — it was a fire — but her mind was kind of warped."

I sensed we were treading on rocky terrain. "If you don't want to talk about it, you don't have to."

"It's okay. I'm over it now."

That obviously wasn't true. She didn't look over anything.

"My brothers had a harder time with what happened," she explained. "I knew there was something wrong when she came back, that she wasn't the same. I kept my distance, but there were times I was tempted to embrace her. Then she turned on me and it was all over. I had a choice: sacrifice her or my brother. I kept my brother ... even though he's a total pain in the butt."

I laughed despite myself. "How many brothers do you have?"

"Four. All older. I guess, technically, my brother Aiden is the same age. We're twins."

"That's nice. Are you close? I never had a brother or a sister. My father didn't remarry, so it was just us."

"I'm close with all my brothers. They're all buttheads of the highest order, but I'm close with them."

"That must have been hard for Griffin. Taking on a girl with four older brothers had to be terrifying."

Aisling's expression softened at the memory. "There were a few tense moments. He held his own. I think that's the only reason we survived. My father says I needed someone strong enough to tell me no, and I think I needed someone strong enough to tell him no. We both got what we wanted."

"That's good." I ignored a pedestrian flipping me off from the sidewalk as I crossed over the final street that led to the docks. "What can you tell me about souls?"

The question clearly caught Aisling off guard because she shifted on her seat. "What do you mean?"

"You said that Jacob's soul should've been absorbed before we had a chance to see him the other day. I'm not familiar with the process of collecting souls, so I don't know exactly what that means."

"We have scepters. They're about a foot long." She demonstrated with her hands. "We press a button and absorb the souls. Then we transfer the souls to a transportation device in my father's office, which moves them along for the next leg of their journey. That's it."

"You mentioned something about souls going crazy if they're not collected. I'm not sure I understand that part."

"Souls aren't meant to stay behind. They become lonely, and a little crazed, if they do. Not all souls, mind you, but most of them. Those are the souls you hear about haunting a house or doing something wacky at a cemetery. They can't seem to help themselves."

"Why would Jacob's soul remain behind?"

"I don't know."

I debated how far I should push things. Finally, I decided I had no choice and went for it. "My grandmother – the one I didn't know about who left me the lighthouse – she's still hanging around. Her soul, I mean. She pops up for visits and even makes tea for me sometimes."

"She makes tea?" Aisling furrowed her brow. "I've never heard of a soul making tea."

"I'm worried," I admitted, tapping on the brake as we hit the docks. "You said souls go crazy if they're left behind. I asked my grandmother about it, and she said she's not beholden to the same rules as everybody else. Do you think there's a chance she might lose her mind?"

Aisling looked caught. "I don't know." She shrugged. "I don't know enough about witches and what happens to them when they pass to answer that question. I could send a message to my father, I guess. He might know."

"You don't have to do that."

"He's not speaking to me, of course," she muttered, talking to herself more than me. "He's furious I got pregnant before we got married. He thinks it reflects badly on him as a father, when in reality it was just a birth control fail. Besides, we're married now. I don't see what the big deal is."

"I think that fathers always worry," I offered, slowing the cart and killing the engine. "I think we should walk the rest of the way."

"You know how I feel about walking."

"I don't want to get arrested. I don't think Galen will find it amusing."

"You'd be surprised." She unfastened her safety belt and hopped out of the cart. "I've been arrested a few times since I started dating Griffin, and he got over it pretty quickly."

"Galen says you have weird things on your record."

"He ran me? Wait … I seem to remember him admitting to running me now that you mention it. I guess I forgot."

"We couldn't figure out why you could see Jacob."

"Oh, well, that makes sense." She fell into step with me. "Let's just say I had a colorful childhood and leave it at that, shall we?"

"What if I don't want to leave it at that?"

"Then you might hear a few stories that will leave you wondering if I'm sane."

"I'm already wondering that."

"Well, then you might like them."

WE SPENT A FULL HOUR wandering the docks looking for Jacob. If he was there, he was well hidden. We came up empty.

"Well, that was a bust." I wiped my sweaty palms on the seat of my capris and hopped into the driver's seat of the golf cart. "I thought if we could find him that he might be able to give us an idea where to look. I guess that was a stupid thought."

"It wasn't stupid." Aisling fanned her red face. "But if you ask me you're looking in the wrong place. We need to find your reaper. Odds are he already collected Jacob's soul. That means we won't be able to find it. If he hasn't sent the soul to the other side yet, maybe we can convince him to release it long enough for us to talk to it."

Hmm. I hadn't even considered that. "Do you think that's possible?"

"I think that's about the only place we have left to look."

"Good point." I tugged on my bottom lip as I considered our next problem. "I have no idea where this reaper lives. And I can't remember his name."

"Adam Grimport," Aisling supplied. "Galen said his name over dinner last night. I remembered it."

"Do have any suggestions about where we might find him?"

"Actually, I do." Aisling grabbed her oversized purse from the floor of the golf cart and rummaged inside until she came back with a tablet.

"Are you going to call someone?"

She nodded. "I'm going to call my brothers and see if they can run the information for us. The reaper network is standard. That means we have access to the address. We just need to get it and then you can program the address into your GPS and we're good to go."

"You're really good at this." I smiled at her. "I'm not sure I would've even thought of that."

"Yes, I'm a queen amongst mortals." Aisling smiled as she placed a Skype call on her tablet. The man who answered on the other end practically took my breath away despite the frown on his face when he caught sight of the person calling him. He was tall, his shirt off and hair wet. It appeared he'd just gotten out of the shower. He boasted Aisling's black hair and purple eyes, and he looked as annoyed to see her as she was to see him.

"Braden," she growled, causing me to bite the inside of my cheek to keep from laughing.

"Aisling." His voice was grim. "Why are you calling me from your honeymoon? If you think I want to sit here and listen to all the kinky stuff you're doing with Griffin, you're wrong. I know you might get your kicks from torturing me, but I refuse to listen."

"I don't want to torture you, Braden," she snapped. "I need some information."

He sobered. "For what? You're supposed to be on your honeymoon. You're not supposed to be doing anything that requires information."

"You're not my keeper."

"You need a keeper," Braden shot back. "I'm serious. "You've only been gone a few days. Did you miss us so much that you felt the need to call and torture us just so we wouldn't forget what a pain you are?"

"No," she sneered. "I didn't call for you. You just happened to pick up. Where's Redmond? Or Cillian, for that matter? I'll even take Aidan or Jerry over you at this point."

"I'm the only one here."

As if on cue, a second voice popped up from Braden's side of the conversation and another Grimlock — this one with slightly longer hair and broader shoulders — grinned when he realized his sister was on the call and nudged Braden out of the way with his hip.

"I thought I heard my name. Hey, kid. How is your honeymoon? And if you answer that with anything resembling a dirty remark I'll rip Detective Dinglefritz's head off when he gets back. By the way,

Dad is still freaking out about you being pregnant. We've managed to calm him down a bit, pointed out that he'll love spoiling a baby, but he's still agitated, so I'd keep Griffin away from him for another couple of weeks."

Instead of being amused — like me — Aisling merely rolled her eyes. "He'll get over it, Redmond. I'm not exactly happy about the situation either. I can't drink on my own honeymoon and I couldn't enjoy the boat trip he set up for us because they have rules."

Redmond's smile slipped. "I'm sorry. That sucks. Do you want me to get Dad and have him place a call? He's good at getting people to change their minds on stuff like that."

"It's fine." Aisling waved off the suggestion. "I got seasick the moment I tried to step on the stupid thing anyway. I think I'm better on bigger ships."

"Bigger is better," Redmond agreed. "I've been trying to tell Braden that for years, but he argues the other side for obvious reasons."

"I'm going to beat the crap out of you for that," Braden warned. "I'm not kidding."

"Hey!" Aisling clapped her hands to get their attention. "I hate to interrupt your little testosterone competition, but I need you guys to look up the local reaper on Moonstone Bay. His name is Adam Grimport."

"Why do you need a reaper address?" Braden asked as Redmond started typing on his phone.

"Because a dude died here and we need to see if we can talk to his soul for a few minutes."

"But you're supposed to be on your honeymoon," Braden persisted. "You're not supposed to be worrying about souls."

"Just ... mind your own business," Aisling snapped. "I'm not asking for a big favor. It's, like, two minutes of work. Give me a break."

"I'm telling Dad." Braden folded his arms over his chest. "I'm serious. I'm telling him and you'll be in big trouble when you get home. No more ice cream bars for you."

I was intrigued. "What's an ice cream bar?"

"Only the best thing ever," Aisling said. "I'll describe it for you on our way to Grimport's house. Redmond, did you get the address?"

"Yeah." He returned to the screen and rattled off the information. I quickly input the address into my GPS. "Listen, Ais, I want you to have a good time and you've clearly made a friend so that's good, but you're supposed to be relaxing. Why aren't you relaxing?"

"Who says I'm not relaxing?"

"I've met you."

She huffed out a sigh. "It's fine. I'm hanging with Hadley, and we're not getting into trouble. At least not major trouble. You have nothing to worry about."

"Hadley is hot," Braden hissed, earning a grin from Redmond.

"She *is* hot," Redmond agreed. "Too bad we weren't there with you. Then we could show her how real men operate."

"Oh, please." Aisling rolled her eyes so hard I was surprised she didn't tumble out of the cart. "Her boyfriend is so big he could crush both of you with one arm. Now stop being crude."

"If we're not crude we have absolutely nothing to offer the conversation," Redmond said.

"Exactly. On that note ... ." Aisling reached for the button to disconnect the call and then stopped herself. "Do me a favor and tell Dad I'm having a good time, and that I said thank you for everything." She was much more serious than she had been seconds before. "Tell him I'm sorry he's so disappointed in me."

Redmond sighed. "He's not disappointed. He's just freaked out. He thinks he's too young to be a grandfather. He'll get over that quickly — you know he can't stay mad at you — and you'll be the favored child again before you know it."

"I hope so. I'll want to be spoiled before this baby comes and sucks up all my limelight."

Redmond barked out a laugh. "Something tells me there's plenty of limelight to go around. Either way, be safe, kid. Have fun. Don't worry about Dad. Getting pregnant is one of the more normal things you've done, if you want to know the truth. Everything will be fine."

"I hope so."

"I *know* so. Have fun. Put this behind you ... and don't get into trouble."

"I never get into trouble."

"Yeah, your hot friend Hadley is in for a world of hurt. It's too bad. She really is pretty." He winked at me and then waved. "I'll see you soon, Ais. Have a good time. Put everything else behind you. You deserve it."

IT TOOK ME ONLY TEN minutes to find Grimport's house. Nobody had cars on the island, so there was no vehicle in the driveway that could confirm he was home. I knocked loudly on the front door, but no one answered. I repeated the process twice more, but everything inside the house was eerily still.

"I don't think he's here."

"Maybe we can go inside, find his scepter and let the soul out on our own," Aisling suggested.

"I don't think that's a good idea."

She already had a tool in her hand and was working on the door. "We'll be in and out before you know it."

"But ... that's breaking and entering."

"You say that like it's a bad thing."

"I can't break the law." I squared my shoulders. "I'm serious. I'm dating the sheriff. That will not go over well."

"It will be fine. No one will even know we were here." Aisling made a triumphant sound in the back of her throat as she threw open the door with a dramatic flair. "Ha! I told you I could do it."

I didn't remember arguing that point with her. "Just because you can do it doesn't mean you should."

"Well, it's done now. I ... ." Aisling tilted her head to the side as a whiff of something awful flowed out of the house and hit our noses on the other side of the threshold. "Uh-oh."

"Uh-oh is right." I waved my hand in front of my nose. "He needs to clean his house. That is awful. I can't believe the neighbors haven't complained."

Aisling poked her head through the doorway and frowned. “We need to call your boyfriend.”

“No way. We can’t tell him we broke in.”

“I don’t see where we have a choice.” Aisling extended a finger toward a huge lump lying on the floor between the living room and kitchen. “The reason your grim reaper was late yesterday is because he’s dead ... and I don’t think he died of natural causes.”

My heart started pounding. “Are you sure?”

“I’m no expert, but that knife in his chest makes me think it wasn’t a heart attack.”

“Oh, geez!” I fumbled for my phone. “How are we going to explain this to Galen?”

“Leave that to me.”

8

EIGHT

I was right about Galen melting down. The look on his face when he parked in front of the house and strode in our direction promised mayhem.

"He's attractive!" Aisling, seemingly unbothered by what was stomping in our direction, sat in a lounge chair in the shade of the porch and rested her feet on the metal railing. "He's big – like, huge. Do you ever worry he'll crush you?"

That was the exact worry flitting through my head. I opted for damage control right out of the gate. "I'm so sorry about this. I had no idea this is how things would go."

Galen pulled up short at the bottom of the steps. I was at the top, so I was taller than him. I didn't feel it gave me much of an advantage.

"You had no idea that breaking into someone's house was a bad idea?" He was incredulous. "Really?"

Shame burned my cheeks. "I swear it wasn't my fault."

"If you want to blame someone, blame me," Aisling suggested. "It was my idea to go inside."

"Really?" Galen flicked his eyes to her. "And why did you think it was a good idea to go inside?"

"Because we're trying to find Jacob Dorsey's soul to ask him if he knows what happened to him, and I figured that Adam Grimport absorbed the soul, which means there was a chance he hasn't transported it yet. Unfortunately, I'm pretty sure the reason we saw Jacob's soul at all is because it was never absorbed in the first place. That means he's still running around out there, which isn't a good thing."

He narrowed his eyes to dangerous slits. "I don't believe you answered the initial question. Why did you break into the house?"

"I was going to search for his scepter to see if I could access the soul."

"That's not really an answer." Galen folded his muscular arms over his chest. "Why did you break in instead of calling for me?"

"Because I felt like it."

I pressed my lips together and stared at my shoes. Aisling had a way about her, and clearly didn't respect law enforcement. She didn't seem to be worried in the least that Galen would slap a pair of handcuffs on her delicate wrists and haul her away. Me, on the other hand, I'd been taught to fear the police to a certain extent. I did not want to spend the night in jail. No way, no how, nothing doing.

"You felt like it?" Galen's tone was like ice. He steamed cold when he was furious, which always set my teeth on edge.

"That's what I said."

"I can't even ... ." He broke away from the steps and dragged a hand through his hair, annoyance playing over his handsome features. "Is this how you do things in Detroit?" He asked, swiveling back. "If so, I can see why you've been arrested so many times."

"And you've only seen my official record," Aisling taunted. "You should see the stuff my father managed to keep from going to court. That's even more enlightening."

"Enough!" Galen held up his hand. "I don't want to hear another word from you. You're in big trouble. You could be charged for the stunt you pulled. Do you realize that?"

"You're not going to arrest me."

"And why not?"

"Because you have bigger problems," Aisling replied pragmatically.

"You have two dead men, both with tiki masks placed over their faces and knives plunged into their chests. Because they died similarly, it's apparent you've got a serial killer running loose. Or at the very least a spree killer."

Galen's mouth dropped open. "Now you're an expert on killer psychopathy?"

"I watch a lot of very insightful television."

"I just ... how does anyone put up with you?"

"I'm an acquired taste. Ask Griffin." She lowered her feet to the cement. "Listen, we weren't trying to foul up your investigation. We were trying to help. There's no reason to get all worked up and growly. It was an honest mistake. We didn't touch anything other than the front door, so no harm, no foul."

"I don't even want to look at you." Galen lifted his hand so he could hold it at an angle and obliterate her face from his sightline. "You no longer exist. I'll let your husband handle you."

Aisling's smirk disappeared. "Wait ... did you call Griffin?"

"Of course I called him. Once Hadley told me what was going on I figured he had a right to know. He's a cop. It's common courtesy in our field to call when someone's wife has been arrested for breaking and entering."

"Oh, you big tattletale." She slapped her hands on her knees, fury positively rolling off her in waves. "Do you know what you've done? He's going to be all 'I told you so' and 'What have I told you about inserting yourself in police investigations?' That's on top of 'You're supposed to be on your honeymoon, not causing trouble.'"

I had to bite my bottom lip to keep from laughing at Aisling's imitation of her husband. The voice was wrong but the tone was spot-on.

"I'll never live this down," Aisling groused, shaking her head. "This bites."

"Well, maybe you'll think about that before breaking into someone's home next time." Galen swaggered up the stairs and stopped next to me. "You're in trouble, too."

"I was trying to help."

"I know. You're still in trouble."

"I guess that means I'm not getting the ice cream again today, huh?"

His lips quirked, but he managed to maintain a straight face. "I guess you'll have to wait and see." He lightly brushed his hand over my shoulder as he walked past me and glanced inside the house. The odor was growing now that the seal had been broken. Soon it would be impossible to remain on the porch.

"See, he's dead." Aisling moved to the spot behind Galen's right shoulder and stared into the house. "I think he's been dead several days."

"Oh?" Galen hiked an eyebrow. "Are you an expert on decomposition, too?"

"You'd be surprised at the things I know."

"Well, you can know them over there." He reached into his pocket and retrieved his cell phone. "I need to call for the medical examiner. I also have to think of a reason why you two were here. Thanks for that, by the way."

"You're welcome." Aisling was blasé. "Would you like me to give you a feasible reason why we were here?"

"No." He paused. "Maybe."

"Just put on your report that I wanted to talk to the island reaper because I was curious. Say we saw something odd through the front window and tried to go inside to offer help. It's not that difficult."

"You're an expert on alibis, too, I see."

She nodded without hesitation. "That's one I'll claim. I've been arrested a few times. I know how to handle alibis."

"Just go over there." He wiggled his fingers. "I can't wait until Griffin gets here to handle you."

"You're still a tattletale."

"I can live with that."

GRIFFIN DIDN'T LOOK ANY happier at the turn of events than

Galen did when he arrived. His eyes were keen as he searched the crowd — the medical examiner's team consisted of six people and the looky-loos from the neighborhood had already turned out, so the number of bodies on the lawn had grown considerably. The moment he caught sight of Aisling sitting under a tree in the middle of the yard his expression shifted from worried to relieved, and then to furious.

"He's here," I told Aisling, inclining my chin toward the driveway. "He looks extremely pissed off."

"He'll be fine." Aisling didn't move her back from the tree. The heat was oppressive — even by Moonstone Bay's standards it was a scorcher — and the only spot that offered even a modicum of comfort was in the limited shade under the leafy branches.

"What are you doing here?" Griffin led with his fury and stalked to us. "Exactly what were you thinking breaking into a dead man's house?"

"We didn't know he was dead when we broke in," I offered helpfully. I was much more nervous than Aisling, even though she was in the hot seat.

"Oh, well, you didn't know he was dead." Griffin hunkered down so Aisling had no choice but to look directly into his eyes. "What is wrong with you? Why would you do this? We're supposed to be on our honeymoon."

"Oh, I knew you were going to take that tack." She screwed her face into a pout. "Just because it's our vacation, that doesn't mean I can't help Hadley search for a murderer. I'm trying to help people."

She looked earnest when she delivered the words. I was impressed.

"Oh, that's a load of bull," Griffin snapped, his temper getting the best of him. "If you think I'm going to fall for that, you're slipping. You can do way better than that."

"Fine. Since you abandoned me to go on a boat ride, I was on my own when I realized I was dehydrated and needed a drink," Aisling offered. "I happened to run into Hadley at a local watering hole, and she volunteered to drive me around in her very cool golf cart so I could cool down. You know how much I love a good breeze. Anyway, we just happened to be close to here when I sensed death inside and we had to check. I can't help it that I have a giving heart and want to do right by others."

Griffin growled. "That was weak ... and don't blame me for taking that boat ride. You insisted that you wanted me to go so your father wouldn't have completely wasted his money."

"Because he's so upset with me." Aisling widened her lavender eyes. "I don't want him to be upset because I'm a daddy's girl and need his support for what's going to happen. I don't know how to be a mother. I need my daddy, and that was the only way I could think to make him happy."

"Knock it off." Griffin extended a warning finger. "None of that will work on me. I don't even know why you're trying to get me to fall for it."

I had no idea why she was putting him through the paces either, but it was a masterful display. I had to give her credit, she was good at thinking up lies on the spot.

"Fine." Aisling exhaled so heavily her black bangs fluttered. "I was bored, Hadley suggested an adventure, I found out she had a golf cart, and I was all in."

"That's better." Griffin sat on the ground next to her, his hand immediately going to her red face. "You're warm."

"And here I always believed you thought I was hot."

"Not funny." He grabbed the bottle of water sitting beside her on the ground. "This is not cold. I need to get some cold water into you." He shifted his eyes to the ambulance sitting on the driveway. "Maybe they have something."

He didn't wait for a response before heading in that direction. Aisling watched him go, her expression unreadable.

"You're good in a crisis," I noted. "I tend to babble when I get into trouble like that."

She merely shrugged. "He's going to let me get away with pretty much everything right now, no matter how annoyed he is."

"Because you're carrying his baby?"

"That and because I had to kill my mother less than two weeks ago. He'll give me all sorts of wiggle room."

"And you're going to take advantage of his giving heart?"

"Of course I am. There's a reason I always get what I want." Aisling offered Griffin a wan smile as he returned with a cold bottle of water. "Thank you. You're the best husband ever."

"I know you think you're putting one over on me, but you're not," Griffin countered. "Once I get you in some air conditioning we're going to have a big fight. Don't think you've slithered your way out of it. I'm simply not going to risk it when you're dehydrated and baking in hundred-degree weather."

Aisling's smile slipped. "It's my honeymoon. I don't want to fight."

"You should've thought about that before you broke into a murder victim's house. By the way, where is your lock pick?"

She feigned ignorance. "What lock pick?"

"You know what I'm talking about."

"I'm afraid I don't."

"Fine. I'll simply frisk you when we get back to the hotel."

"Now that is talk for a honeymoon."

GRIFFIN SEPARATED FROM AISLING long enough to converse with Galen in the shadows at the front of the house. They had their heads bent together and looked serious. I was uncomfortable watching, but Aisling seemed amused.

"Griffin looks like a little kid standing next to Galen," she mused. "I mean ... he's not a small guy. He's tall and strong. Galen is huge, though. Seriously, aren't you ever afraid he'll crush you?"

"It's never come up," I said dryly. "I think I'll be okay."

"Yeah, well, look at them." Aisling's lips curved as she shook her head. "They think they look all manly as they talk dead bodies and tiki masks, but they're totally whipped. Neither one of them yelled about what happened. They did a little smoldering, but that's easy to ignore."

For my part, I was under no delusions that Galen wouldn't resort to yelling later. He was simply waiting until we didn't have an audience. "I don't think they're done."

"Oh, they're done."

"Griffin says he's going to yell at you when you get back to the hotel."

"I'm not afraid of him. He's a big pussycat. I'll just call my dad and tell him Griffin is yelling at me and let them take out their frustrations on each other. Then they'll both forget they're angry with me."

"I don't think your father is angry with you." I'd never met him, so I couldn't say that with any degree of certainty, but I recognized what she was projecting. She was letting fear of being a mother take over. She was clearly fast on her feet, but baby talk seemed to be paralyzing her. "You'll be fine. Besides, I think you're right about Griffin. He won't yell long. Just remind him you're carrying his child every time he opens his mouth and he'll back off quickly."

"That's actually a good idea." She brightened. "Speaking of good ideas, I need to head over there and talk to those guys. Can you help me up? I think my butt is numb."

I grabbed her arm and helped her to her feet. "Why are you going over there? I don't think it's a good idea. That'll just remind them that they're angry."

"As much as I'd only like to worry about myself, I have a certain duty ... and I definitely need to talk to them." Aisling scuffed her feet against the ground as she closed the distance. Griffin sensed her before Galen bothered to look, but neither man appeared happy to see her.

"Sit in the shade, Aisling," Griffin ordered. "I'll be there in a few minutes and we'll head back to the hotel. Stay out of the sun."

She ignored the order and focused on Galen. "So, I don't know if you've thought about it or not, but you have bigger problems than a dead reaper."

Galen blinked several times before speaking. When he finally opened his mouth, his voice was rough. "Really? What are you an expert on now?"

"Being a reaper," Aisling replied without hesitation. "You said you only have one on this island. He's in there dead." She jerked her thumb toward the house. "I think he's been dead for a few days, but you don't have to tell me I'm right."

"Thanks for giving me permission to keep the specifics of my investigation under wraps," he drawled. "Was there anything else?"

Aisling bobbed her head. "You have one reaper and he's dead. That means you have no one collecting your souls. You might not realize it, and you don't have a lot of deaths so it probably won't become a problem right away, but the longer you go without a reaper the more souls you'll have running around willy-nilly."

Galen opened his mouth to say something that I was certain would be nasty, but he snapped it shut, flicking his eyes to Griffin as he shifted from one foot to the other. "I didn't think of that. I don't even know what to do under these circumstances."

"I can contact my father and make sure he knows," Aisling offered. "He's with the reaper council. They should be able to get someone here relatively quickly. That doesn't change the fact that we know one soul is running free and there might be more joining him. You need to find his scepter."

"Why?"

"Because I can use it to absorb Jacob if we can find him again. You don't want his soul running free for too long. It will cause problems."

"And what does his scepter look like?"

Aisling described the device for him, and when Galen disappeared inside the house a second time it was with a huff. He was gone a full ten minutes, and when he returned he looked even unhappier than before – if that was even possible.

"I can't find a scepter," he announced. "In addition to that, it looks like he had a computer that's been taken. There's no tablet or anything else around. I'm betting that means his equipment was stolen."

"So what do we do?" I asked, my stomach clenching. "What happens if we get overrun by ghosts? Will they become dangerous?"

Aisling didn't immediately answer as Griffin absently rubbed her shoulders, instead pressing the heel of her hand to her forehead. "I think I need to call my father to get some advice."

"Then do it," Galen prodded.

"He won't be happy."

"He'll be fine," Griffin soothed. "It's not as if this is the worst thing you've ever done. Heck, it's not even the worst thing in the last thirty days."

"True enough. I guess I shouldn't wait. We definitely need direction."

9

NINE

Aisling insisted on searching the house herself, which annoyed Galen to no end. When I pointed out she would be better at recognizing things, he responded with an agitated growl but let her inside. She stopped by the body long enough to give it a long look and then proceeded into the bowels of the house. After twenty minutes, she declared the scepter nowhere to be found.

"I believe that's what I already told you," Galen pointed out once we were back on the front lawn.

"Yes, but now we can say it with authority."

He slid his eyes to Griffin. "How do you live with her?"

Griffin shrugged. "I think she's kind of cute." He cast Aisling a fond look. "She's also in big trouble. We're heading back to the hotel so she can call her father and we can discuss the proper way to enjoy a honeymoon."

Aisling's scowl was pronounced. "I know how to enjoy a honeymoon. You get naked and eat a lot of ice cream."

"Then we'll try that." Griffin slipped his arm around her back and prodded her forward. "We'll be in touch once we hear something from Cormack. I don't know enough about the inner workings of reapers to say how he'll react, but I'm pretty sure Aisling is right about this. You don't want a bunch of souls running around your island ... it might turn off the tourists."

"We'll meet for dinner," Galen said. "I know a nice place that won't be overrun. It has good food. I need a few hours to deal with this."

"Understood." Griffin offered up a half-salute before dragging Aisling out of the yard.

I watched them go, amused at the way they interacted. He said something she didn't like, causing her to groan, but her smile returned when he poked her side and leaned his head close and whispered something to her.

"They're kind of sweet, huh?" I shifted my eyes to Galen and found him frowning at me. "Or ... she could be the Devil. I think it's entirely possible."

"She's definitely the Devil," he agreed. "You and I need to talk later. I don't have time now because I have my second dead body in as many days, but as soon as we both have a free moment there are things we should probably discuss."

My shoulders slumped. "Are you waiting for air conditioning to yell, too?"

"No. I said we're going to have a discussion. I don't foresee yelling."

I didn't believe him. "Have I ever told you how handsome I find you?"

He shook his head. "We're going to talk. That's all there is to it." He leaned down and gave me a soft kiss. "I think you'll survive."

"I guess." I leaned in and gave him another kiss. "I really am sorry. I didn't know she was going to break in until she already had the door open. She has fast hands."

"And a mouth that doesn't quit."

"I kind of admire that about her."

"I'm definitely limiting your time with her." He stroked his hand down the back of my head. "What are you doing the rest of the afternoon?"

"The plan was to research the tiki masks. I guess that's still the plan. I'm going to have to think of another way to approach it, though."

"Just be careful. Don't go looking for trouble. We have a murderer on this island, and because we don't know what's triggering the kills everyone is a potential victim."

"I'll be careful."

"Good." One more kiss and he sent me on my way with a wave. "I'll be in touch about dinner. We'll work in our conversation around that."

"I can't wait."

INSTEAD OF HEADING BACK TO the lighthouse, where I was certain Wesley and May were up to their usual hijinks, I headed for the beach. While out and about with Aisling earlier, I'd noticed a familiar van parked next to one of the tiki bars, and I was certain I would find the area jack-of-all-trades hanging there.

I wasn't disappointed.

Booker (no last name that I'd been able to ascertain) was sitting at a table drinking an iced tea when I walked through the door. He had his toolbox on the floor next to his feet, and his eyebrows hopped when he saw me.

"Well, well, well," he drawled, a sly smile splitting his handsome features. "If it isn't my favorite witch."

"If it isn't my favorite cupid," I shot back, enjoying the way his cheeks flooded with color as he slipped lower in his seat.

"Don't say that so loud," he admonished, glancing around to see if we'd drawn attention. "You know I don't like talking about ... it."

The "it" he was referring to was the fact that he was a cupid, something I'd only learned about a few weeks before. He'd rather begrudgingly admitted it when my questions about his nature became too invasive. After dropping the hammer — and helping me out with a murderous witch — he'd taken to lurking in the shadows for a bit. I understood why he was embarrassed and wanted to keep to himself. Most females threw themselves at him because they couldn't help it, his pheromones apparently too great to resist, but I was seemingly immune. Still, I liked him. We'd built up a solid friendship. I had no intention of letting him hide forever.

"I'm sorry." I held up my hands in capitulation. "I thought everyone on the island knew."

"The locals know. The tourists don't. And I'd like to keep it that way."

The restaurant was mostly empty, so I didn't think there was danger of his secret spilling. Now wasn't the time for that argument, though. "So ... what do you know about tiki masks?"

The shift clearly threw him for a loop. "Excuse me?"

"Tiki masks," I repeated, as if it was the most normal topic in the world. "What do you know about them?"

"I know that they're creepy decorations if you get drunk enough."

"They have meaning, though." I wasn't sure of much, but I was certain about that. "There are different types of masks for different things."

"I'll have to take your word for it." He leaned back in his seat and rubbed the back of his neck. "Why are you asking about tiki masks?"

I told him what had happened during the last twenty-four hours, leaving nothing out. That included Aisling, because she had too big of a personality to be ignored. "So, as you can see, I need to know what the tiki masks mean. They're obviously important to whatever ritual this guy has going."

"Uh-huh." Booker scrubbed the sides of his face. "Wow. Everything with you has to go to a weird place. I don't understand that."

Oh, if he wanted to play it that way, I could take it to an even weirder place. "Do you have wings? I mean ... cupids must have wings, right?"

His scowl was back. "Fine. You're totally normal. I was wrong when I said otherwise. Happy?"

"I'm happier. I wouldn't say I'm happy. Galen says we need to have a long talk tonight, and I just know he's going to blame me for opening the reaper's house when I had nothing to do with it. That was all Aisling."

"Oh, geez!" He slapped his hand over his eyes. "I miss the days when all I had to do when near a woman is let her rub herself all over me. Those were fun times."

Now it was my turn to scowl. "I thought you didn't want to talk about that."

"I don't."

"So let's talk about what I told you. I need information on those tiki masks."

"They're decorations, Hadley," he snapped, exasperation evident. "The original tiki culture was different, I'm sure, but now the masks are for decorations and nothing else. No one here participates in tiki culture."

"How can you be certain?"

"I ... ." He trailed off and moved his jaw. "You're right. I can't be sure."

I wanted to crow. "Do you mind saying that again into my phone recorder so I can keep it for posterity?"

"Don't push it." He sipped his iced tea and got comfortable. "All I know about tiki masks is that they mean different things to different people. Some are for strength, some protection ... I think there's some earth, air, fire and water stuff thrown in for good measure. I'm pretty sure tiki legends originated in Polynesian cultures. I might be wrong on that, but it feels right."

It did feel right. "Well, I need to learn about these masks. Do you guys have a library here?"

"Of course we do."

"Where is it?"

"It's that small building with the glass ceiling by the beach."

Hmm. I knew which building he was talking about and I was understandably surprised. "That doesn't look like a library. Besides that, it has a sign proclaiming the best coffee on or off the island is sold inside. What kind of library sells coffee?"

"The smart kind. Tourists like souvenirs and drinks. The library is more than one thing. That's how the folks on the library board make money to keep that building. Do you have any idea how many business owners have tried to lease that property?"

"I would think it would be perfect for a restaurant."

"And the DDA wants a library, so we still have a library."

"Yeah. I want to meet these DDA folks everyone keeps going on about," I offered. "I think they sound ... neat."

"Then you haven't been listening. They're not neat. They're ... something else." He shook his head. "As for the masks, they might have some information there. I think you'd be better off researching online, though. The internet is more than just filthy porn these days."

I wanted to smack myself. Duh. Why didn't I think of the internet? I was definitely off my game. "Oh, well, I guess I can go that route. I thought maybe the library would have specialized books or something."

"All that information is available on the internet."

"Then I'll look."

We lapsed into uncomfortable silence. I was about to ask more questions about Booker's cupid leanings when he decided to take control of the conversation himself. "Tell me about the reaper. She sounds fun. What does she look like?"

I shot him a warning look. "She's here on her honeymoon."

"That doesn't necessarily mean anything where I'm concerned."

"Well, it means something to me." I meant it. "They're very much in love ... and she's pregnant."

Booker made a face. "Well, even I wouldn't cross that line. She still sounds interesting. I can't say I ever spent much time around Adam. He was weird. But I've been interested in reapers for years. Very few paranormals have jobs associated with their birthright. The reapers are kind of secretive."

That was the opposite of the conclusion I'd reached. "Aisling talks a mile a minute and she likes to mouth off."

"I'm pretty sure that's a woman thing, not a reaper thing."

"Ha, ha."

"I still wouldn't mind talking to her," Booker said. "You said she was from Michigan? I heard through the grapevine that they've had a wraith problem up there the last few years. I'd like to learn more about that, because we don't tend to get wraiths on the island."

"What's a wraith?"

"A displaced soul who stays behind and sucks the souls of others to survive. They can live forever that way, but it's more of a half-life than anything."

I thought of May. "Do you think May is in danger of becoming a wraith?"

The question caught Booker off guard. "Why would you think that?"

"Because Aisling mentioned that souls shouldn't be left in this world, that they should move on to the next because otherwise they go crazy. I don't want May to lose her mind. I'm just getting to know her. I don't want her to leave yet either."

"I think May is well aware of what she's doing." Booker looked around and chose his words carefully. "She wouldn't have stayed if she didn't think she could handle it."

"I think she stayed for me, to see if I would come."

"That's what I think. But she wouldn't have risked her soul for it. She simply would've waited for you on the other side if that were the case. You could always ask her."

"Yeah, I guess." I slowly got to my feet. "Listen, I know you're embarrassed about the whole cupid thing, but you don't need to be. I'm fine with it. We don't have to talk about it if you don't want to. You can come around again, if you want."

"Are you saying you miss me?"

He looked a little too smug. "I'm saying you can come around again. I promise not to ask questions unless you're ready to answer them."

"I suppose I could answer questions ... later. I don't want to answer them yet."

"Then just come around," I suggested. "We'll have a barbecue or something. Not tonight, because we're supposed to meet Aisling and Griffin for dinner and hear what her father has to say about our predicament, but we'll set something up for later in the week."

"Then I shall be there." He tipped an invisible hat. "By the way, I wasn't hiding from you. I was just ... ."

"I know." I offered him a half wave. "You were giving me some space. I don't need it any longer. I really think I'm starting to get the hang of this witch thing."

"Famous last words."

"We'll see. I think everything will work out the way it should be."

MY CONTENTED FEELING about the way my world was shifting didn't last long. In fact, it lasted only until I pulled into the driveway and found Wesley standing on the front lawn yelling at the house.

"I've had it up to here with you!" He bellowed, holding his hand about a foot over his head. "Right up to here. I've had it! I hope you're happy."

May's voice drifted from inside the house. "The happiest day of my life was when I divorced you."

"Right back at you!" Wesley realized after the fact that I was watching him and he adjusted his frame and tone accordingly. "Good afternoon, granddaughter."

I smiled. I couldn't help myself. "Good afternoon. What's going on with you and May?"

"Your grandmother is a pain in the ass. Pardon my French, but she truly is. There are times I just want to ... ." He broke off and mimed strangling an invisible person.

"I think someone already did that to her." I pocketed my golf cart keys and stood. "Speaking of that, I have a question for you. Now might not be the time, but I'm worried and it's something I can't push out of my head despite what you told me yesterday."

Wesley sobered, perhaps sensing trouble. "What's wrong? You haven't got a killer after you again, have you? If so, I'll start locking you in the house, girl."

I chuckled, amused. I wasn't used to having a grandparent watch out for me. It was kind of nice ... and altogether annoying. "Not last time I checked, but there is a killer running loose. Whoever it is has only taken out men so far, so I think I'm safe, but you should be on the lookout."

"I'm not worried about some killer. I'm too old and cranky to go out that way."

"Yeah, well ... about May. I met a reaper yesterday and she said something that has me worried. She said that souls can't stay behind without going crazy. May isn't going to go crazy, is she?"

"Your grandmother has always been crazy."

I shot him a stern look. "You know what I mean."

"I do, and you don't have to worry." He softened his voice. "Your grandmother was a powerful witch. Her soul is warded. Do you know what that means?"

I'd read about wards in one of May's books, but I couldn't remember exactly what I'd learned. "So ... she's safe?"

"She's safe," he confirmed, patting my shoulder. "She knew what she was doing when she stayed behind."

"Because of me. That's why she did it, right?"

"Not only because of you. She stayed because of me, too."

"All you've done is fight since you were reunited."

"That's how we communicate. Both of us like it."

"Then why didn't you stay married?"

"We were unique individuals who wanted to live a certain way. I know it's hard for you to understand — and that I've been taking over the lighthouse a little more than I should — but things will settle. Despite the fighting, we're not unhappy. In truth, I wish she were still alive so she could throw things when she gets angry."

"I'll bet she'll be able to throw things soon. She's been working on it."

"Good. I like my women feisty." He took me by surprise when he pressed a quick kiss to my forehead. "Now, I'm out of here for the rest of the day. When your grandmother starts complaining that she's bored — and she will because that's what she does — I want you to remind her she kicked me out. This one is on her."

"I'll remind her."

"Good. As for you, stop fretting. You're too much of a worrier. Things will work out the way they should. I promise you that."

"I'll have to take your word for it, at least for now."

"That's fine, but you'll figure it out on your own soon enough. The world isn't exactly how you thought it was before you got here, Hadley. That doesn't mean it's not something better."

His words bolstered my spirits. "Thanks for that. I needed to hear it."

"Don't mention it."

10

TEN

Galen arrived shortly before six. He looked to have showered, his hair wet, and a new pair of khaki shorts and shirt setting off his brown legs and broad shoulders. He smiled when I walked out of the lighthouse, taking in the simple dress and sandals I chose, and leaned against his truck as he folded his arms over his chest.

"You look nice."

"I was just about to say the same about you," I offered as I walked in his direction. "You clean up well."

"Ha, ha." He tapped my chin to lift it and gave me a long kiss. "You smell good. What is that?" He pressed his face close to my neck and inhaled, causing goosebumps to break out across my skin. "Coconut. I love the smell of coconut."

"I do, too." I lifted my eyes and searched his face. "We don't have to go out for dinner. We could stay here and eat soup. Wesley left."

A look of regret crossed Galen's face and caused my heart to plummet. "We have to meet Aisling and Griffin."

"Oh, right." I shook my head, mortified I'd been so forceful. "Of course we do."

He snagged my hand before I could move too far away. "There's a whole lot of night in front of us, though. I'm pretty sure we'll be able to work something out."

"Oh, yeah? What makes you think I'm going to ask you twice?"

"I favor my odds." He pulled me flush to him and offered up a scorching kiss before pulling back, somewhat ruefully. "We should get going before I completely lose my head and take you up on that offer."

"Oh, that offer is off the table."

He gave me a playful swat as he walked me to the passenger side of the vehicle and opened the door. "We'll just see about that."

THE DRIVE TO THE RESTAURANT was short. We could've walked, but because Galen was the sheriff there was every chance he might need his vehicle if another body was discovered before the end of the night. For his sake — as well as my own — I hoped that wouldn't happen.

Galen signaled the hostess as we entered. She was a pretty brunette, all long legs and gaping cleavage, and the look she shot Galen as she gathered menus and gestured for us to follow bordered on salacious.

"A friend of yours?" I asked dryly as we followed.

Galen squeezed my hand. "I'm the sheriff. I'm notorious amongst the locals."

"Right."

The hostess led us to a table on the beach. It was near a huge bonfire. I'd never quite seen a setup like this at another restaurant.

"What's with all the open space?" I asked as Galen pulled out my chair for me to sit. "Is something going to happen on the beach?"

"They dance later," Galen replied simply. "It's an interesting show that I thought you would find riveting. The food is also great." He sat in the chair next to me and focused on the hostess, who was still hovering. "There is another couple joining us. She has long black hair with white streaks and he has brown hair and dark eyes. If you can lead them out to us as soon as they get here I would appreciate it, Jen."

The woman nodded. "Of course. I hope you have a pleasant evening, Sheriff Blackwood."

He gripped my hand tighter on top of the table and smiled. "That's the plan."

I waited until she was gone to speak. "You have fans all over this island, don't you? I mean ... women just throw themselves at you."

"I hardly think she was throwing herself at me."

"If you'd given her an opening that would've been the next step. She didn't care that I was here at all. You might not be a cupid, but you have your own mojo in that department."

"Cupid?" Galen narrowed his eyes. "Should I take that to mean you saw Booker today?"

"I did." There was no sense in lying. "He's still embarrassed I know what he is. I don't get why he's so worked up. I think it's kind of cute. And it's not as if he walks around in a giant diaper or anything."

"You don't know what he does in his private time." Galen ran a hand through his hair. "As for Booker ... our relationship isn't always easy."

"Because he stole all your girlfriends when you were growing up?"

"Hey, I stole plenty of his girlfriends, too. That's not the issue."

"So ... what is the issue?"

"We're simply competitive," Galen replied. "We can't help it. We're both built that way. For the most part, I trust him. He seems to like you and I doubt he would move on you unless you offered an opening."

"Do you think I would offer an opening?"

"No. It's just ... I'm totally better looking than him."

He growled the last part of the statement and made me smile. "You totally are," I agreed. "I think you might be the best-looking man ever born."

"I know you're only saying that to placate me, but I'll take it." He gripped my fingers for a long beat and stared into my eyes. "In case I haven't told you, you look really pretty tonight."

"You have told me, but it's always nice to hear."

We lapsed into silence as we perused the menu, which was large and varied. I was on the second page of offerings when I heard a noise to my left and looked up. Jen the hostess was showing Griffin and Aisling to the table, and she seemed as happy to see Griffin as she was to see Galen.

"Right this way." Jen practically bubbled over as she beamed at Griffin. "The rest of your party is already seated."

I slid Galen a sidelong look. "It seems she's hot for a lot of people."

"She's a siren." Galen's grin reflected amusement. "That means she's attracted to everyone. She can only sleep with someone under the right circumstances, though."

"A siren?" I searched my memory. "Like a mermaid?"

"Kind of, but not really. It's a myth that sirens lured only sailors. They lured all men when they could ... but only unfaithful men."

"Really?" I looked him up and down and then shifted my eyes to Griffin. The Detroit police detective was polite as Jen led them to their chairs, but he didn't give the striking woman much attention as he pulled out Aisling's chair so she could settle before sitting next to her.

"What were you guys talking about?" Aisling asked, grabbing the menu resting in front of her.

"The hostess is a siren," I answered, my eyes on her as she left the beach area. Two men — both with women — were staring hard in the siren's wake. "Sirens kill men if they sleep with them, right?"

Galen followed my gaze, seemingly reading my mind. "Those guys aren't going to die. The siren population on the island is limited. If they stay in smaller groups they don't tend to act out. Jen knows that if she kills someone she'll have repercussions to face."

"But those guys over there, both of them, they're still staring after her and she's been gone for, like, two minutes," I pressed. "I don't think that's a coincidence."

"That's Pat Johnson and Fred Montcalm. They're both known womanizers. They probably hear Jen's song."

I learned something new every day on this island "What song? I didn't hear a song." I turned to Aisling for confirmation. "You didn't hear a song, did you?"

She shook her head. "I don't even know what we're talking about."

"The hostess," I volunteered. "Apparently she's a siren and she can kill men by having sex with them."

"Really?" Aisling was officially intrigued. "Did you hear a song around her?" she asked Griffin.

He shook his head. "No. Was I supposed to?"

"Only men who cheat on women hear it," Galen explained. "I don't think he's the cheating sort."

"Definitely not," Griffin agreed, moving his hand to Aisling's back and idly rubbing. "I can barely keep up with Aisling. Besides, I've been threatened with great bodily harm – and a really terrible death – by her father and brothers so many times I already know what sort of fate awaits me if I ever hurt Aisling."

"Griffin isn't the cheating type," Aisling volunteered. "But to be fair, not long after we started dating I did think he was cheating on me with his sister."

Now it was Galen's turn to make a face. "Gross."

"It was definitely gross," Griffin agreed. "It also isn't how she's making it sound. I was at lunch with my sister. Aisling had never met her, and assumed I was on a date. I was not dating my sister."

"You always have to make that clarification," Aisling muttered, shaking her head. "It's almost as if you're embarrassed to have people think you're dating your sister."

"And how would you like it if people thought you were dating one of your brothers?" Griffin shot back.

"That has happened numerous times. Even though we all look like we clawed our way out of the same test tube together, people have occasionally asked me about my boyfriends."

"I saw two of her brothers when she Skyped them," I offered. "I can vouch for the fact that they look a lot like her. It was pretty eerie. Those are some dominant genes."

"You should see them all together," Griffin said. "Aisling's brother Cillian has long hair, and I'm not kidding, I once thought he was her from behind. I almost grabbed his butt."

Aisling snickered. "He was traumatized. He hid from Cillian for hours."

"It sounds like your family is close," Galen noted. "I'm guessing you work and play together."

"I think co-dependent is the word you're looking for," Griffin corrected. "They all feed on one another. Which brothers did you meet, Hadley?"

"Um ... Redmond and Braden."

"Well, Redmond is the oldest, so he spoils Aisling almost as much as her father does, and Braden ... well, Braden is the most like Aisling. That means they fight. Constantly."

"We haven't fought since the wedding," Aisling countered.

"You haven't seen him since the wedding."

"And we haven't fought in all that time. That's simply the point I was making."

"Whatever." Griffin turned his full attention to the menu. "What's good here?"

"Everything is good," Galen replied. "The sushi is amazing. Do you like sushi?"

Aisling made a face. "I can't eat sushi. I'm pregnant. The mercury could kill the baby. I read it on the internet."

"Oh, well, then we know it must be true," Griffin teased, leaning close and pressing a kiss to the corner of her mouth. He seemed to be in doting mode despite his earlier anger. It was interesting to see. "Aisling didn't like sushi before she got pregnant. There's no way she's going to eat that."

"I like my seafood cooked," Aisling explained. "Although ... ooh. They have prime rib."

Griffin perked up. "Where are you seeing that?"

Aisling pointed at his menu. While they were distracted by food, I flicked my eyes to Galen. He seemed as amused by Aisling and Griffin as I felt. As if he could sense my eyes on him, he slowly turned to me and smiled.

"What?"

"Nothing." I hurriedly shook my head. How could I explain to him that it gave me hope to see them together? They'd clearly weathered incredible odds and come out the other side with their humor and love intact. That was the one thing that worried me about discovering I was a witch. I wondered if I would be able to find the balance necessary to keep him and myself happy. If Aisling and Griffin were any indication, it was possible. "You look really handsome tonight, too."

His smile was indulgent as he gripped my hand. "We won't stay out too late tonight." He lowered his voice as he leaned closer, his lips brushing the ridge of my ear. "I want you to see the show because I think you'll find it interesting. After that, we're out of here."

His tone thrilled me. "Okay."

"As for the prime rib, they're right. It's very good."

"I guess I'm getting the prime rib."

Everyone ordered the same thing — prime rib all around — and after our drinks were delivered talk turned to the obvious topics of the day.

"What did your father say?" Galen asked, getting right to the heart of the matter.

"He said he's going to cut Griffin's hands off when we get home because it's obviously his fault I got pregnant before we were married," Aisling automatically answered. "Griffin says he's not afraid of my father, but I have my doubts."

Griffin scowled. "He's talking about the dead reaper, not your father's insistence that I'm some dirty pervert."

"I know." Aisling's smile was so wide it almost split her face. "I couldn't help throwing in the other part because it makes me laugh. I keep picturing my father chasing you with a pair of gardening shears. It will be like a bad cartoon."

"Ha, ha." He poked her side, smirking as she squirmed. "As for your reaper, Cormack did some research while we were on the phone. He said your reaper was highly regarded in the business for a long time, which is why he got the plum position on Moonstone Bay."

"I had no idea that Moonstone Bay was considered a plum position," Galen quipped. "I guess I can see it, though. It's an island and there's not a lot to do. It's more like living a constant vacation and having your day occasionally interrupted for work."

"Basically," Griffin agreed. "Cormack said that Grimport had been here a good eight years or so and they never had a lick of trouble with him. He's placed calls to the other bigwigs in the office and they're going to figure out what to do. For now, he said to hope that someone else doesn't die overnight."

"What happens when a reaper dies?" I asked. "I mean ... does a reaper need to be reaped?"

Aisling nodded, her expression distant. "Yeah. Because reapers usually come in families, though, another reaping family is called in to reap. We get lists. Can you imagine if you got your mother's or father's name on your list? You would spend all your time trying to save them and it would be chaos."

Something occurred to me. "Is that what happened to your mother? You said she died but wasn't really dead. Did you try to beat the list?"

Aisling's head shake was slow. "No. We thought she was dead. It was the other reaper family that pulled the shenanigans."

"And they're being punished," Griffin said, shifting closer to her. "Your mother is gone. She's where she was always supposed to be from the start. Things are back the way they should be."

His tone was heavy, causing my heart to roll. I didn't know the specifics of the story, but it was obvious whatever happened almost ripped a hole straight through the middle of Aisling's family. I couldn't help feeling sorry for her.

"Things are the way they should be," Aisling agreed, forcing a smile. She seemed determined not to dwell on her family woes. "Anyway, my father is talking about having a scepter overnighted here so I can take possession. It's the only thing he knows to do in the short run."

"How will that work?" Galen asked. "Will you start getting the lists?"

"No. That's another problem. When we told my father that Grimport's equipment seemed to be gone he was almost more worked up about that than the missed souls. No matter how diligent we try to be, occasionally a soul gets missed. That's part of the game. But if someone has Grimport's equipment they can look at his files. It's a concern, and I'm pretty sure the reaper council is going to send a team to handle it."

"Will you know the team?"

"I don't know. My father said he would send a message to let me know what was happening. For now, I'm getting a scepter tomorrow morning. I'm not to go looking for the souls, but if they pop up I'm to absorb them. My father says he doesn't want me running around looking for souls on my honeymoon."

"I would prefer that, too," Griffin agreed. "I want you to stick close to me."

"Oh, don't start that." Aisling adopted a whiny tone. "I'm a grownup. I think I've proven that I can take care of myself."

"You've been injured, like, thirty times since we met, and a few of those were serious," Griffin argued. "I'm not risking that on our honeymoon. I'm putting my foot down."

"You're putting your foot down?"

"I am and it's going to be glorious."

Aisling, Galen and I snorted in unison, causing Griffin to glower.

"Hey, I can put my foot down," Griffin snapped. "I've done it before and it worked out well. I'm not afraid to do it again."

"Of course." I fought to hold back a giggle. "You're going to put your foot down."

"And it's going to be glorious," Galen echoed, smirking. "I look forward to seeing it."

"I get absolutely no respect," Griffin complained.

"Until it's time to put your foot down I suggest we talk about something else," Galen offered. "Tell me how the reaping business works."

Aisling was blasé. "Okay, but it's nowhere near as interesting as you think it's going to be."

"I still want to hear about it. Lay it on me."

11

ELEVEN

The "show" Galen referred to was something to behold.

After we finished our dinner, and three of us indulged in cocktails, the staff started setting up close to the fire. What followed was a rollicking good time, with loud music, fire dancers and multiple performers wearing tiki masks.

I really was entranced.

"What do the tiki masks mean?" I asked Galen, who was snuggled close at my side.

"I think they mean different things. Some are for protection and strength, others represent the elements, like fire and water."

"Were different masks placed on each body?"

"I don't remember looking. I'll check tomorrow."

"It might help if I had photos of both masks."

"Okay." He brushed his lips against my cheek. "For now, just enjoy the show. We'll worry about work tomorrow."

Next to us, Aisling squealed (a sound that seemed out of place coming from her snarky mouth) when one of the fire dancers got close. She was laughing so hard her shoulders shook, and Griffin wrapped himself around her as a form of protection, whispering something in her ear that made her smile broaden.

They were in tune with one another, completely lost in the moment. It was as if they were the only two people in their little world. When I shifted my eyes to Galen, I found he was watching me instead of the dancers. It made me feel a little self-conscious. "What?"

He shook his head. "Nothing. You should watch the show, not them."

"I like them."

"Me, too."

"Aisling drives you crazy."

"She does, but I can see why he loves her. She's mouthy ... and opinionated ... and full of herself. She's also clearly loyal and absolutely adores him. Men like to be adored."

"Oh, really?" I was amused. "Do you think I adore you?"

He shrugged. "I am adorable."

"That wasn't what I asked."

He sighed as he slipped a strand of hair behind my ear. "I think I adore you. I don't want to pressure you to feel the same way about me because we haven't known each other all that long. We'll get there."

Hmm. I couldn't help but wonder if the question made him feel exposed. If our roles were reversed, I would've felt exposed. That was simply the natural order of things. "I adore you ... and it's only partially because you're smoking hot."

His grin was mischievous and flirty. "Thank you for that. We still have to talk about this afternoon. I haven't forgotten."

My smile faltered. "I thought we were being all romantic and stuff. You can't lecture me one second and expect to get my hormones pumping the next."

He chuckled. "I believe I can pump up your hormones regardless. I won't ignore my duty as your boyfriend. You can't break into houses. I'll have to arrest you if you do it again."

"But I didn't break in. I'm not the breaking-in type."

"I'll still arrest you."

I jutted out my lower lip. "Fine."

He kissed me despite my pout. "I'll bail you out if I have to arrest you. Don't worry about that."

"Oh, well, that makes me feel so much better."

"I know it makes me feel better." He slung an arm around my shoulders. "Now, watch the show. I'll handle your hormones in a little bit. If I start now, we won't make it five minutes before you're dragging me out of here."

He was awfully full of himself. "I'll have you know that I can resist your wiles. I'm a strong and independent woman. Your wiles are no match for me."

"Ah, a challenge. I love a challenge."

"So do I."

"I guess we'll have to wait to see who is victorious."

Something told me we both would be victorious.

Finally.

BY THE TIME WE MADE it back to the lighthouse two hours later, I was ready to admit defeat. My hormones were officially rioting, ready to take over the prison, and Galen was all too happy to cede to their demands.

By the time we hit the front porch and I fumbled for my keys, we were a mess of hands and kisses. There was no stopping us this time. I had no doubt about that. Wesley was absent and May would simply have to make herself scarce.

It was time. My hormones, just like the tiki gods we'd watched dance, demanded a tribute.

We almost tripped into the living room when I finally managed to get the door open. Galen caught me around the waist before I fell — which would've been mortifying given the fact that I was trying to be sexy and self-assured — and he made sure to lock the front door before prodding me toward the stairs.

May, floating at the edge of the room, merely widened her eyes when she saw us. "Well, well, well. I see someone took my words to heart."

I couldn't even remember what she'd said to me because my brain was so fuzzed. "Have a nice night," I murmured, as Galen crowded me onto the first step.

"Maybe you should head out to the farm and bug Wesley," Galen suggested. He was positively panting. "You might want to stay out there the entire night."

"I don't have to visit Wesley to make myself scarce." May's smile was fond. "You guys have fun ... and be safe!" She raised an admonishing finger. "Don't make me haunt you for stupid reasons, Galen."

"I wouldn't dream of it." Galen's eyes flashed as he started climbing the stairs. "You know your way out."

"I do." She waved brightly before disappearing. "Have fun!"

I probably should've been embarrassed by the scene, but I had other things on my mind. "We're done arguing about breaking and entering, right?" I was breathless.

He nodded. "Totally done. There's something else I want to discuss with you now."

"Which is?"

"I think it's going to lose something in the telling. That means I'll have to show you."

I WOKE LATE THE next day, the sun from my bedroom window already kissing my bare skin. Galen was still asleep beside me, his chest rising and dropping at even intervals. He looked relaxed, his morning stubble making him even more attractive than usual ... if that was even possible. He resembled a Greek statue, a perfect man carved from pure marble and put on display.

And for now at least, he was all mine.

I brushed my finger against his cheek, grinning when his reflexes kicked into gear and he grabbed my wrist before I could pull away.

"What are you doing up so early?" he growled, his eyes still closed. "I must not have done my job if you're ready to play some more."

"It's almost nine."

His eyes snapped open and he looked to the bedside clock for confirmation. "Oh, well, crap."

"I think you're going to be late for work."

Instead of jumping out of bed, he slid his arm around my waist and tugged me to his side, his blue eyes searching as they locked with mine. "How did you sleep?"

"Hard. Did I snore?"

"If you did, I didn't hear it. My snoring drowned out your snoring."

"Yeah, well ... it was nice." I felt a little ridiculous saying it, but I couldn't stop myself. I almost wanted to gush. The events of the previous evening would be seared into my memory for a long time to come.

"Really nice," Galen agreed, his lips curving. "So nice I think we'll need a repeat."

"Now? I thought you had work."

"I'm the sheriff around these here parts." He adopted an adorable southern drawl. "That means I call the shots."

"I guess I could be persuaded."

WHEN WE FINALLY ROLLED out of bed, Galen headed straight for the shower. He seemed happy, relaxed and in no mood to get clean on his own. "Come on." He crooked his finger for me to follow. "I'm not done with you yet."

My cheeks heated as I watched him. "You'll never make it to work at this rate."

"Work is highly overrated."

I couldn't argue with that.

EVENTUALLY WE MANAGED TO get dressed and head downstairs. I immediately went to the refrigerator so I could do something with my hands — other than run them over his muscled chest — and he set about making coffee. He whistled as he worked, something that amused me. We were both feeling chummy when we sat on the stools at the kitchen counter and started talking about the day ahead.

"I'm assuming you're going to do more research on your tiki mask project," he said.

I bobbed my head. "That's the plan."

He handed me a mug of coffee and leaned forward to kiss me before I could sip it. "Try to stay out of trouble ... and no breaking and entering."

"That's also the plan."

"If you run into your buddy Aisling, make sure she knows that breaking and entering isn't allowed on this island. Apparently she forgets."

I nodded as I gulped the too-hot coffee. "I have to wonder how many homes she's broken into over the years. She seemed totally comfortable with it."

"My guess is that it's part of the deal with reapers." Galen sobered, but he kept his hand moving up and down my back. "She probably has to break into places to collect the souls, and she has to do it on the down low. I heard reapers have rings that make them invisible."

That was interesting. "Invisible? She can make herself invisible? That's a neat superpower."

"It's the ring, not her. Reapers don't have special abilities, other than seeing souls, but a lot of paranormals have that ability."

"You can see souls," I mused. "So can I. Is that normal in paranormal circles?"

"Actually, it is." He kissed the tip of my nose. "I don't want to be a demanding man, but I thought you were making breakfast."

"Oh." I hopped to my feet. I'd completely forgotten my task after moving the eggs and hash browns to the counter. "I guess I got distracted by how pretty you are."

"I think that was supposed to be my line." He followed me to the stove and grabbed a frying pan from the rack hanging over my head. "I'll help. You shouldn't have to do all the work."

"I think you just want to stay close."

"I think you're right. In fact ... ." His mouth was over mine again. I didn't have a chance to sink into the kiss, though, because the swinging door that separated the kitchen from the hallway opened to allow Wesley entrance. He didn't look remotely happy.

"Oh, geez." He slapped his hand over his eyes. "It's almost noon. What are you people doing in here? I can't even ... . Somebody shoot me now."

"My gun is locked in my truck," Galen replied evenly. "I can get it if you really want me to shoot you."

"What I want you to do is stop groping my granddaughter in front of the stove," Wesley complained, banging his shin on a stool when he refused to uncover his eyes and watch where he was walking. "Dagnabbit!"

I bit my bottom lip to keep from laughing. Technically, it wasn't funny. In a slapstick movie way, though, it was downright hilarious. "Are you okay?" I choked on the words.

"Oh, don't bother." Wesley slowly lowered his hand, his eyes mutinous as he glanced between us. "I take it you're going to be a regular fixture around here both night and day now, Galen."

"I was always going to be a regular fixture around here, Wesley," Galen replied calmly. "Your protective grandfather routine was never going to change that."

"Yeah, well ... I wasn't really trying to keep you away." My grandfather plopped himself on an open stool and regarded us with dark eyes. "I simply wanted to make sure you were serious. You have a certain reputation around the island."

"That reputation wasn't exactly earned," Galen argued. "Some people assumed I was a ladies' man when I really wasn't."

"Yeah, yeah." Wesley waved off the comment and focused on me. "Are you going to start calling me 'grandpa' now?"

I wasn't expecting the question. "Oh, well ... ."

"I figure now is the time to ask because you're so embarrassed you'll likely agree to anything."

He wasn't wrong about that. "I'm going to try," I said after a beat. "It's new for me. I want to get to know you, spend time with you. I figure it will happen when it's supposed to happen."

"Just like everything in life," Galen teased, poking my side.

"Oh, good grief." Wesley made a face that bordered on comical. "You guys are fluttery flirts this morning. I don't want to watch this. Where's May?"

"She disappeared when we came home last night," I replied. "I haven't seen her since."

"I believe she wanted to give us some privacy," Galen supplied pointedly. "You might want to consider that, too. Maybe, I don't know, call ahead before stopping by to make sure we're not busy or something."

"It's almost noon," Wesley pointed out. "How was I to know you'd still be lazing about?"

"I guess that's fair." Galen dumped the entire bag of hash browns into the skillet. "How have things been with you otherwise? How are you getting along with May?"

"That woman ... I swear she'll be the death of me."

He said it with a certain fondness that made me realize he was fine if he went during the middle of an argument.

"I don't understand why you two divorced, because you're clearly still tipped over one another," I said. "I mean ... why not stay together? Work it out and the like."

"Because we realized we both needed our own space," Wesley replied, nodding his head in thanks when I delivered a mug of coffee to him. "I love my farm. I like working out there and enjoy the solitude. Your grandmother always loved this lighthouse. I loved it, too, but I was fine walking away from it. She never could.

"We were better splitting our time with each other, spending a few days together and then a few apart," he continued. "The rest of the people on the island didn't get that, thought there was something wrong with us. It was simply easier to divorce, separate our finances, and then date. I guess that would be the best word for it."

I could think of a few other words, but I wisely kept them to myself. "Well, if you guys were happy living your lives that way, more power to you. Still, it might benefit everyone if May occasionally visited your farm."

My cheeks heated as I held my grandfather's gaze. I needed to get the words out — and now — if there was ever going to be any peace in the lighthouse.

"I like having you here and getting to know you, but ... sometimes it's a little weird," I admitted. "Maybe we should come up with a schedule."

Instead of being offended, Wesley merely sighed. He rolled his neck until it cracked and then nodded. "This is your home now. May gets that. I guess I've still been thinking of it as her home. You have a right to your privacy."

"I still want to see you," I said hurriedly. "I want to spend time with you, get to know you. It's just ... I want a balance. I don't mean to hurt your feelings, but we have to find a compromise that works for everybody."

"And we will." Wesley patted my hand. "I never got to see you when you were young, so it's hard to shake the idea that you're a little girl. I know in my head that you're an adult. My heart just needs to catch up.

"As for May and me, I'll talk to her about visiting the farm more often," he continued. "She prefers the lighthouse, but she needs to give you some privacy, too. The good news is, she likes messing with some of my workers. That will keep her busy at least four or five hours a day."

I smiled. "We'll figure it out."

"We will," Galen agreed as he flipped the hash browns. "We're all in this together. We'll come up with a solution that works for all of us. I mean ... how hard can it be?"

He probably jinxed us with the question, but I was in too good a mood to call him on it. "How does everyone want their eggs?" I asked, moving up beside him. "We can have a big breakfast together and then start making plans. How does that sound?"

"Sounds great," Wesley nodded. "I like my eggs basted."

"You've got it."

12

TWELVE

I felt as if I was walking on air when I headed downtown, navigating my purple golf cart with ease. I headed to Lilac's bar, parked in the tiny lot designed with golf carts in mind, and took a few extra minutes to collect myself before entering.

I couldn't stop smiling. That would be a dead giveaway to Lilac, who was seemingly more invested in my sex life than I was. Okay, that was an exaggeration, but there were times it felt like that.

Instead of smiling, I adopted what I hoped she would take as a distracted expression. I wanted her to think I was busy, that I had a million things to do, and answer the questions I intended to pepper her with as quickly as possible. With that in mind, I squared my shoulders and walked through the door ... only to practically trip over my feet when I realized Aisling and Griffin were sitting at the center table with Lilac, the three of them laughing so hard I thought there was a possibility the walls might tumble thanks to the echoes.

"That is hilarious!" Lilac swiped at the tears freely running down her cheeks. "I mean ... hilarious. What did your father do when he picked you up at the police station?"

Oh, good. Aisling was telling stories about her multiple arrests.

That would naturally be of interest to Lilac. She wouldn't ask about my night with Galen if she was focused on Aisling. Whew!

"He didn't say much," Aisling replied, playing with her straw wrapper as she stretched out her legs. "Griffin was there — that was essentially the first time they met — and my father didn't want to let his anger show in front of a police officer."

"What did you think?" Lilac asked Griffin as I took one of the open seats at the table. "Did you think she was crazy?"

Griffin slid Aisling a look as he cupped her hand in his. "I don't know what I thought at that point. I barely knew her, but I was attracted to her. I think the attraction started the second she opened that sarcastic mouth of hers. Her father is a scary guy, though. At least I thought he was on that first meeting."

"What are we talking about?" I asked brightly.

"Aisling was telling the story about how she was arrested for getting in a hair-pulling contest with the worst woman in the world and how Griffin met her father for the first time at the police station after the fact," Lilac replied, giggling. "Her brothers were arrested, too. Apparently her father keeps several thousand dollars in cash at his house just in case his children are arrested."

I smiled. "That sounds kind of ... freaky." I tried to imagine my father bailing me out of jail. He was a lawyer, but he didn't handle criminal cases unless they were of the high profile variety. "My father probably would've left me to rot."

"My father threatens that all the time," Aisling offered. "He's never once done it. I doubt your father would either."

"My father is very by the book."

"My father wears a three-piece suit to work every single day and has a butler. He still bails me out of jail. Of course, I've ended up behind bars at least three times because he was the one who called the cops on me."

"Aisling has a habit of stealing his vehicles," Griffin explained.

"Hey, if he hadn't treated me differently because I have a vagina rather than a penis none of those things would've happened."

"Fair enough." Griffin stroked his hand over her back. They were lovey-dovey, slightly facing each other, and again I was struck by their bond. Griffin was a police officer, and they were telling stories about Aisling's arrests. Their bond had to be absolutely unbreakable to survive something like that.

"Why are you so late getting here?" Lilac asked, flicking her eyes to me. "You're usually out and about before ten. In fact ... ." She trailed off, her eyes narrowing. "You had sex."

I was mortified. "W-what? I ... w-what?"

"That was a really poor comeback," Aisling shook her head. "You need to work on your poker face. You definitely had sex. You've got that whole glowing all over thing going for you."

I was desperate to get all three sets of eyes off me. "I have no idea what you're talking about. In fact, we should definitely talk about something else. Let's go back to Aisling getting arrested. That was a fun story."

"No way." Lilac shook her head, vehement. "I want to hear how your first night with naked Galen went. I hear he has magical hands."

I slapped my hand to my forehead and averted my gaze. "I can't even ... ."

Aisling was more pragmatic with her approach. "I didn't realize you guys hadn't done the deed. I thought you'd been dating for a bit."

"Only a few weeks," Lilac said on my behalf. "I would've jumped him after the first date, but people say I have impulse control problems."

"People say that about me, too," Aisling said. "When they say it, I just punch them in the face." She mimed letting loose a short jab. "Not that it's any of my business ... ."

"Which has never stopped you before," Griffin interjected.

Aisling ignored him. "Not that it's any of my business," she repeated, "but how could you wait that long? I pretty much slept with Griffin on our first date. My father had a meltdown when he heard the next day."

There was far too much to absorb in what she seemingly thought a simple statement. "You told your father?"

"I told my brother ... who told my other brother ... who told my other brother ... who told my father. By the time Griffin swung back around they were all calling him Detective Dinglefritz and threatening to bury him alive."

"Ah, fun times." Griffin grinned at the memory. "And we didn't sleep together on our first date. We technically didn't have a first date. I threatened to arrest you, you got arrested by someone else, I checked on you, then I saw you kill a wraith and thought I was losing my mind. Then we fell into bed."

"And then you disappeared the next morning," Aisling reminded him.

"I needed to think. I hate it when you tell that story." Griffin made a face. "I didn't disappear. I needed to think because I didn't know the paranormal world. I don't think that's uncalled for."

"Of course not." Aisling's tone was placating, but her expression was full of mischief. "It wasn't uncalled for in the least."

"Besides, it wasn't as if I was gone very long," Griffin added. "I couldn't stay away from you. You hooked me from the first, and I was a goner after that."

"Yeah. I kind of liked that part." Aisling grinned as she poked his side, her eyes drifting to the door as it opened. She didn't recognize the figure strolling into the bar, but I did. Still, she seemed impressed by what she saw. "Hello," she muttered under her breath, causing me to smother a smile as Booker headed toward our table.

Griffin slid her a sidelong look. "What did you just say?"

Aisling managed to regain a modicum of control over her mouth. "I didn't say anything. You're hearing things."

I shared an amused look with Lilac as Booker grabbed a chair from a nearby table and slid between Aisling and me. "Hello," he drawled, greeting me with a wink. "You look all ... shiny ... today." He tilted his head to the side as my cheeks started to burn.

"She finally got up close and personal with Galen," Lilac explained, making things worse. "She's embarrassed and doesn't want to talk about it."

"You're embarrassed?" Booker didn't bother hiding his amusement. "Is that because he's bad in bed? Don't answer that. I'm going to tell him you said he was no matter your response."

I found my voice. "Don't you dare!"

"Oh, chill out." He waved a hand and focused on Aisling, who was watching him with a moony look. "Who's your friend?"

"This is Aisling."

"Ah, the reaper." Booker's smile widened. "I hear you have a mouth like a sailor, and suck souls for a living."

Aisling didn't immediately respond, instead lifting her nose to scent the air. I found her reaction strange. Apparently, so did Griffin.

"What are you doing?" Griffin asked, annoyance bubbling up. "You realize I'm sitting right here, right? If you're going to check out another guy on our honeymoon, you should at least be subtle about it."

Something occurred to me, and my mouth dropped open as I shifted my eyes back to Booker. "Is this because you're ... you know?"

Booker scowled. "I thought we agreed not to talk about that."

"I said I would wait to talk about it," I clarified. "I didn't say I would let it go forever. Besides, she wasn't acting weird — er, any weirder than normal — until you walked through the door. Now she's all hot and bothered."

"I'm not hot and bothered," Aisling said, annoyance creeping in. "It's just ... he smells like ice cream."

That was news to me. "Uh-uh. He smells like sweat. He works outside a lot."

"No, he smells like ice cream." Aisling was firm. "Like ice cream with melted caramel on top ... and sprinkles ... and whipped cream ... and maybe some maraschino cherries."

Griffin was beside himself. "That's your favorite ice cream dish." His eyes were accusatory when they locked with Booker's more neutral orbs. "What's going on here?"

Booker heaved out a sigh and held up one hand as though halting traffic. "It's not her fault," he said finally. "I didn't think a reaper would have this reaction, but it's probably because it's the first time she's been close to me. The initial reaction will fade."

"She's pregnant," I reminded him. "Her hormones are all out of whack."

"Oh, I didn't consider that." Booker was intrigued as he leaned forward. "What's with her eyes? They're purple."

"Her whole family has purple eyes," Griffin replied, sliding his arm around Aisling's waist to anchor her to him. "What's going on?"

"You have to tell him," I prodded. "He's a cop. He'll probably shoot you if you don't."

"Oh, good grief." Booker wrinkled his nose. "Listen, it's a chemical thing. It will be over in five minutes. I have a certain effect on women."

"Does he ever," Lilac drawled, grinning. "I've known him forever, and women have been throwing themselves at his feet that entire time. It is ridiculous ... and sometimes funny if it happens to a woman I don't like."

"Seriously." Aisling inhaled deeply. "How can you smell like ice cream?"

"I'm going to shoot you," Griffin warned. "I don't have a gun, but I have a rich father-in-law and he'll get me one. Plus, I'm married to a reaper. I'm assured they know how to get rid of a body."

Aisling giggled as she squirmed in her chair. Her eyes had taken on a hazy quality that made me mildly nervous. "Do you ever dip yourself in chocolate? Roll around in a bed full of sprinkles? Ooh, how do you feel about waxing yourself with hot caramel?"

"That will be enough of that." Booker extended a warning finger. "You're making me uncomfortable. Sexual harassment is a real thing, and I'm more than a piece of meat."

"You're definitely not a piece of meat," Aisling agreed. "Meat doesn't belong anywhere near whipped cream."

"What are you?" Griffin barked. He was familiar enough with the paranormal population to realize right away that something otherworldly was happening.

"I'm just a handyman," Booker lied.

Griffin narrowed his eyes to dangerous slits. "Don't make me smack you around."

"As if you could take me."

"Booker." My voice was low and full of warning. "You have to tell them. It's only fair."

"Fine." He scorched me with a look before focusing on Griffin. "I'm a cupid. There, are you happy?"

Whatever he was expecting, that wasn't it. Griffin's forehead wrinkled as he absorbed the news. "Like a cherub? Do you wear a diaper and shoot people with arrows?"

Aisling barked out a laugh. "That is hilarious. Although ... do you?" Her eyes darkened. Apparently the initial flood of Booker hormones was dissipating. "I have a few people I would like to shoot with arrows. Do you have a way of doing that?"

"I don't shoot people with arrows," Booker countered, his temper short. "I don't know why people think that."

"Blame Valentine's Day," Griffin volunteered. "That fat little baby cherub isn't doing you any favors."

"Yeah, that guy." Booker made a face. "Basically I'm simply a normal man, who is often so desirable that I do have to beat women off with a stick."

"Ooh. Do you sell your sweat as musk?" Aisling asked, brightening. "I've been wondering what I should get my brothers as souvenirs. Cillian has a girlfriend and Aidan is gay, but Braden and Redmond would be all over that."

Booker was incredulous. "You want me to bottle my sweat?"

"More than anything."

"Just cool it." He shook his head and his lips twitched. "I heard you were full of yourself and said whatever came to your mind. I guess the rumors about your personality weren't exaggerated."

"Not even a little." Aisling looked proud as she leaned back in her chair, her face no longer flushed. Griffin still didn't appear happy, but he also didn't look as if he was ready to jump to his feet and rip Booker's head off his shoulders at any second. "What's it like being a cupid?"

Booker shrugged. "I don't know. It's not like anything."

"You must have some special powers," she persisted. "Other than simply making women lose their heads and drool, that is. What can you do?"

"I have a few talents in my arsenal," he replied, leaning back in his chair. "I've always been curious about reapers. What can you do?"

"I can see souls and absorb them. That's about it."

"I hear you're a special reaper," Booker pressed. "I hear you've been at the center of several very big fights the past two years."

Aisling was instantly suspicious. "How did you hear that?"

I was equally curious. "Yeah, how did you hear that?" I echoed.

"I know people." Booker's eyes never left Aisling's face. "I hear you took down a couple of reaper families, wiped out a bunch of rogue reapers, got in a gargoyle war, took down a very dangerous witch named Genevieve Toth, and put a huge dent in the wraith population in Detroit. While all of it sounds interesting, I'm most interested in Genevieve."

"Who is Genevieve?" I asked.

"You knew Genevieve, didn't you?" Aisling asked. "Don't bother denying it. I can tell. If you're going to take up for her, well, stuff it. I'm not sorry about what I did. She had it coming."

"I didn't have any love for Genevieve," Booker countered. "In fact, she killed my great-uncle about sixty years ago. I thought she was dead, lost to time, but I guess not."

"She killed a lot of people's uncles." Aisling was grim. "I'm sorry she took yours."

"That was long before my time. My family remembers, though. My father will happy to hear she's gone. How did she die?"

"My father beheaded her with a really big sword."

Booker stilled. "Is that a euphemism?"

"No."

"I'm dying to hear the story."

Aisling leaned back in her chair and ran her tongue over her teeth, internally debating. "Okay. I'll tell you the story of Genevieve Toth if you tell me about being a cupid. I am equally curious to know what you're capable of."

"Because I smell like ice cream?"

"Actually, now you smell like tomato juice."

Lilac snorted. "What? How is that possible?"

"I'm pregnant. My cravings change on a whim."

"I'll tell you what I can tell you," Booker hedged. "But only if you get your husband to stop glaring at me. Seriously, dude, I have no interest in your wife."

"Hey!" Aisling was offended. "I'm totally desirable."

"I don't believe that's the point, baby," Griffin growled.

"I'm still desirable."

"Of course you are." He slipped a possessive arm around her back, practically daring Booker to fight his claim.

"I only want to hear about Genevieve," Booker promised. "She lived on this island for ten years. This was one of the places she escaped to when she wanted people to believe she was dead."

I had no idea who Genevieve was, but I was fascinated. "I wouldn't mind hearing it either," I offered.

"I'll tell the story." Aisling was resigned. "The ending, even though she had it coming, isn't entirely happy."

"It's not sad either," Griffin pointed out. "You survived. We won. We found each other."

"Yeah, but a lot of other people lost their lives along the way."

"That's how it goes," Booker said. "Tell the story. Something tells me your unique spin on things will make it all the better."

Aisling's smile widened. "I'm really starting to like you."

"Don't push things, baby," Griffin warned. "I'll still kill him."

Booker didn't look frightened in the least. "Yeah, yeah. Lay it on me. And don't leave anything out."

13

THIRTEEN

Booker and Griffin ultimately found common ground and started engaging in conversation. Within an hour, they were downright friendly and some of the additions Griffin made to Aisling's very long story were absolutely hilarious. Once she wrapped up, and Booker was convinced there was no more information to glean on the subject of Genevieve Toth, he invited Griffin to a nearby golf course ... and that's when the conversation truly got interesting.

"I don't think I should leave you." Griffin was adamant as he folded his arms over his chest and evenly met Aisling's gaze. "We're on our honeymoon. I'm pretty sure that means we're supposed to be fused together for the rest of the week."

Aisling made an exaggerated face. "You mean you want to babysit me."

"I don't believe that's what I said."

"It's what you mean, though." Aisling refused to back down. "You don't think I'm capable of taking care of myself."

"Don't do that." He extended a warning finger and wagged it in her face. "That won't work on me. I'm onto your tricks."

"What tricks?"

"You're trying to bully me into leaving you," Griffin replied, matter-of-fact. "The thing is, it won't work. We're on our honeymoon."

"Yes, but I hate golf."

"I don't have to golf."

"You love it. That's one of the few things you do with my father that he doesn't want to kill you over."

Griffin heaved out a sigh. "I'm not leaving you. I left you yesterday for a few hours and look what happened."

Aisling wasn't the type to admit defeat, even when caught. "That was a fluke. What are the odds I'm going to stumble over another body today?"

"Do you really want me to answer that question?"

"Just go." Aisling made a face. "I want you to have fun. My activity is limited thanks to your offspring taking over my body like the creature in *Alien,* so I think you should take Booker up on his offer."

Griffin's eye roll was exaggerated. "Listen here, missy ... ."

Aisling cut him off with a wave of her hand. "I want to talk to the girls," she said pointedly, gesturing toward Lilac and me. "I don't often get to hang around with women. You know I don't get along with any of the women at home. I want to take advantage of this situation until they realize they don't like me."

She was up to something. I couldn't quite identify what, but she was definitely up to something.

"I don't know." Griffin rubbed the back of his neck as his gaze bounced between faces. "What are you going to do today, Hadley?"

The question was a trap of sorts. I sensed it. "Well, I plan to get some iced tea here and then probably head back to the lighthouse to conduct a little research in my library. Aisling is welcome to come with me. She'll probably love the lighthouse. The view is breathtaking from the library."

"See." Aisling's smile was pretty, with just a hint of manipulation darkening the corners. "I'll be perfectly fine. You'll only be gone a few hours."

Griffin looked to Booker for confirmation. "Are you sure we can get on and off the course right away?"

"I know the woman who runs the course," Booker replied, his smile wide. "She thinks I smell like milk and cookies."

Griffin returned the smile, legitimately amused. "Okay. I'm going to hit the course and let you do ... your girl thing. You're right about not having female friends. You're overloaded with testosterone. Even your best friend is a man.

"That doesn't mean I believe you're going to behave," he continued, leaning forward and pinning her with a dark look. "If you act out and do something you're not supposed to do, I will punish you."

"You mean you're going to do something worse than forcing me to deliver a watermelon through my ... you know what?"

Griffin sighed. She was clearly using her fear of giving birth as a weapon. "Have fun." He forced a smile. "If you get in trouble, I'm calling your father. He's not afraid to yell at you."

"I won't get in trouble." Aisling's smile was sweet. "I give you my word."

Griffin gave her a kiss and hug, and went on his way. Booker gave me a wave and a whisper, explaining that I owed him for taking Griffin off our hands and he expected me to return the favor.

Once they were gone, Aisling waited five minutes before hopping to her feet. "Let's go."

"Where are we going?" I asked.

"We're going to the hotel they're building," she replied. "Odds are, that's where Jacob died." She pulled what looked to be a long flute-like device from her pocket. "My father sent a scepter. If we're lucky, he'll be at the hotel site and we can question him before absorbing him."

"Oh." That sounded like a good idea. "My golf cart is outside."

"Great." Aisling beamed. "I'm driving."

"Why do you get to drive?"

"Because I'm pregnant and it's going to hurt when I deliver."

"How long are you going to use that as an excuse to get whatever you want?"

"Until it stops working."

. . .

AISLING'S DRIVING SKILLS left a little (actually, a lot) to be desired. She had a lead foot and didn't care about sticking to paved surfaces. The highway between the lighthouse and the hotel wasn't busy, so she wasn't forced to pull to the side very often, but she swerved in and out of the dirt multiple times. She seemed to be having a good time, though, so I let it go.

When we parked at the new hotel site I was surprised to find at least thirty people working on the foundation — they were pouring concrete and taping off portions of the expansive basement to make sure nobody actually wandered into the wrong areas.

"Do you know these people?" Aisling asked.

I shook my head. "I'm new. I ... ." I broke off when I recognized one familiar face. We had met once. I questioned him after one of his workers broke into the lighthouse not long after I moved to the island. He seemed nice, bright and friendly. And he was our best shot. "I know him."

Aisling followed my gaze. "Great. Get him over here."

"He's working."

"Tell him I'm pregnant and the baby might fall out of me if I'm in the heat too long. Trust me. That will work. Men don't want to see a baby fall out of anywhere. It terrifies them."

She was something else. There was no doubt about that. I almost had to admire her manipulative mind. "That's kind of mean."

"Do men have to squeeze a watermelon out of their hoo-has?"

"No."

"That's what's really mean. Making men bend to my will isn't mean. It's ... necessary."

I realized I was bending to her will when I raised my hand and waved for Martin Gullikson to join us. If he was surprised to see me, he didn't show it. He merely smiled, returned the wave, and headed in our direction.

"You're kind of terrifying when you want to be," I noted, cringing when Aisling smiled.

"I'm an artist," Aisling explained. "I simply work with different ranges of being spoiled instead of oils."

"Good to know."

Martin was all smiles when he greeted me, offering a half-hug even though we weren't especially well acquainted. I was learning fast that Moonstone Bay was a small community where everyone knew everyone else's business. I either had to get used to it or leave ... and I had no intention of leaving.

"Hey, Martin." I hoped I sounded friendly rather than expectant. "This is Aisling Grimlock. We were just passing by when we saw the construction. We have a few questions."

"Questions?" Martin furrowed his brow. "I didn't realize you were in hotel management. I don't know if the staff for this place is already in place, but if you're interested, I can get you the owner's name."

I realized what he was referring to. "Oh, I'm not interested in hotel management. That's not what the questions are about."

"Oh." Martin was even more puzzled than when he started. "I guess I'm confused."

"Jacob Dorsey," Aisling interjected, refusing to pussyfoot around the topic at hand. "He was found on the docks, dead. We understand he was working out here at the time of his death."

"Ah." Martin nodded once and motioned to several plastic chairs placed under a large weeping willow. The spot was clearly a break location for some of the men, and I was eager to sit after the harrowing golf cart ride with Aisling behind the wheel.

"Can I offer you anything to drink?" Martin asked. "I only have water, but it's hot out here."

"Water is great," I said, bobbing my head. "Aisling is pregnant and needs to keep hydrated."

She shot me an unreadable look. I wasn't sure why she was so worked up. She's the one who wanted to use her pregnancy as a weapon. I was merely following her lead.

"You look great for a pregnant woman," Martin said as he handed her a bottle of water from the nearby cooler. "People say pregnant women are beautiful, and I happen to agree. You're glowing."

Aisling narrowed her eyes. "I'm also married."

I shot her a look and shook my head. "Ignore her. She's crabby after the drive." Keeping up with Aisling's moods was like dealing with a temperamental toddler. I couldn't help feeling a jab of sympathy for her poor father. He had to be a ragged man after dealing with her for almost thirty years. "We're more interested in Jacob. Is it possible he was killed out here?"

"Galen has already been out here asking about that," Martin volunteered. "He was out here yesterday, in fact."

Uh-oh. I could only hope Martin didn't call Galen to ask why I was asking questions about his investigation. "We're trying to track down information about the tiki masks in an effort to help," I explained. "Galen has a lot on his plate — what with two deaths now — and I'm trying to help in any way possible."

"I heard about the masks, but only vaguely." Martin screwed up his face in concentration as he thought. "Jacob was quiet, kept to himself. He was thrilled about the baby, and instead of staying here for lunch he headed home every day to check on Casey. He loved her more than anything, and they were so excited for that baby. It's sad that he never got a chance to meet the child he wanted so badly."

"It's terrible," I agreed, my heart rolling. "I can't imagine what poor Casey is going through."

"She's strong. She'll survive because she has to. And she'll take care of that baby, but it's not right that Jacob never got to see his own child. It breaks my heart."

"It breaks everyone's heart," Aisling said. "What about the people who used to own this land, though?" She had limited patience and was the type who pushed hard when she wanted something. "My understanding is that some sort of tribe lived out here and they didn't want to give up the land."

"The Maboli tribe. I don't think they're technically a tribe. They created their own ... community, I guess would be the right word ... about eight or ten years ago. It's hard to pin down. The members aren't ethnically related."

He was trying to explain something without coming right out and saying it. I hated that.

"I'm not sure I understand," I hedged.

"He's saying it's a cult," Aisling surmised, her head clearly busy as she pressed the sweating water bottle to her forehead. "He's basically saying a group of people came out to the beach, set up a commune, and then melted down when they were asked to move. Am I right?"

"I think you're breaking it down into simple terms when it's a complex issue, but you're essentially right."

Aisling nodded, tapping her bottom lip. "And where was this cult forced to move?"

"About five miles inland."

"Can you show us on a map?"

"I guess, but ... why? You shouldn't go out there. They've been angry ever since this development was approved. Locals are giving them a wide berth, and for good reason."

"Oh, we're not going to visit them," Aisling said, her smile firmly affixed. "We just want to know where they are so we can tell Galen."

Martin was confused. "I'm sure he knows."

"We want to make doubly sure. It's the baby that really wants the information," she added, causing me to widen my eyes. "The baby is worried ... which means I'm worried."

Even though Martin was clearly dubious, he readily agreed. "Of course. The baby knows best, right?"

"Absolutely."

THE GOLF CART needed gas, so I directed Aisling to Wesley's farm. It was the only location I knew in the area where we could fill up, and I wasn't surprised to find Wesley sitting on the front porch when we pulled into his driveway.

"Well, there she is." He beamed at me as he slowly got to his feet. "Who's your friend?"

"This is Aisling Grimlock." I stretched my muscles as I climbed out of the golf cart. The trip up the driveway had been dusty, and

Aisling, being a pedal-to-the-metal girl, kicked up even more dust than was necessary. "She's a reaper ... and she's on her honeymoon."

Wesley made an exaggerated show of checking the driveway behind us. "Where is her husband?"

"He's golfing with Booker."

"That doesn't make sense to me, but I'll let it go." Wesley shook his head as he gestured toward the front porch. "I'll get a pitcher of iced tea. Does anyone need anything else? Aisling?"

"I'm fine." Aisling swiped at the dust on her face, leaving a grimy streak as she smiled at my grandfather. "I love your place. I bet you don't get many visitors out here."

"Not many," Wesley agreed. "That's the reason I like it."

He was back in a few minutes, a pitcher and three glasses perched on a tray. Aisling was already sitting, opting for a spot in front of the box fan he had resting on the ground, and leaning back so she could stretch out her long legs.

"So, what are you girls doing with your afternoon?" He asked as he poured the iced tea. "Are you showing Aisling the sights?"

"We stopped by the new hotel construction site," I said. "We're looking for Jacob Dorsey."

Wesley stopped in mid-pour. "Jacob is dead."

"Yes, but his soul is still roaming around. Aisling's father sent her a ... what did you call it?"

"Scepter," Aisling supplied, eagerly taking the glass of iced tea and gulping half of it down before continuing. "It's to absorb souls. Your reaper is dead and was already dead before Jacob was killed. That means you have at least two souls running around that need to be reaped."

"Huh. I never really thought about that." Wesley was thoughtful as he met my gaze. "You went to the hotel site looking for Jacob? I'm guessing you didn't have any luck."

"He's not there," I replied. "Do you know anything about the Maboli tribe? Martin Gullikson mentioned it when we were out there. They sound like potential suspects in Jacob's death. Martin seemed nervous to talk too much about them, but I'm kind of intrigued. They don't sound like a tribe."

"That's because they're not a tribe." Wesley's voice took on a certain edge. "They're something else."

"I told you." Aisling crossed her legs at the ankles and allowed the fan to hit her full-on. "It's a cult, isn't it?"

Wesley sighed. "I don't know that I would use that word."

"What word would you use?"

"Cult. I don't want to make them sound interesting, though, because it's important you stay away from them. There's a reason they're segregated from the rest of the population."

"And what reason is that?" I asked, my stomach twisting at Wesley's look of consternation.

"They're dangerous. That's the reason it took so long to get them off the property in the first place. They were making threats against the DDA ... and any surveyors who went up to take a look at the property. They claimed they had divine rights to the property through the spirits ... it was a whole big thing."

"They sound like the types who would kill people and leave tiki masks on their bodies," Aisling noted. "I think they're exactly who we should be looking for."

"And I think you should mind your own business," Wesley fired back. "You need to behave yourselves and let the professionals handle this one. Galen knows what he's doing. Let him do his job and stay out of it."

Instead of capitulating, Aisling narrowed her eyes. "Have I mentioned that I'm pregnant? The baby doesn't like it when other people tell me what to do."

"Have I mentioned I didn't just fall off the turnip truck? I've dealt with pregnant women before. You can't pull that one on me."

I pressed my lips together, sensing a potential fight. Instead, after a moment's contemplation, Aisling merely shrugged.

"Fine. We won't visit the cult. I don't suppose your library has any research books we could check out? That's a way for us to look things up without finding trouble."

"Actually, it probably does." Wesley relaxed a bit, a smile creeping over his features. "I'm the first person who shut you down on the baby thing, aren't I?"

Aisling nodded without hesitation. "Don't worry. I'll be able to keep using it with my husband, father and brothers. You're simply an anomaly."

He chuckled. "I think I kind of like you, even though you drive like a maniac. Who taught you to drive a golf cart?"

"My father."

"He should have his license yanked."

"You're not the first person to say that. I'll make sure to bring it up next time I talk to him. It's always funny to watch steam come out of his ears."

"Yup. I definitely like you." Wesley's grin was wide when he glanced at me. "You attract weirdos, Hadley. Your grandmother was the same. You get that from her."

I had no idea if that was a good or bad thing, but I thanked him all the same. "Can we get gas before we leave? I need to make sure we make it back to town without incident."

"Absolutely. Help yourself. That's why I bought you the golf cart."

"It's the best gift ever," Aisling enthused, her smile widening. "I'm going to ask my father for a golf cart when I get home."

"Don't you live in the Motor City?"

"Yes. That doesn't mean I can't have a golf cart."

"Fair enough."

14

FOURTEEN

Aisling had a unique take on life.

Basically, it went something like this: Whatever she wanted to do, she did. Whatever she thought came spewing out of her mouth. Rules had no place in her world. Oh, and she was in charge no matter the fact that I'd been on the island longer.

Once Wesley warned us about visiting the Maboli tribe — or cult — I figured we would take a leisurely ride back to town and get some iced tea ... and maybe some ice cream.

Aisling had other plans.

"What are we doing here?" I hissed when she parked in the shade and climbed out of the golf cart.

"We're spying on the cult," she replied without hesitation, swiping the back of her hand over her forehead while grabbing a bottle of water from the cooler Wesley had supplied in an effort to make sure we were comfortable for the return to town. He might've found Aisling annoying, but part of her charmed him. I figured that had to be her super power.

"How do you even know if we're in the right place?" I asked, bewildered as I glanced around. "Wesley said it was out here, but he didn't say exactly where."

"You weren't listening," Aisling chided. "He said there were signs everywhere that the cult was taking over the valley."

"When did he say that?"

"When you were in the bathroom."

"But ... what signs are there that this is the spot?"

Aisling lifted her finger and pointed up, toward a sharp rock face. When I looked up, my mouth fell open as I saw what looked to be some sort of pictograph etched into the wall. It featured several rather crude figures engaged in sexual acts. And they looked to be wearing tiki masks.

"Huh." I tilted my head to the side as I regarded the images. "I don't think that's anatomically correct."

"You're looking at it the wrong way." Aisling moved my head to the other side. "See."

"Oh." My cheeks heated. "I don't think we should be here."

"Listen, whinebox, we're here and there's no harm looking around." Aisling was adamant. Her expression changed when something occurred to her. "You were the sort of kid who actually showed up for detention, weren't you?"

"I didn't get detention."

"Why not?"

"Because ... I simply didn't. Oh, don't look at me that way." Now it was my turn to make a face. "You think I was a goody-goody, but that's not true. My father was busy all the time. I didn't want to bother him because he didn't have my mother to help him. That doesn't make me a goody-goody."

Aisling was incredulous. "My parents had five children, and we were all animals, according to my father. We all got arrested. We all fought. Redmond used to grow pot in the basement and Braden accidentally brought a prostitute home when he was sixteen. It's not your job to make life easier for your father. It's your job to keep him on his toes."

"I think we grew up with very different fathers."

"Maybe. It's still not your job to live for him ... or Galen, for that matter. If you're worried he'll get angry, suck it up. It's clear he's head over heels for you. He won't suddenly change his mind because we did a little spying. You need to let worries like that go."

I opened my mouth to respond, but she was already moving. "Come on." She gestured for me to follow as she headed for a clump of trees. I'm dying to see if this is a freaky cult or a boring one."

"Are there boring cults?" I found I was hopeful as I followed her.

"I'm sure somewhere out there there's a cult that worships watermelons or something. I don't think this is going to turn out to be that sort of cult."

I studied the pictograph. "No. I don't think so either."

"HOLY WOW!"

Aisling seemingly had a nose for trouble. She tracked down the cult in ten minutes. We heard their voices before we saw their faces, and she drew me into a bower of trees before we were spotted.

"I know, right?" Aisling was as amused as me when she spotted the group. They were dressed in normal clothes, some more raggedy than others, and they all seemed to be wearing different color armbands. "I bet the armbands change color depending how high you make it into the organization."

That made sense. "There are more women than men."

"I think that's the standard for cults." Aisling furrowed her brow as she leaned to the right. "Look over there." She pointed toward what looked to be a rather ornate chair set apart from everybody else. It was in the shade, and the man who sat in it had long, dark hair that brushed his shoulders. He also had a beard shot through with more gray than black. "I bet he's king of the cult people."

I followed her finger and frowned at the man. Three women kneeled on the ground before him, as if in supplication. "Why do you think they're doing that?"

Aisling shrugged. "I think he's king, and women here are possessions."

"We don't know that," I stressed.

"No, but I think we have a good idea. The women outnumber the men at least three to one. I mean ... I guess it's possible there are more men and we can't see them because they're not here — maybe they have jobs or something — but that's not the feeling I get.

"Look at the guys," she continued, inclining her chin. "They're all more important than the women, but subservient to the big man on the throne. I wonder how he managed to work that. He doesn't seem to have security around, but the others essentially bow to him."

Now that she mentioned it, the chair he occupied did look like something of a throne. "How did you think they survive out here?" I was genuinely curious as I craned my neck to scan the acreage. "Do you see any buildings?"

"Huts."

"What?"

"Huts," Aisling repeated, shifting her finger. "They're hard to see, but if you look between the tree canopy in that direction you'll see about fifty huts."

I had to squint to make out what she was pointing toward, but sure enough, once my eyes adjusted, I saw the huts. "That's weird, right?"

"It's part of the show," Aisling replied, her eyes back on the leader. "I'm curious what they do out here, what their tenets are."

"What do you mean?"

"All cults have underlying tenets. Usually they're set up by charismatic men. That means women are subservient. It's not an overnight thing, though. The beliefs of the leader are slowly revealed over time. It's easier to get people to give an inch than a mile, so the leader nudges them along inch by inch until they accept him as a true leader, a prophet who sees more than anyone else.

"From the outside looking in, that person would appear crazy to almost everybody," she continued, licking her lips. "What most people don't understand is that the cult members have been conditioned for an extended period of time and that they didn't suddenly turn crazy overnight."

"So we have to figure out what this cult believes," I mused, dragging a hand through my hair. "I don't think they're simply going to tell us."

"No," Aisling agreed. "I ... ." She broke off, a horrified expression flitting across her face as a new noise filled the air.

"What is that?" I was alarmed when I shifted, my eyes immediately falling on a struggling pig that was being led from the forest. I had a very bad feeling about what was to become of it. "Maybe we should get out of here."

The disgusted look on Aisling's face told me she felt the same. "I don't want to know what they're going to do to that pig."

I didn't either. In fact ... . I stopped myself from fleeing the area at a dead run and focused on the leather leash they had affixed to the pig. They were dragging the poor animal toward the middle of a circle that was created when some of the women started dancing.

"They're going to sacrifice it," Aisling hissed, grabbing my arm. "I can't see that. It will make me sick ... or angry. You wouldn't like me when I'm angry."

"Okay. I just ... hold on." I wasn't an expert at magic by any stretch of the imagination. Still, I had it at my disposal. It was there, and I was desperate to trip over something that would help me aid the pig. I couldn't stand the idea of it being slaughtered as part of some perverse ritual.

And, yes, I eat meat, so I'm something of a hypocrite. Seeing it slaughtered is something else entirely.

I closed my eyes, exhaled heavily, and searched for a wisp of the magic I knew was there. Galen had helped me access it the first time I purposely tried to use it. We created a water spout ... and then I passed out. It was kind of a sensual evening. The few times I'd been able to use my powers since then had been a little different, but I knew the magic was there.

"What's that?" Aisling's voice was barely a whisper when she realized what I was trying to attempt.

"I just need to ... ." I pushed with everything I had, sending out a sharp tendril of fire that flew the distance between the pig and me.

The magic slammed into the leash tethering the animal, and the second the pig realized it was free it took off.

The cult members took a moment to realize what was happening, and then started exclaiming at once. Two men immediately gave chase, but the pig had a head start and wasn't about to lose its chance for escape.

The man on the throne started barking orders to the women, who scattered after the men, and then he very slowly shifted his eyes over the trees until they landed on us. My heart rolled when we locked gazes and I slowly got to my feet.

"We really need to get out of here," I said as I wiped my sweaty palms against the front of my pants.

Aisling's gaze was withering. "Oh, you think?" She leaned over and scooped up a huge rock.

"What are you doing?" I was understandably confused. "You're not going to throw that at the pig, are you?"

"No, I'm going to throw it at the guys heading in our direction."

"What guys?" The question was barely out of my mouth before I heard a noise behind me. I turned to find two huge men pushing through the trees. They'd obviously seen us and were on their way to collect us.

There was no way I could allow that to happen. "Move!" I attempted to prod Aisling to start running, but she had other plans. She firmly planted her feet, drew back her arm, and let the large rock fly. It hit the first man square in the middle of the forehead.

His eyes widened at the impact and he dropped like a stone. The second man was caught in a moment of confusion, and that's when Aisling grabbed my arm and tugged.

"Now we need to run," she hissed.

I couldn't agree more and scrambled after her.

"Don't look back," she ordered. "Whatever you do, don't look back."

WE MADE IT BACK to the golf cart without incident, and I didn't put up a protest when Aisling jumped into the driver's seat. That lead foot of hers was going to come in handy.

"Head back to Wesley's," I ordered when we hit the road. "He's closest, and they won't dare attack on his property."

Aisling absently nodded as she glanced over her shoulder, her eyes going grim. "We have company."

I turned to stare and my stomach threatened to revolt when I realized that several men were following us on scooters.

"What are we going to do?"

Aisling didn't look nearly as worried as I felt. "What other magic tricks do you have up your sleeve?"

"I don't know. I didn't even know I had that one until I tried. I'm new at this."

"Well, do you think you can try something on our friends back there?"

She was calm but I knew she was just as worried as I was. "I can try."

"Good. I suggest trying something with fire."

"Why?"

"Everyone is afraid of fire."

She had a point. I screwed my eyes shut, rubbed my hands over them, and focused on my breathing.

In and out.

In and out.

There was a spark.

I saw it out of the corner of my eye, a little orange ember.

I breathed again and the spark grew.

I continued the process until the ember was almost as big as my head. Then I debated how to deliver it.

"Now!" Aisling snapped, causing me to lose control. The firebomb I was building rushed out and careened toward the men, who were gaining on us. I had a brief moment to marvel at the size of the magical burst before it slammed into the road between two of the riders, causing them to veer off into the trees.

"Very good," Aisling approved, tugging the steering wheel to the left. We were at Wesley's driveway. She remembered the route — which was fairly impressive given the circumstances — and I was so relieved when I saw the house appear on the skyline that I almost cried.

The feeling didn't last long, because the second thing I saw when we crested the hill was Galen's truck. He stood next to the porch talking to Wesley, and his eyes went to the size of saucers when he realized we were tearing up the driveway ... with several scooters giving chase.

We skidded to a stop, allowing him and Wesley to stalk in our direction. When the scooters caught up, Galen turned his attention to the drivers and positioned himself between them and us.

Galen greeted the leader, who had somehow jumped on a scooter and managed to catch up, with a nod as he planted his hands on his hips. "Taurus. Is something wrong?"

"Taurus? Like the bull in astrology?" Aisling scoffed. "That is so lame."

Taurus openly glared at her. "These ... women ... crossed the boundaries and stole our sacrifice."

"Oh, yeah?" Galen cocked an eyebrow. "What boundaries? You don't own any land. Last time I checked, you were squatting on government land. So, technically, they weren't on your land."

"The gods gave me that land," Taurus challenged. "You can't take it back."

"The DDA allows you to live on that land because it's not being used for anything else right now," Galen clarified, refusing to back down despite the dark looks the other riders gave him. "You don't own that land. If you try to hurt people who visit the land — which is allowed — I'll be forced to intervene and remove you. Is that what you want?"

"The gods won't smile on your efforts," Taurus replied. "They'll punish you."

"Oh, what a load of hogwash." Aisling shook her head. "I don't know how you managed to convince people to follow you, but you're a nutball. We saw what you were going to do to that pig, which makes you a sick nutball."

Galen slid his eyes to me. "What pig?"

"The tribute," Taurus spat. "They used magic to free it."

"You used magic to save a pig?" Galen's expression was unreadable, but I was almost certain I saw the hint of a smile.

I nodded. "I couldn't watch it die."

"She also tried to blow us off the road," Taurus added. "The gods won't smile upon that either."

"Oh, shut up, freakazoid," Aisling ordered, shaking her head. "We know exactly what you're doing out there, you pervert. There's a reason the women vastly outnumber the men. Although, now that I think about it, where are the kids? If there's a bunch of fornicating going on out there — which is obviously the number one thing on your mind — what happened to the kids?"

Galen's eyes briefly locked with mine. "That's a good question, Taurus. I know you're supposed to have a few kids living out there. Where are they?"

"They're not present for the rituals," Taurus replied, disdain practically dripping from his tongue. "They're all alive and accounted for, Sheriff Blackwood. You don't have to worry about that."

"Perhaps I'll stop by tomorrow and check, just to be on the safe side," Galen suggested.

Taurus didn't as much as flinch. "That's certainly your prerogative. I'm assuming you'll stop by after these two are punished."

"And what should I punish them for?"

"Trespassing."

"We already covered that. They weren't trespassing."

"One of them threw fireballs at us on the road," Taurus snapped.

"Really?" Galen's eyes locked with mine. "Is that true?"

"They were chasing us," I explained. "We thought they were going to hurt us."

"I've got this." Aisling held up her hands and strolled to a spot several feet in front of Taurus, her expression challenging. "Prove we threw fireballs at you."

"Excuse me?" Taurus's eyebrows winged up. "We saw them."

"Do you have proof of these alleged fireballs?"

"Of course not. But we saw them."

"That means it's your word against ours. You'll have to come back with more proof if you expect us to be arrested."

"Who said anything about arresting anyone?" Galen challenged.

Aisling ignored him. "Until then ... toodles." She offered Taurus a small wave that was meant to antagonize. "See ya, wouldn't want to be ya."

Galen sighed as he pressed the heel of his hand to his forehead. "I don't understand how she hasn't pissed off the wrong person and gotten herself killed yet."

I didn't understand that either.

"She's going to give me an ulcer," he muttered, shaking his head.

I graced him with a wan smile. "The good news is that we're okay. That's the most important thing."

"You're still in trouble."

Rats. I should've seen that coming. "You know, this is not my fault."

"That's starting to be your refrain. You're still in trouble."

15

FIFTEEN

Galen's fury once the tribe members left was something to behold.

He started out by pacing, gesturing wildly as he muttered to himself. Eventually that turned into barking out short, pithy sentences. Finally he started ranting ... and that's when I grew incredibly uncomfortable.

"I don't know what you were thinking," he complained, hands fisted at his sides as he walked back and forth. "I simply don't understand it. I mean ... what is wrong with you?"

I realized he was staring at Aisling when he asked the question, which made me feel guilty. "I was in on it, too," I offered lamely.

"Oh, I know." His tone was grave. "But something tells me she instigated this little outing."

Instead of being upset, or reacting out of contrition or fear, Aisling merely accepted the bottle of water Wesley supplied and propped her feet up in the shade of his front porch. She didn't appear remotely sorry for what transpired, which was fairly impressive given Galen's righteous anger.

"Aisling just wanted to see the tribe," I offered. "She thought it would be a learning experience."

"She wanted to stick her nose into an investigation she has nothing to do with," Galen corrected. "She's a busybody."

"You say that like it's a bad thing," Aisling drawled, earning a sidelong look from Wesley, who clearly found her amusing.

"It is a bad thing!"

"From where I'm sitting it's a good thing," she countered. "Now you know exactly who you're dealing with. And, if you have any questions, I can say without reservation that they're psychos. They were going to kill a pig until Hadley let loose some of her mojo and freed it. That was impressive, by the way. Although not nearly as impressive as that ball of fire thing you did on the road."

"Now we're talking." Galen arched an eyebrow as he pushed some of my wayward hair from my face. "Your creepy new friends mentioned it, too. I'm dying to hear about this ball of fire."

"I don't know how to explain it," I shrugged. "It just sort of happened. They had scooters that were faster than my golf cart, and Aisling suggested I try magic. I'm still not sure how it happened."

He stroked his hand down the back of my head and flashed a smile. It wasn't one of his "make my stomach go gooey" smiles, but it was legitimate all the same. "That's pretty impressive. I'm proud of you."

"Really?" I went warm all over, which was mortifying. "Well, thanks."

"I'm still angry," Galen said, giving the ends of my hair a light tug to get my attention. It didn't hurt, but his eyes were serious. "You could've been hurt, Hadley. Do you have any idea what that tribe is capable of?"

"No. Do you?"

"Actually, no one knows much about them." Galen heaved a sigh as he moved to the porch, giving Aisling a wide berth as he grabbed one of the bottles of water Wesley supplied. "Their origins are ... murky."

I took a bottle of water and cracked it open, drinking a third of it before continuing. "Do you know what's going on up there? We only watched them for a little bit, but I can tell you it's creepy."

"Speaking of that ... ." Galen trailed off and focused on Aisling.

"What?" She held her hands palms out and shrugged.

"Booker is bringing your husband out here. I called Wesley when I couldn't find Hadley in town. He told me what was going on. I called Griffin, who happens to be with Booker, before leaving. They're on their way."

Aisling scowled. "Thank you, Sheriff Tattletale."

"If you think that bothers me, think again. I have no problem being a tattletale."

"You wouldn't have survived five minutes in my family," Aisling grumbled, shaking her head. "Rats were locked in the basement ... with the snakes."

"I'm sure that means something to you, but it means absolutely nothing to me."

"It means ... ." Aisling must have realized she was about to go off on a tangent because she caught herself and shook her head. "It doesn't matter. Griffin will yell for five minutes and get over it. It's fine."

"He seemed pretty angry to me."

"Yes, but I've got an ace in the hole ... almost literally."

"And what's that?"

Aisling gestured toward her stomach. "I'm carrying his baby. He turned me into a human incubator before my wedding. He'll let me slide."

"I don't think you're that charming."

"Care to place a wager on it?"

"Absolutely." Galen nodded his head without hesitation. "If I win and you're in trouble, then you have to stop roping Hadley into your crazy schemes."

I balked. "Hey. I wasn't roped in. We went to the site of the new hotel, looked for Jacob's soul, and then Aisling suggested we see if we could track down the tribe. It was harmless. She couldn't possibly know it would go the way it did."

"And I think you're making excuses because you find her entertaining," Galen shot back. "That tribe is not to be trifled with. There are horror stories about them."

"I want to hear those horror stories." Aisling leaned forward. "Seriously. Do they involve ritual sacrifice and sex games?"

Galen narrowed his eyes. Even though he found Aisling beyond annoying, he was clearly intrigued by her words. "What did you see out there? That was going to be my question before we got derailed by a bet we didn't finish."

"Oh, you're such a whiner." Aisling made a face as Wesley snickered into his water bottle. "If I get in trouble I won't tap Hadley for any more adventures."

"Thank you."

I was about to ask where my desires fit into the equation, but Aisling barreled forward.

"If I win, you have to back off and stop acting like a teenaged girl who just missed curfew," she said. "Hadley is an adult and can make her own decisions."

"I was just going to say that," I pointed out. "You can't control my actions, Galen. I wanted to go with her."

He stared at me for a long beat. "I still want to beat her."

I couldn't contain my laughter. "Fair enough."

Aisling didn't act bothered by his tone. "You won't beat me. Trust me. I know what I'm doing. As for what we saw up there, it was odd. We saw only two or three men and then that Taurus guy. That's not his real name, right?"

"His real name is Barry Wentworth," Galen replied, drawing me into the shade so I could sit between him and Aisling. "He grew up on the island. In fact, he was ahead of Booker and me in school. He was a senior when we were sophomores, and even then he showed cult leader tendencies."

"He clearly has that charisma thing going for him," Aisling agreed. "Most cult leaders have enough charisma that they convince their followers that they're geniuses. I'm sure your buddy Taurus did that. When did he change his name?"

"You seem awfully interested," Galen noted. "Why? What do you know about cults?"

"I don't know if you would call it a cult, but when my mother came back she amassed an army of wraiths and rogue reapers to help her." Aisling was calm as she wiped the palms of her hands against her knees. "I started learning things about behavior even if I wasn't in the mood for a lesson. I understand about warning signs."

Galen furrowed his brow. "Hadley told me about your mother, and I read a little bit about it in the file I requested on you from the reaper council."

"You requested a file on me?" Aisling's eyes flashed with annoyance. "Why?"

"I wanted to make sure you weren't a suspect."

"Oh, whatever!" She waved her hand and flicked her eyes to the driveway at the sound of a vehicle. Booker's ancient van sped into view, and the nerve that worked in Aisling's jaw told me she was preparing for another round of fighting. "You knew I wasn't a suspect in Dorsey's death. You're just as much of a busybody as me."

"I most certainly am not."

"Yeah, yeah." Aisling slowly got to her feet as Griffin jumped out of the passenger side of the van. His brown hair was tousled — my guess was from the multiple times he swiped his hands through his hair during the ride — and he looked frustrated as he strolled toward the porch.

"Are you okay?" He pulled Aisling in for an extended hug before releasing her. He didn't sound angry as much as relieved. Of course, the anger could very well be a secondary emotion and the explosion might still be coming.

"I'm fine." Aisling flashed a tight smile. "Whatever stories you've heard have been exaggerated."

"I only know that you were missing." Griffin moved his hands up and down her slim back as he rubbed his cheek against her face. "I figured you were out for a ride on the golf cart because you seem to love that thing so much."

"I do! I'm making Dad buy me one when we get home."

"And where will you drive it?"

"I'll figure out a place."

"Well, there are worse things for your father to spend his money on." Griffin pressed a kiss to her forehead. "I'm glad you were just out here for a visit. Next time, though, text me."

"Okay." Aisling beamed as she stared into his eyes. It was a nice moment ... which Galen ruined by clearing his throat and tapping his fingers on the table.

"I think you're leaving some vital information out of your story, Aisling," he drawled. "Would you like to tell Griffin what you were really doing, or shall I?"

Griffin's eyes darkened. "Do I even want to know?"

"Probably not," Aisling replied, tugging him toward the table so she could reclaim her chair. "You'll be forced to listen to what I'm sure will be an exaggerated story by King Tattletale, though, so you might as well make yourself comfortable."

After a brief introduction to Wesley, Galen launched into his tale. When he was done, he watched Griffin closely for a reaction. He was expecting one thing and Aisling another, and he was clearly desperate to beat her at her own game. Instead of yelling at Aisling — or forgiving her — Griffin focused on me.

"You can make fireballs with your mind?"

My cheeks flooded with warmth. "I guess. Today was the first time I tried."

"That's neat. I'm glad Aisling can't do that. Her temper would turn her into the kid from *Firestarter* and I would eventually have to arrest her. It's cool that you can do it, though."

"That's all you're going to say?" Galen's frustration came out to play. "She spied on a dangerous cult."

"That's hardly the most dangerous thing she's done this month," Griffin countered, collecting Aisling's hand and pressing it to his chest as he grinned at her. "In fact, compared to what went down two days before our wedding she's being downright angelic."

"Oh, good grief." Galen made an exaggerated face as Aisling preened. She graced her husband with a soft smile before flicking a triumphant look toward Galen. She waited a few seconds, until her silent gloating was complete, and then turned serious.

"You were about to tell us about the cult," she prodded. "I want to hear about them. You said the leader was in school with you and the guy who smells like tomato juice."

Booker shook his head. "Pregnancy hormones must be making you want wacky things, huh?"

"No. I love tomato juice year round."

"You're a weird woman."

"And you sit over there," Griffin warned, pointing toward the opposite side of the table. "We may be golfing buddies, but she's still my wife."

"Whatever." Booker rubbed his forehead as he sat between Galen and Wesley. "You guys fought with Barry? That was probably not a smart move. That guy has always been crazy."

"He definitely has," Galen agreed. "He wasn't normal when we were in school. As I was telling you, we were several years behind him, but even then you could see the way he herded people."

"Herded?" Griffin cocked an intrigued eyebrow. "That's an interesting way to put it."

"I don't know how else to explain it," Galen said. "He managed to convince people to essentially worship him, even in high school. He had a whole harem of girls chasing him around."

"Was he spouting this tribe nonsense back then?" Aisling asked, practically purring when Griffin started massaging her shoulders. "Right there, baby. You're the best husband in the world."

Griffin smiled indulgently. "I'm glad you finally acknowledged it."

Galen's expression reflected overt annoyance, causing me to pat his knee under the table. When his gaze slid to mine, his expression softened, though only marginally. "I don't know how to explain the things Barry did when we were in school. To my knowledge, he was a garden variety shifter and nothing more."

"A bull shifter?" Aisling asked, legitimately curious.

"Actually, he can shift into any animal he wants. He can't turn into other humans – which is a unique gift – but he's not hampered otherwise. He usually chooses a bull. Why?"

"His name. Taurus is the bull in astrology. That means he's known for being reliable, practical, ambitious and sensual."

Galen snorted. "You don't believe in astrology, do you?"

"Do I personally believe in astrology? I don't know." Aisling was matter-of-fact. "I think the question is, does Barry believe in astrology? My guess is yes."

"I guess that's a fair point," Galen hedged. "What else do you know about Tauruses?"

"I know a lot, because my best friend Jerry happens to love astrology."

"Love it," Griffin echoed. "It's ridiculous how much he knows about everyone's astrological signs."

"He imparts his wisdom to me all the time," Aisling added. "One of my brothers is a Taurus, so I've heard Jerry recite the information numerous times. Tauruses are patient and persistent. I'm guessing those are necessary traits for a cult leader."

"He calls himself a tribal chief," Galen corrected. "You have to be careful how you refer to things around him. He doesn't take it well if you use the C-word."

"Well, I don't think he's going to take it well if he sees me again regardless," Aisling said. "As for Tauruses, they're also stubborn, self-indulgent, lazy, materialistic and possessive. I think all those things play into being a cult leader."

"What did you see out there?" Galen asked, his eyes on me. "I need specifics."

"Not much," I replied. "We found a spot on top of a hill and hid in some trees. At first we heard tribal music, some drums and a thrumming island beat. Then we saw people. They were dressed normally, but they all seemed to be wearing armbands."

"I think the armbands signify what level they're on," Aisling offered. "I know a thing or two about cults — mostly because I watch a lot of television — and the way a leader exerts control is by creating a caste system. The women far outnumber the men, by the way. We barely saw any men until it came time to run."

"Looks can be deceiving," Galen intoned. "There are definitely men out there. How many, I can't say. Barry recruited both men and women. The men he went after were strong ... and most of them were struggling with substance abuse problems. He offered them a way to detox if they pledged their support."

"Detox?" I absently scratched my cheek, considering. "How did that work?"

"My understanding is that he locked his recruits in one of those huts they've built out there, surrounded it with followers so there was no getting away, and conducted a forced detox. The participants were so strung out by the end they thought he was a god and agreed to stay with him."

"How many people does he have out there?" Griffin asked.

"I have no idea. That's the problem. No one has ever come back, and we can't watch them closely enough to get a proper number."

"Wait ... no one has ever come back?" That didn't sound right. "Even cults don't have complete loyalty. Someone must have defected."

"Not that I'm aware of."

"That means that if someone tried to leave, he or she was probably stopped before they could make their escape," Griffin noted. "Do you have any missing people that you can tie to that group?"

"Loads," Galen confirmed. "At least thirty. We have no proof, though, and more than once Barry has produced the person we thought was missing when we went out to check on the group. I think there are certainly some people no longer with them, but my hands are tied for procedural reasons. We can't do anything without proof."

"So, what do we do?" I asked.

"We don't do anything." Galen's voice grew stern. "You need to stop poking your nose into this before things get dangerous. Do you understand?"

He sounded as if he meant business. Of course, he was my

boyfriend, not my keeper. "You lost the bet," I reminded him. "I don't really have to stop doing anything."

His expression darkened. "Don't push me."

"I was just going to say the same thing to you. I'm an adult. I'm able to make my own decisions."

Galen didn't immediately respond, which allowed Aisling time to stand and dust off her hands.

"Well, my work here is done." Her grin was broad. "We need to head back to the hotel so I can shower. I've had a long and dusty day."

"Okay." Griffin stood, along with Booker. "I'm sure we'll see you guys later."

Galen didn't look at him because he was focused on me. "You can count on it."

"Great. Um ... we'll see you later."

"Good luck, Hadley," Aisling called out. "Just remind him that you hold the keys to his sexual happiness now and it would be better for all concerned if he just rolled over and showed you his belly."

I pressed my lips together to keep from laughing at Galen's furious face.

"You told her?" He scowled. "We seriously need to talk."

"I think we do," Wesley agreed, his gaze equally dark as he leveled it on Galen. "We definitely need to have a talk about your intentions regarding my granddaughter. I didn't bring it up over breakfast, but I'm bringing it up now. I have some questions."

Wow! And here I thought this day couldn't get any worse.

16

SIXTEEN

I drove the golf cart back to the lighthouse, Galen following behind. He was still angry, but was doing his best to contain his emotions. He pulled into my driveway after me, watched as I hopped out of the cart and waited for me to walk to him.

If he wanted to be stubborn I could play that game as well as anyone. In hindsight, I understood Aisling and I probably did a dumb thing. I decided to offer him an olive branch of sorts. I trudged to the driver's side window, which he'd lowered, and adopted my best "we made things official last night so you have to forgive me" smile.

"You're not coming inside?"

"I have work to finish," he replied, his expression unreadable. "I was in the middle of paperwork when I rushed out to Wesley's place."

"Oh, well ... thanks for coming to my rescue. It was much appreciated."

His eyes flashed. "Don't take that tone with me." He extended a finger. "I have a right to be angry."

"Did I say otherwise?"

"No, but you're giving me *the look*."

"I have no idea what look you're talking about."

"Yes, you do." He exhaled heavily and shook his head. "You could've been hurt, Hadley. We have no idea what those people are capable of. Don't you understand that I would be very upset if something happened to you?"

My heart rolled at the admission. "I'm sorry." I mostly meant it. "I didn't mean to upset you. It's just ... I get carried away sometimes. Aisling has all this energy and she does whatever she wants. I like that about her."

"Aisling definitely does what she wants." His lips curved down. "She also has a very strong support system, including four brothers and a father who have bailed her out her entire life. She has a false sense of security that doesn't work here because she has no brothers or overprotective father to swoop in here."

"I still like her."

"I know you do. The thing is ... I happen to like you. Like ... a lot. I don't want you getting hurt. I can't take that."

"I'll do better." At least I hoped that was true. "It seemed like a good idea at the time. That's the only excuse I have."

"Well, it wasn't a good idea."

"No." I was sheepish. "I guess not."

"Still, you handled yourself well ... and even saved a pig." He was cracking a smile when I risked a glance at him. "You're strong, Hadley. Really strong. But you don't know everything, and what happened today could've gotten away from you."

I recognized the wisdom behind his words. "I guess I didn't realize exactly what was going on out there. How was I supposed to know that they were sacrificing animals?"

"You could've asked."

"Next time."

"Next time?" He shook his head and drew a deep breath. "I don't want to fight, but I'm not completely ready to make up either. I have to get back to work."

"Okay." I deflated a bit. "Will I see you later?"

"Yes."

I shouldn't have been as thrilled by his immediate answer as I was. I simply couldn't contain myself. "Great."

"We have an outing," he cautioned. "They're having a fundraiser for Casey at Lilac's bar ... to help pay for the funeral and get her some extra money for baby expenses going forward. I have to go, and I expect you to be my date."

"I want to help Casey ... especially since I made that crack about her being your ex-girlfriend."

"Then I will pick you up at six."

"Okay." I watched him for a beat. He didn't put the truck into reverse and pull out, but he didn't lean close to kiss me either. He simply sat there. "So ... um ... is there something else?"

"I don't know. Is there?"

Ah, well, crap. He expected me to make the first move. I hated that. "I guess there is." I rolled to the balls of my feet, leaned through the window and pressed a firm kiss to the corner of his mouth. "You won't stay angry very long, will you?"

His expression turned rueful. "Probably not, but I plan to hold out for at least another few hours."

"Fair enough." I stepped back and waved. "I'll see you later, Sheriff Blackwood." I added a wink and swing to my hips just because I could.

He sighed. "You're going to be the death of me. I can feel it."

"What a way to go, huh?"

I WASN'T SURE what to expect from a fundraiser — especially one under such somber circumstances — so I opted for a plain spaghetti strap dress in a muted blue and a matching pair of sandals. By the time Galen picked me up, I was officially nervous. I didn't know the people of Moonstone Bay all that well.

"What should I expect?" I waited to ask the question until we'd parked close to Lilac's bar and Galen was helping me out of his truck.

"From what?" he asked, confused.

"From this." I gestured toward the bar. It was early, but given the people milling about outside I was convinced it was already packed. "What are we supposed to do?"

"It's just a fundraiser. Lilac donated the food and liquor. We'll pay for tickets when we go inside. Then we eat, drink and converse with others. It's not a big deal."

"I've never been to a funeral fundraiser. That's not exactly how we do things in Michigan."

"Ah, well ... don't act like a ninny and you'll probably be okay."

I was affronted. "I never act like a ninny."

"Not often, but it all depends on your buddy."

"Which buddy? Lilac? She doesn't act like a ninny either."

"I was talking about your reaper buddy."

"Why would she be here?"

"I don't know, but she's headed in this direction." He pointed toward a familiar couple on the opposite side of the road. Aisling wore a purple dress that matched her eyes, and Griffin had a firm hold on her hand as they waited for the light to change so they could cross. There was next to no traffic on the island, so I never understood the crosswalks. People obeyed them, though, so I followed suit.

"Hey, guys." Aisling was all smiles as she neared. She seemed to be in a good mood. She'd clearly showered because all the dirt and grime from our earlier adventure was absent from her features.

"Hey. What are you guys doing here?"

"We saw fliers for the event in the hotel lobby," Griffin volunteered, transferring his hand to the small of Aisling's back. "We thought we should put in an appearance."

"You didn't know the victim," Galen pointed out.

"No, but I feel as if I know him," Aisling replied. "Besides, his soul might show up here. I have my scepter in my purse. I wasn't kidding about the ramifications if his soul runs around too long unattended. His wife is supposed to be here, so I figure there's a good chance he'll show up."

"And what will happen if he does?" I asked. "How will you absorb him without anyone noticing?"

"I'm sure I'll figure something out. The island is full of mostly paranormal beings, so I'm not sure about the rules on secrecy. Did your former reaper work in front of an audience?"

"I rarely saw Adam," Galen replied. "I don't recall ever watching him absorb a soul, but I guess it's possible."

"Yes, well, his soul is out here, too, at least probably," Aisling said. "I have no idea if the rules are the same for a reaper who dies – you know, the going crazy thing – but we should probably try to find him, too."

"I believe that's your job," Galen argued.

"I'm on my honeymoon. I don't have a job. I'm trying to help because I'm benevolent of heart and mind. I can stop trying to help if you're so inclined."

Galen's smile was back as he gripped my hand tightly. "I don't understand how anyone puts up with you." He looked to Griffin for insight. "Seriously, how have you not killed her?"

Griffin was blasé. "She has some very attractive qualities."

"You realize you're looking at her legs when you say that, right?" Galen barked.

"I love the whole package." Griffin prodded Aisling in front of him and lowered his voice. "If you keep pushing her the way you are, she'll fly off the handle. I happen to like you, but if that happens you're on your own."

"I'm not afraid of her," Galen scoffed.

"You should be."

EVEN THOUGH THEY WEREN'T locals, Griffin and Aisling fit in seamlessly with the Moonstone Bay crowd. I felt a pang of jealousy at the way she chatted with two men I'd never met. She seemed friendly, as if she'd known them her whole life, and I was frustrated because I was still so nervous around the paranormal crowd.

"You need to relax," Booker advised as he moved up beside me, a plate of appetizers in his hand. "People can sense the tension rolling off you from across the room."

That sounded unlikely. "I'm not tense." I smoothed my dress and fussed with my hair. "What? I'm not."

"You're afraid the people on the island won't accept you, but that's not true. You're May's granddaughter. You're accepted on those grounds alone. If you want to make friends, you have to loosen up."

"I'm plenty loose."

"That's the word on the street." He gave me a saucy wink to let me know he was kidding. "Look at your friend Aisling." He inclined his head toward the center of the room. "She doesn't know anyone and she's the life of the party."

"I know. I'm jealous."

He snickered. "Look more closely. She only plays well with men. Do you see any women around her?"

I hadn't even considered that. "I guess not."

"That's because the other women don't like her." He gestured toward the far corner, where a group of Moonstone Bay's finest gossips had their heads bent together. They occasionally cast a look in Aisling's direction, and I was sure they were talking about her. "Aisling feels more comfortable with men. That's probably because she was raised in a house full of them."

"Her best friend is a man, too. She mentioned it earlier today. Jerry."

"I don't see how her husband puts up with a male best friend, but he seems as enamored with her as everyone else."

"Yeah." I smiled as Griffin watched his wife wow the room. "What do you think she's doing over there? She never struck me as the life of the party, and yet she seems to be having a great time."

"She's looking for information on Jacob, trying to figure out where his soul might be. It's obvious she's trying to steer the conversation toward Jacob. She's very good at manipulating people. I have to hand it to her. They have no idea what she's doing."

"Yeah, well, I guess I should walk around and mingle."

"Relax," Booker ordered. "You're already one of us, whether you realize it or not."

. . .

I SPENT THE NEXT HOUR chatting with a variety of people. Even though I felt self-conscious, no one treated me as if I were an outsider. The more people I talked to, the more comfortable I became. I was feeling pretty good about myself when I happened to stop by the appetizer table and noticed Griffin and Galen talking on the other side. They hadn't noticed me – and I was curious – so I decided to listen. In a casual and unobtrusive way, of course.

"Where's your lovely wife?" Galen drawled.

"Hanging out with the members of Jacob's construction crew. She's trying to get leads on where we might be able to track down Jacob's soul."

"She seems awfully dedicated for a woman who is supposed to be on vacation."

"No, it's not that. She knows what can happen to a soul that's not treated properly. She saw it happen to her mother. She wants to help if she can."

"What's the deal with her mother?" Galen lowered his voice. "I've heard you mention her a few times. That sounds like an ugly business."

"It was. I don't want to spend a lot of time talking about it because it makes me upset — and she's nowhere near over it — but suffice to say she understands about souls, and what happens if they're fragmented. Her mother's soul split when she died the first time. The pure half, the part that was really her mother, moved on. What remained behind had her mother's memories but none of the emotions that should've been there."

My heart rolled at the thought. Aisling made jokes about her mother, the occasional crack about a tortured soul, but she never delved into the deep stuff. I was starting to understand why.

"I'm sorry for that. How did the rest of the family take it?"

"Aisling knew when she came back that she wasn't right. She tried to work around it for her brothers' sake, but she couldn't accept what she was being told. In the end, she had a choice to make: save one of her brothers — the one who gives her nothing but grief — or save the shell of her mother."

"I'm guessing she saved the brother."

"Yes, and he's still not over it either. He was the one closest with their mother. He's trying to accept everything that happened, but it's hard on all of them. The honeymoon couldn't have come at a better time. I want Aisling to deal with her emotions about what happened away from her brothers and father. She should have a chance to feel what she wants to feel without them influencing her."

"And what does she feel?"

"Sadness ... and relief."

"Is that why you let her get away with murder?" Galen sounded legitimately curious. "I mean ... I don't want to tell you your business, man, but you need to put your foot down with that woman. She wears trouble like other women do earrings."

Griffin chuckled. "You have no idea."

"And yet you seem fine with it."

"I don't know that 'fine' is the word," he countered, shifting from one foot to the other. "She is who she is and I wouldn't trade her for anything. I fell in love with her because of who she is. I don't want to change her now that we're married."

"She's pregnant," Galen reminded him. "If she gets hurt ... or falls down a hill ... or gets in a golf cart accident, she could lose the baby. Is that what you want?"

"Of course not." Griffin's gaze darkened. "I don't ever want her in danger, but she finds trouble. I can't change that. If I try, I'll become bitter and then I'll turn on her. It will destroy our marriage.

"I fell in love with a strong woman," he continued. "So did you. No, don't bother denying it. I see the way you look at Hadley. You might not quite be to the 'love' part of your relationship, but you're well on your way.

"She's strong, too," he said. "Sure, she's a little unsure right now. Aisling says it's because she recently discovered she was a witch. My understanding is that she was freaking amazing this afternoon and saved my wife and unborn child, along with herself. You have to be proud of that."

"I didn't say I wasn't proud." Galen sounded frustrated. "I want her to be able to take care of herself. She doesn't know the ways of the island yet. She could get in real trouble if she's not careful. I won't always be there to get her out of it."

"That's the thing about being with a strong woman. They don't always need you to get them out of trouble. Sure, I've been with Aisling a few times and helped. She's been with me a few times and helped, too. Once she stood in the rain when a magical storm was trying to make me kill her. Armed only with her mouth and heart, she somehow broke a spell she had no business breaking.

"If the rules had stuck the way they were supposed to stick, I would've killed her," he continued. "But I didn't. She saved both of us. She had the strength inside her the entire time. Hadley has that strength, too. You have to trust her."

"I do trust her," Galen supplied. "I just don't want to lose her."

"You have to learn to balance the fear and find your faith." Griffin was solemn. "When I finally did that with Aisling, it was as if the world became easier to live in. Our life isn't perfect, but I know she can take care of herself. I don't want to change her. I fell in love with who she is. If you want to change Hadley, you should probably get out now. That's not fair to her."

"I don't want to change her," Galen huffed. "I like who she is. I just want to protect her."

"That's man thinking, as Aisling would call it. Just because they're women doesn't mean they can't take care of themselves."

"I guess, but ... you still worry, don't you?"

"All the time. But I have faith. I've seen what she can do. She's a hundred wonderful things wrapped in one small package."

"And that package is all mouth," Galen complained.

"Yes, well, the mouth is an acquired taste."

"She does have a way about her."

17

SEVENTEEN

Griffin caught me eavesdropping, but didn't say anything. He merely smiled and winked while keeping Galen busy so I could make my escape. I found Lilac on the far side of the room talking to Casey, so I decided now was as good a time as any to pay my respects.

Casey, her face sallow, had shadows under her eyes big enough to hide in. I was hesitant as I approached, but my resolve was firm.

"I'm so sorry for your loss."

She furrowed her brow as she looked me up and down, waiting until Lilac made a discreet escape to speak. "I feel like I should know you, but ... I don't. I'm sorry." Her voice was soft, barely audible.

"Hadley Hunter." I extended my hand. "We met on the dock the other night. I ... um ... you probably don't remember me. You had other things on your mind."

"On the dock." She nodded slowly. "Right. You're Galen's girlfriend."

"Among other things."

"I didn't mean that in a dismissive way."

"I didn't take it that way." I forced a tight-lipped smile. "People have been talking about your relationship with Jacob, how you were high school sweethearts and stuck together through thick and thin. I'm so sorry."

"Yes, well … ." She broke off, her voice cracking.

I gave her a moment to recover, tilting my head to the side when I heard the distinctive sound of drums. "What's that?" I swiveled and looked over my shoulder, but the jukebox was playing the same melancholy music as before.

"What's what?" Casey asked, confused.

"The drums. Do you hear drums?"

She shook her head. "Am I supposed to hear drums?"

"I … I guess I must be hearing things." The drumming had since faded, making me think perhaps the sound came from a passing shuttle or golf cart. "How are you feeling otherwise? I mean … how is the baby?"

"He … or she, we never did find out … is doing okay. The doctor wants me to take it easy. I'm not sure that's possible. Not with Jacob's killer running loose. I mean … what's to stop whoever did this from coming after me?"

"I'm sure you're not a target." I meant it, but even as the words left my mouth I realized how ridiculous they sounded. Of course she would be afraid. The husband she'd loved since childhood was coldly stolen from her. Anyone would be frightened under those circumstances. "Maybe your parents can stay with you or something."

"They have been, but my mother is suggesting I move in with her until after the baby is born. That way I can go there after leaving the hospital and have help under the same roof."

"That sounds like a good idea."

"I don't know if I want to do that." Casey's eyes turned glassy. "Jacob and I shared that home together. We did the baby's room together. It seems like that's where I should be. I don't know. Maybe I'm being ridiculous."

"You're going through a lot," I offered. "You should do whatever feels right to you. Jacob would want that. I didn't know him, but everything I've seen indicates that he would want that more than anything."

"You're probably right." Casey turned wistful as she looked toward the window. The second she closed her eyes, I heard the drums again. This time they were accompanied by chanting. I couldn't make out the words, which were muffled and overlapped one another, but a chill ran up my spine as I tried to calm myself.

"I should probably get back. I just wanted to tell you how sorry I was about your husband."

"Thank you so much."

I left Casey, gratified that her mother appeared to be walking across the room to comfort her daughter. That allowed me to walk through the front door and plant myself on the sidewalk. I listened as hard as I could, hoping to pick up the chanting and drums again so perhaps I could follow the sound to the source, but I heard nothing even though I waited for what felt like a really long time.

"What are you doing out here?" Galen asked, his eyes filled with concern as he took in my drawn countenance.

"I'm kind of afraid to tell you."

"I want to build this relationship on trust."

"Oh, yeah?"

"Yeah."

"Okay, well, first I should tell you that I was eavesdropping when you were talking to Griffin," I announced, rubbing my hands over my stomach as I tried to shake the remaining chills left by the chanting. "I heard you ask him about putting up with Aisling's mouth and I listened as he told you that strong women need to be given freedom to do stupid things."

Amusement slid across his handsome features. "I don't believe that's what he actually said."

"It's close."

"No, he said he fell in love with a strong woman and doesn't regret it. He said I wouldn't regret it either — which I believe — and he also said that his wife is a royal pain in the behind."

"I think you embellished that part."

"He said it with his eyes, not his lips."

I couldn't stop myself from laughing. "Nice save."

"I thought so."

I licked my lips and prepared to tell him the second part. "I heard something weird when I was trying to talk to Casey. The thing is, I don't know if I really heard it. I'm afraid I imagined it."

"What did you hear?"

I explained about the chants and drums. He made me reenact the drum sounds twice, which is when I caught on that he was having a bit of fun with me. Still, when I finished, he was somber.

"Aisling mentioned they were playing drums at the Maboli campsite. Was it the same sound?"

"I don't know. I think the rhythm was different. If you're asking if the sounds came from the same drums, I have no idea."

"Well, it's weird, but I don't know what we can do about it." He opened his arms and pulled me in for a hug, swaying back and forth as he considered our options. "I guess we can't do anything but wait."

"I guess." I gave him a quick kiss on the cheek, surprising both of us. "Thanks for not thinking I'm crazy."

"I would never think that."

"Lesser men might."

"I'm not a lesser man." He held out his hand. "Come on. Let's go in and say our goodbyes. I think we could both use a break from all this for the rest of the night."

"What did you have in mind?"

His smile was impish. "I'm betting you can figure it out."

"It's like you were reading my mind."

WE WERE BREATHLESS AND giddy when we got back to the lighthouse. Wesley's truck was in the driveway and he was sitting in the living room playing a board game with May when we practically fell through the door.

Galen caught me before I could hit the floor, his lips pressed to mine, and he made a face when Wesley growled in disgust.

"Don't even think about it," he warned, extending a quelling finger with one hand while he kept his other arm wrapped around my waist. "I don't want to hear one word. We're going upstairs ... to bed ... and you're not going to say a thing about it."

"Aren't they cute?" May beamed. "They remind me of us when we first got together. We couldn't keep our hands off each other either."

Wesley scowled. "I don't think it's appropriate. You should drop her off and go home, Galen. She's going to get a bad reputation."

"Oh, that memo was sent in high school," I said, laughing when Galen rubbed his cheek against mine. "It's okay. I don't really mind having a bad reputation."

"Well, I mind."

"It's not your house," Galen pointed out, refusing to release his grip on me. "I get that she's your granddaughter and you have certain ideas about how she should act, but it's not the fifties and she's an adult. Besides that, you don't live here."

"He's right about that, Wesley," May intoned. "She's an adult."

"How can you be okay with this, May?" Wesley was incredulous. "They're not married."

"Neither were we."

Wesley's eyebrows flew up his forehead. "That was a secret! You swore to take it to your grave."

"And I did." May did a little twirl under the light so she could emphasize the fact that we could see through her. "They're adults. They're responsible. Let them have their fun."

"Well, I can't stay here for this." He got up on shaky legs. "I have to leave."

"I'll see you tomorrow ... I'm sure." I was firm as I held his gaze. "It's going to be okay. I swear it."

"Whatever." Wesley was morose as he started putting away the board game. "Just wait until I'm out of here."

"Hurry," Galen suggested, dragging me toward the stairs. "Oh, and lock the door on your way out. There are killers out there ... and I'm not entirely sure that Hadley hasn't inadvertently made herself a target with her visit out to the sticks today."

"I'll handle the locks." Wesley pinned Galen with a dark look. "You'd better be good to her. I'll blow your kneecaps off if you aren't."

"I swear I'll be good to her. You don't have to worry about that. I *want* to be good to her."

"That's what I'm afraid of."

"Get over it."

I WOKE TO THE WARM feeling of Galen's breath on my forehead. We were wrapped around each other, the sheets pulled up to our waists, and the sun was filtering in through the window. It was an absolutely perfect morning.

"Hey." He stirred, brushed a kiss against my forehead as he moved to stretch. "How are you?"

"Pretty good." I meant it. I felt good, rejuvenated even. There was something about being close to him that charged my battery, so to speak. I didn't know how to explain it.

"What are you thinking?" he asked, dragging me back to reality.

I shrugged, embarrassed to be caught thinking such ridiculously schmaltzy thoughts. "I was thinking that it's nice waking up with you."

"It is nice," he agreed, smoothing my hair. "But that's not what you were thinking."

"If I tell you what I was thinking I'll never live it down."

"Now I definitely want to hear it."

"Uh-uh."

He resorted to tickling, refusing to let up even though I shrieked and fought back. I was laughing so hard I was crying when he was done, but still I refused to give up my secret.

"I thought we agreed to tell each other the big stuff?" he challenged.

I shook my head. "This isn't big. It's ... mushy."

"I want to hear the mushy stuff."

"We can't tell each other everything." I was perfectly serious as I pressed my hand to his chest to make sure he didn't get any ideas about continuing the tickle attack. "We can tell each other the big things, and that should probably be a rule. But you have to allow a girl a little mystery."

Galen didn't look convinced. "I'll tell you what I was thinking if you tell me what you were thinking."

"I already know what you were thinking."

"And what's that?"

"You were thinking that you want to play a game before breakfast. I know which game ... and I'm fine with it."

Torn between the cutesy offer and chasing the truth, he finally heaved a sigh. "Fine. Keep your secrets. I'll get them out of you eventually."

"That's not going to happen."

"We'll just have to see about that."

MAY WAS IN THE KITCHEN when we made our way downstairs and she looked happy, bubbly even, when she saw us together.

"So cute," she chortled, grinning. "I love how cute you are together."

"And we love hearing how cute we are," Galen teased, pulling the carton of eggs from the refrigerator and handing me the bag of shredded potatoes. "I, for one, can't tell you how much I love hearing about how cute I am."

"You were a darling boy," May agreed, pouring tea for both of us as she watched us navigate the stove together. "I remember when your mother brought you by one day for a visit and you gave me a flower. You said it was for the prettiest woman on the island."

Galen smiled. "I probably stole the flower."

"You did ... and from my own garden. You were a charmer and a half as a boy, and you've grown up to be even more charming as a man."

"Oh, did you hear that?" I drawled. "You're charming. And here I thought you were just good at flirting."

"I have many talents." Galen winked at me before focusing on May. "Did you talk to Wesley after he left last night?"

She nodded, sobering. "He likes you, Galen. You don't have to worry about that. He's always liked you ... even when you used to sneak onto his property to drink in the fields."

"I didn't realize he knew that was me," he said, shaking his head. "I always thought I got away with that."

"He let you get away with it because he knew you weren't really doing any harm. He believes you're a strong man, with good values and a stalwart heart."

"Then what's his problem?" Galen challenged. "He's been giving me grief for days about spending time with Hadley. He had to know it was coming to this. From the moment I laid eyes on her, she's all I can think about. It's not as if I've got five women twisting in the wind or anything."

"Of course not. It's just ... when Emma left the family it was because of a man. We never got to see Hadley grow up because our daughter put distance between us. Now we have Hadley back and here you come. He's worried you'll steal Hadley."

"I have no intention of stealing Hadley."

"And I wouldn't let him if he tried," I added. "I want to know you and Wesley. Galen won't steal me. I can't pretend to understand why my mother did what she did. I didn't know her, not even for a second. I'm not her. That's the only thing I have to offer on that front. I have no intention of going anywhere."

"And Wesley will come to realize that." May smiled as her gaze bounced between us. "Seriously, you two are just adorable."

"That never gets old." Galen took to cracking eggs and flicked his eyes to me. "What are your plans for the day?"

I sensed trouble. "I don't know. I promise not to go back out and visit the cult, if that's what you're worried about."

"Well, I know you'll end up with Aisling."

"How do you know that?"

"Call it a hunch."

"Even if I do you have nothing to worry about," I promised. "We'll be good little girls and not get into trouble."

"Right."

"I swear it."

He turned to face me, his expression serious. "I don't want to rain on your parade. I simply want you to be safe. As long as you promise to stay away from the tribe, I promise not to give you grief."

It seemed too easy. "Seriously?"

"Yes."

"Why are you being so agreeable?"

"Because he's adorable," May answered for him.

"Because Griffin said something to me last night that stuck. He said he fell in love with Aisling because of her mouth. Trying to change her after the fact isn't fair to her ... or him. That means it's not fair to you, or me, for that matter. I don't want to change you."

That was a relief. I most certainly didn't want to be changed. "I happen to like you the way you are, too."

"Great." He gave me a soft kiss. "Compromise might be fun. I'm looking forward to trying it."

"So am I."

"It's going to be a good day."

"Definitely."

"So cute," May bubbled, shaking her head and smiling. "I wish I had a camera.."

"Let's not push things," Galen hedged. "Just stick with how cute I am for now."

"I can do that."

18

EIGHTEEN

Compromise is a funny word. I thought it meant Galen would stop constantly worrying about where I went and what I planned. He thought otherwise.

Thirty minutes after breakfast I heard voices outside, and when I went to the window I found Griffin and Aisling, hand-in-hand, walking up the driveway.

"Huh."

"Who is that?" May asked, floating behind me. "They don't look familiar."

"Aisling and Griffin. They're here on their honeymoon."

"Oh, the reaper." May looked intrigued. "I knew our reaper, of course, but she looks a lot more fun."

"Oh, you have no idea." I moved to the door and tugged it open before they could knock, smiling as I ushered them inside. Even though I was suspicious and had tons of questions, Griffin beat me to it.

"This place is great." He was enthusiastic as he released Aisling's hand and started prowling around the living room. "It's so ... interesting. The building looks absolutely huge, but inside it's kind of homey."

"It's definitely homey," I agreed, casting him a sidelong look before focusing on Aisling. "Not that I'm not happy to see you, but what are you doing here?"

"Oh, Galen didn't tell you?" The fire in Aisling's eyes told me that she was on the verge of losing her temper. "It seems my husband and your boyfriend had a long talk last night."

"I know. I was eavesdropping. You don't have to worry. You came out smelling like a freshly-baked doughnut during the conversation."

Confused, Aisling knit her eyebrows. "Are we talking about the same conversation?"

"No," Griffin answered for me, his hands busy as they moved over the bookshelf May had built into the wall sometime in the past. "Hadley was gone before we started talking about our plans for the day."

Our plans? Hmm. I wasn't expecting that. "You have plans with Galen today?" I asked.

"He does," Galen confirmed, strolling through the door and pulling up short when he saw what Griffin was doing. "Isn't that neat? It's recessed into the wall and there are carvings inside. Whoever did this for May did a heckuva job."

"It's very cool," Griffin enthused. "Baby, we should consider something like this for our condo. Now that the baby is coming we won't have nearly as much room as we originally thought when we bought it."

Aisling scowled. "Just another reason I want to collect all your sperm and set them on fire," she groused.

Galen stared as I chewed my bottom lip to keep from laughing.

"I see you're in a good mood," he said, shaking his head. "What's wrong with you?"

"Nothing," she answered hurriedly, her eyes flashing. "Why does something have to be wrong? Perhaps I'm simply not quite awake yet because it's barely dawn."

"Ignore her," Griffin suggested, his eyes plastered to the shelf as he admired the craftsmanship. "She's a bear in the morning until she gets her caffeine. And we woke up to information from her father that put her in an extremely foul mood."

"At least your father is talking to you," I said brightly.

"Yeah, well he's not really talking as much as emailing lists of things I can't eat or drink now that I'm pregnant. Caffeine is one of those things."

She lapsed into silence a moment, morose, and then she exploded before I could think of something comforting to say.

"He expects me to go nine months without caffeine. No rare steaks either." Aisling looked positively apoplectic. "No deli meat for sandwiches because of the listeria. No smoked seafood. No raw eggs. No soft cheeses. Apparently there's nothing I can eat."

"I think you're overreacting," Griffin shot back. "I saw that list of cheese you can't eat and the only one on it you've ever tried is feta. You'll simply have to go without Greek salads until the birth. You usually eat chili dogs and fries when we're at the Coney, so I think you'll somehow survive."

Aisling growled. "It's not that I can't do it. It's that I have to do it. I didn't expect this. I just ... thought we would have more time."

Her eyes briefly turned glassy, making me think she was going to burst into tears, but she caught herself before Griffin could pull her close for a hug. He wrapped his arms around her even as she fought him, pressed a kiss to her forehead and rocked back and forth.

"I know you didn't expect this. I didn't either. We'll be okay. It's not as if we're alone. We'll figure things out. You need to tell me what you're feeling instead of bottling it up. When you bottle things up you end up exploding ... and then I end up exploding. Let's try to stay away from explosions."

I felt intrusive staring at them so I tilted my head and indicated Galen should follow me back into the kitchen. When we were clear of the scene in the living room, I gave him a serious look. "I don't understand any of this. Why are you taking Griffin with you?"

"Because he's worried Aisling will get herself in deep trouble and wants to end this as soon as possible," Galen replied without hesitation. "During your eavesdropping yesterday, you missed the part of the conversation when he admitted that he wants to wrap himself around Aisling and act as a human shield to protect her and the baby."

"She won't like that."

"No, definitely not." Galen's expression was hard to read as he glanced back toward the hallway we'd just escaped through. "You want to learn things because you're curious by nature. Aisling wants to be in the middle of things because she's used to being the center of the universe. Griffin is a detective with keen instincts, and I could use the help. I think we can arrange this so we all benefit."

I wasn't as easily convinced. "So ... what's the plan? Are you going to try to lock us into the lighthouse or something while you guys do all the heavy lifting?"

"Not even a little. You guys can go wherever you want ... as long as you stay away from the tribe. I have no idea what they're capable of, and if they see you again things might get bloody."

"I protected us yesterday. I can do it again if it comes to it."

He extended a warning finger, his expression fierce. "You promised!"

"I did ... and I'll keep that promise. I'm just reminding you that I managed to keep us safe yesterday."

"And I'm very proud of you. That doesn't change the fact that there are more of them than you realize and they could've easily outnumbered you if Barry had decided to call in reinforcements. I prefer you steer clear of them today."

In truth, I had no interest in getting up close and personal with the neighborhood cult leader ... or any of his rabid followers. It wasn't a hard promise to make. "We're not going back out there." I was firm. "We're going to hang out here, try to find some information on the tiki masks, and maybe grab lunch downtown. Now that Aisling can't eat deli meat, we'll probably have to eat out."

"Yeah. Who knew deli meat was such a death trap?" He pulled me close and gave me a long kiss, his eyes going heavy and hooded when I finally caught my breath enough to meet his gaze. "I'll text you a few times throughout the day. Please text back so I know you're not in trouble."

"I will."

"Try to keep Aisling from doing anything stupid."

"I'm not a miracle worker."

"That's not what you told me last night."

My cheeks burned. "I … ."

"You're cute when you're tongue-tied." He gave me another kiss before taking a step back. "As long as you guys stick close to town you can have your run of the place. Just don't go beyond the township limits. That's all I ask."

"I'm sure we can follow your rules."

"I'm sure you can, too. I'm not sure about your buddy."

Now that he mentioned it, I wasn't sure Aisling was capable of following rules either. I decided to change tacks. "Everything will be fine. I have everything under control. You have nothing to worry about."

"I'M BORED."

Aisling lasted exactly ten minutes in the third-floor library before she chucked the book I gave her for research and stretched to stare at the ceiling.

"I'm trying to find the meaning behind the tiki masks," I explained. "If you don't want to help, you don't have to. My bedroom is a floor down if you want to take a nap."

Aisling made a horrified face. "I'm not sleeping in your bed. I saw you and your flirty love monkey this morning. I know exactly what you were doing last night and I wouldn't touch that bed with Taurus's imaginary ten-foot pole. I don't want your sex cooties."

She was definitely in a mood … and it just so happened to be an irritating one. "You know, you don't have to stay here."

"According to Griffin, I do. He's worried, but he won't come right out and say it."

Her scowl told me everything I needed to know. "He's worried because of what happened yesterday?"

"That and other things." Aisling was dejected as she rubbed her hands over her face. "When my father sent the list of things I could and couldn't eat, he was reading through it and I could tell he'd never considered any of it. He's just as freaked out as me, which isn't good."

"I have news for you; he's been just as freaked out as you since the beginning. He's simply better at hiding it."

"I guess. He's usually the steady one — except for rare occasions — so I'm not used to having to console myself. He spent twenty minutes reading that list and then he got on the internet and did his own research. Neither one of us knows what we're doing."

"I'm sure that can be said for most first-time parents. You'll figure it out."

"Yeah." She blankly stared at the ceiling for an extended beat and then swung herself into a sitting position. "What are you researching?"

"The tiki masks," I said again. "I think they were chosen for a specific reason. The problem is, I can't find any books that help. I don't know where to look. There's a library down on the beach, but I haven't visited it yet. The way it was described makes me think it's a coffee shop more than anything else."

Aisling made a face. "No coffee shops. If I see other people with caffeine I might be forced to choke them to death. On the research front, though, I might have an idea."

AISLING BORROWED MY COMPUTER to make a Skype call, and the man who answered looked sleepy and annoyed. I recognized right away that he had the same dark hair and purple eyes as Aisling. Unlike her other brothers, though, he had shoulder-length hair and he wasn't alone in bed when he accepted the call.

"Why are you calling me from your honeymoon, Ais?" Cillian Grimlock growled. Aisling swore up and down before placing the call that he was her favorite brother. Not only that, he was supposedly a whiz when it came to research.

Right now, he looked like a shirtless underwear model in his boxer shorts. His tousled hair was all over the place and he scrubbed his cheeks as he carried his computer away from the bed — and the sleeping brunette in it — and settled at his desk.

"Is something wrong, Ais?"

"Why would anything be wrong?" Aisling adopted an air of innocence that didn't quite fit her personality. "Why would anything possibly be wrong? We simply need information on tiki masks. Can you get that for us?"

"Probably," he hedged, uncertain. "Do you want to tell me why you need this information? I was under the impression that you were supposed to be soaking up the sun and reveling in the fact that you're now Mrs. Griffin Taylor."

Aisling's eyes narrowed to glittery purple slits. "Do you want me to smack the crap out of you when I get home?"

"You can't wrestle. You're pregnant. I heard Dad with Braden and Redmond last night going through a list of things you can't do. By the way, sock hockey is off the table, and you're only allowed to absorb souls in quiet and safe neighborhoods."

Aisling's mouth dropped open. "Excuse me? He can't do that!"

"What's sock hockey?" I asked.

"Only the best game ever," Cillian replied. "It's brutal, though. Dad doesn't want us accidentally jostling the baby loose."

"That won't happen. I mean ... will it?" Aisling screwed up her face in disgust. "There are too many new rules, Cillian. Everything is changing."

Sensing the shift in his sister's mood, Cillian sobered. "Ais, don't you dare cry. I won't be able to take it if you cry."

"I can't seem to help it. I've cried three times since we left on our honeymoon ... and for no good reason. I can't explain it."

"I believe it's hormones." Cillian was pragmatic as he dragged a hand through his hair. "Maya is a nurse. You can talk to her if you're nervous. She's excited to be an aunt, and she was telling Dad, Braden and Redmond to chill out last night. For the record, they did not listen."

"Who is Maya?" I hated feeling out of the loop.

"Maya is Cillian's girlfriend and Griffin's sister," Aisling explained. "She's the chick in the bed."

"Who had a double-shift yesterday and needs her sleep," Cillian said. "Keep your voices down."

"Yeah, yeah." Aisling waved off the admonishment. "Can you help me with the tiki mask research or not?"

"I guess." Cillian didn't look thrilled at the suggestion. "May I ask why this is so important?"

Aisling related the events of the last few days to her brother. It was a tidy condensation that left a few things out of the telling ... like the fact that I used magic to scare off the members of the tribe who gave chase. All Aisling said was that Galen happened to show up and left it at that. It was a curious choice, but I didn't question her on it.

"So what you're basically saying is that you went on your honeymoon and stumbled across a murder mystery," Cillian muttered after a beat. "Only you would allow something like this to happen."

"Hey, I didn't go looking for it. Trouble simply seems to find me."

"Yes, because you're a pain in the behind." He exhaled heavily as he looked over his shoulder to make sure Maya was still sleeping. "I'll look for you, Ais. It would help if you could get me descriptions of each mask."

"I'm the one who saw them," I offered. "I can put together quick sketches and email them if it helps."

"It will," he confirmed. "I'll do what I can and put together a packet of information. I'm assuming you don't want Dad to know what you're up to. That's why you're calling in the middle of the night, right?"

"It's almost ten, Cillian," Aisling drawled. "It's hardly the middle of the night."

"I've been working the late shift with Maya so we can spend time together. It's the middle of the night to me."

"Then I'm sorry for waking you." Aisling looked genuinely contrite. "Before you go, though, how is everyone else? I mean ... how is Jerry?"

"Jerry has been shopping for onesies and decorations for the baby's room," Cillian replied. "He's excited to be an uncle. So is Aidan. They've already discussed getting baby monitors that stretch to their condo so they'll be able to help you."

"That sounds sweet," I prodded Aisling, grinning. "And here you were worried you wouldn't have any help."

"That's not all I've been worried about," Aisling grumbled, shaking her head. "I'm worried I won't survive childbirth. That's the real worry."

Cillian snickered. "You know what's weird? Maya was saying just last night how that's a regular worry for expectant mothers. Dad said Mom thought the same thing — at least with Redmond. By the time you and Aidan came around, she was over thinking she would die in childbirth. I think that's a normal fear."

"Yeah, well, it doesn't feel normal." Aisling turned pouty. "It doesn't help that Dad is mad at me."

"He's not mad. He's ... surprised. We've had a lot to deal with the last few weeks, Ais. Mom's soul crossed over to help us. Then that thing that we thought was Mom did what she did. You got married. The baby was simply an element we weren't expecting. That doesn't mean we're not happy."

Aisling turned suspicious. "Why are you happy?"

"Because I'm going to be the best uncle in the world. We all are. We'll spoil the crap out of that kid. That includes Dad. Just you wait."

"I hope so." Aisling remained melancholy a moment before recovering and changing the subject. "Did you know I can't eat deli meat?"

"Who do you think did all that research, Ais? Dad asked for it, so I did it."

"So you're the reason I can't eat deli meat. I'm going to make you pay when I get home. And since you guys can't fight back, it's going to be fun."

"Who said we can't fight back?"

"You might jiggle the baby loose if you do."

Cillian's smile slipped. "You're going to use that baby against us?"

"Don't act so surprised. I was always going to use the baby against you. As for now, we'll email copies of the masks to you. See what you can come up with."

"What are you going to do?"

"We're going to try to find our missing souls," Aisling replied without hesitation. "They must be around here somewhere."

"Be careful. If you get in trouble and Dad has to swoop in and save you, he won't be happy."

"What else is new?"

19

NINETEEN

May was fascinated with Aisling.

Of course, so was I.

There was something about the woman that defied conventional thinking. On paper, I shouldn't have liked her. She was egotistical, blunt and spoiled to the core. Unlike others of her ilk, she recognized all those things in herself and didn't apologize. That was probably why I liked her so much.

"Tell me about your life growing up," May insisted as I worked on the sketches to email Cillian. "As the only girl, you were probably treated like a princess."

"Not exactly a princess," she hedged.

"You grew up in a castle, right?" I prodded. "I think that's what Griffin said."

"It's not a castle, although it does have turrets. It's just a big house in an older neighborhood. It's really close to the lake, and only the uber-rich can afford to live there."

"Still, it must have been fun," May pressed. "To have all those brothers. There was a time I thought I wanted a houseful of kids. We were only blessed with my daughter Emma, and we loved her to distraction. I think more children would've been fun."

I had never really thought to ask May about that. I only knew the bare bones of the story, that my mother had grown up on Moonstone Bay and moved away to marry my father. There had been some sort of fallout because May and Wesley wanted her to return home, but she died before they could reconcile. My father decided to cut them out of my life — which I was still mildly bitter about — and then I got a letter not long after May's death telling me I'd inherited a lighthouse. Things moved fast after that, so I only learned the story in bits and pieces. I made a mental note to sit down and ask May about the rest of her life when we had time.

"We had fun as kids," Aisling volunteered. "We ran all over the neighborhood, terrorized everyone we could find and fought with each other nonstop. I'm sure my parents had plans to be strict, and maybe they even carried them out when it was just Redmond. We came in a clump, though. One day they had one baby, the next they had five. I think they learned to pick their battles."

"That makes sense." May bobbed her head. "Are you close with your father?"

"Yes, but he's not really talking to me right now."

"I'm sure he'll get over that. Are you sure you're not exaggerating things?"

"He was pretty angry. He chased Griffin. I'm not making that part up."

"He was probably surprised. A baby is a joyous occasion, and you're married. You seem to have a good head on your shoulders. There's nothing to worry about."

Aisling cast my grandmother a look. "You're pretty good at this. I have one set of grandparents still alive on my father's side of the family and they're nowhere near as cool as you. But I have to ask, why did you decide to stay behind? Don't you want to cross over?"

"Maybe one day," May replied. "I want to spend time with Hadley first. And, well, Wesley isn't ready for me to go. I'm not ready to leave him either. I figure when it's time I'll know it."

"Fair enough. I think it's cool that you and Wesley got divorced and still acted as if you were married on the weekends." I'd related the story of my grandparents' rather infamous love affair to Aisling as we drove to spy on the cult the previous day. She'd been thrilled … and couldn't stop laughing.

"Sometimes love is a cagey beast," May explained. "I always loved Wesley. I simply couldn't live with him."

"At least you recognized your limitations."

"Is that what you're worried about?" My grandmother's eyes twinkled. "Are you worried you'll have limitations on being a mother because you weren't expecting it? Trust me, my dear, you'll be perfectly fine. In fact, I'll wager that you'll be better at it than you ever imagined."

"I hope so." Aisling flashed a watery smile before focusing on me. "Have you got those drawings done yet? I want to send them to Cillian and then head out. I could use some iced tea."

"I thought you weren't supposed to have caffeine," I challenged.

"They make decaffeinated tea."

"Oh." That sounded perfectly reasonable. "Good point."

"I might not drink it, but they make it."

Yup. It was going to be a long day.

INSTEAD OF HEADING TO Lilac's and allowing Aisling to get buzzed on caffeine, we stopped at the grocery store before I decided to take her to one of my favorite places to visit. She was less than thrilled when I told her where we were going, but her fascination grew when she caught sight of the cemetery … and the absolutely huge walls surrounding it.

"Why is your cemetery locked up like this?" Aisling played with the padlock on the front door. "I mean … isn't the whole point of a cemetery to visit the dead, pay your respects and meander into memories?"

"Yes." I nodded perfunctorily. "I was surprised, too. There's something different about this cemetery."

"Oh, yeah? What's that?"

"Come with me." I led her along the cemetery wall. It was a big plot, so it took a few minutes. By the time we crossed to the back of the graveyard she was grousing about the heat and humidity. That ceased when she caught sight of the viewing window, which allowed as many as three people to sit in front of it and watch the show at night.

"What the ... ?" Aisling strode forward and stared through the window, baffled. "I don't understand."

"I didn't either when I first got here." I sank onto the bench and looked through the window. There was no movement on the other side, not even a stray animal. I knew that would change as soon as the sun set, but we wouldn't be around for that happy occurrence. "Someone cursed the cemetery."

"Who?"

"I don't know. Galen says nobody knows. They're trying to counteract it, but they haven't been able to yet."

"And what does the curse do?" Aisling gave up trying to find anything of interest on the other side of the glass and settled next to me. "Something tells me that you're extremely interested in this curse. I know I am. The only curses I've come into contact with have been terrible ... like storms that turn people you love into monsters. What's the deal with this curse?"

"At night, once the sun sets, the people in the graves get up and start walking around."

"Get out!"

"It's true." I rubbed my sweating palms over my knees. "It's fine to wander around the cemetery during the day. At night, though, it's filled with zombies and it's dangerous. That's why they put up the high wall."

"Huh." Aisling rubbed her chin. "How long has this been going on?"

"Several years."

"Do you come out here and watch the zombies at night?"

"Yeah." I swallowed hard, my heart giving a little roll before I continued. "My mother is in there."

Aisling snapped her head in my direction, surprised etched over her features. "I thought your mother died when you were born ... and far away from here."

"She did. May and Wesley brought her back here because they wanted the island to be her final resting place. My father allowed it. No one has given me any specifics, but I think my father said it was okay because he knew even then he was going to cut me out of their lives. He wanted to give them something."

"Why don't you just ask him?"

"My father isn't always chatty."

"My father is the exact opposite. He always wants to talk." She pursed her lips as she stared at the window. "So ... you come out here and watch your mother walk around as a dead person pretty regularly?"

"I came a lot when I first found out. Now I try to keep it to once a week. Galen worries otherwise, even though he doesn't come right out and say it."

"She's dead." Aisling adopted a pragmatic tone. "You realize that. Galen is worried you'll get it in your head that she can somehow be saved. It makes you feel close to her, even though it's not really her."

"Yeah."

"It's okay. I get it." Aisling cleared her throat and I could tell she was fighting tears. "The thing that came back with my mother's face was kind of like a zombie, but she had attitude and could think. She didn't exactly try to eat us, but she had a plan to steal my soul to prolong her life. It was essentially the same thing ... without the gross eating of entrails."

"She wanted to steal your soul?" I was horrified. I never knew my mother. I missed her, but it was a different sort of longing, something that only popped up at odd times. How difficult had it been for Aisling, someone who knew and loved her mother, to deal with a monster when it returned?

"She wasn't really my mother," Aisling stressed, taking on a far-off expression. "I knew that the moment I crossed paths with her. She was different, somehow stretched. The problem was, there were glimpses of the real her under the veneer.

"My brothers wanted to believe so badly it almost ripped us apart," she continued. "Especially Braden. He has middle-child syndrome and always required extra attention from her. My father did his best to spread the love, but he was more practical.

"Every day, he would pick one of us as his favorite and give that child more attention," she explained. "With five of us, that meant we essentially had a special day at least once a week. My mother spread herself thin trying to jump from whiny child to whiny child. She recognized that Braden needed more from her."

She was so sad I couldn't help uniting my emotions with hers. "It must have been hard for him when she died a second time."

"It was, but it's for the best. She was stirring everything up and trying to work against us from behind the scenes. Our real mother came back thanks to a spell, and helped us end the woman that had her face. Now she's gone again."

"That's terrible."

"And yet it's better than what you're dealing with," Aisling noted. "You know that thing in there isn't really your mother, right? It's just her body. I'm sure it's terrible because you never knew your mother. All you have are stories from other people, and even though they probably didn't mean for it to happen, those stories are filtered."

"I wish I'd gotten at least a chance to know her."

"I've dealt with zombies before, believe it or not, although not on this scale." Aisling slowly climbed back to her feet and meandered to the window. "I find it interesting that your island government hasn't eradicated them."

"I think they're looking for another way. This island is different from other places."

She snorted. "Trust me. I figured that out the moment we hit the docks. Still, this has to be dangerous."

"I think they've gotten it under control. We're allowed to watch as often as we like. Until they find a way to fix things, it is what it is."

"Yeah, well ... ." Aisling trailed off when she turned, her eyes going to a spot over my shoulder. I instinctively looked in that direction, worried I'd find some of the cult members from the previous day. If they'd followed us, we'd have to fight to escape.

Instead of Taurus's tribe, I discovered the soul of Jacob Dorsey watching us with morose eyes. He looked absolutely beaten down, as if life had shoved him into a slasher movie from which he couldn't escape. My heart immediately went out to him.

"We've been looking for you." Aisling was calm as she regarded him. She had much more experience with displaced souls. It was obvious she knew what she was doing. Er, well, more than me, that is.

"I don't know you." Jacob was uneasy as he glanced between faces. "I don't know either of you and yet you can see me. I don't understand what's going on."

"You're dead." Aisling was matter-of-fact. "Someone killed you several days ago, left your body on the docks. I was there the day it happened. I saw you when I was heading to the hotel. Hadley did, too." She inclined her head toward me, causing Jacob's gaze to float in my direction.

"Hadley." He rolled my name through his head. "Hadley Hunter. You're May Potter's granddaughter."

"That's me."

"And Galen Blackwood's girlfriend. I've heard people mention you. A lot of the women have their noses out of joint because they thought Galen wasn't ready to settle down. Your arrival proved that wasn't true."

"I don't know that he's ready to settle down," I said, embarrassed.

"And I don't think that's important to our conversation," Aisling noted, striding forward. Jacob didn't shy away from her, but he didn't look overly happy that she was invading his space. "What do you remember about your death?"

Jacob held out his hands. "Nothing."

"Then what is the last thing you do remember?"

"I ... was at work." Jacob furrowed his brow as he searched his memory. "I was out at the construction site. We were laying the foundation. It's a big job, took a lot of planning. We had to get the basement exactly right before we could do anything else.

"Once the foundation is set, the construction can really begin," he continued. "I was excited to be part of the team. It meant having steady work for two full years. That's unheard of on Moonstone Bay."

"I can imagine." Sympathy rolled through me at the man's lost expression. "Were you there alone? Were others with you?"

"There were a few people about, but they were getting ready to leave," he replied. "They wanted me to go to the bar with them, but I couldn't. I had to go home. Although ... did I make it home?" He looked upset. "Casey is due to give birth at any time and I promised to go home. I don't want to miss that. I ... um ... I guess now I am going to miss that."

"Casey is okay," I offered hurriedly. "I saw her last night. She misses you terribly. She's upset about everything that's happened, but she's holding it together for your little one. You would be so proud of her."

"I'm always proud of Casey." Jacob mustered a smile, although it didn't make it all the way to his eyes. "I wish I could talk to her again, say goodbye. I've tried. She can't see me."

"Only people with certain gifts can see you," Aisling explained. "I'm a reaper. That's why I can see you. Hadley is a witch. She has a whole bag of magic tricks."

"Can you make Casey see me? Just once? Just so I can say goodbye?"

"I don't know how to do that." I felt terrible. "I'm sorry."

"We can't fix this for you," Aisling supplied. "There's no going back. What we can do is try to help you. It's important to go back to that last day. You said your co-workers wanted you to go to the bar with them. Did they leave you?"

"I told them to. I was packing up the tools and preparing to leave." Jacob's sadness permeated the entire area. "I was almost ready to leave when ... it happened."

"What?" I leaned forward, intrigued. "Did you see who it was?"

"No. I sensed something ... someone. There was a shadow behind me. I got spooked and wanted to hurry and go home. I ... can't remember if I ever made it home, but I want to say I did. But I don't know. That's all I remember."

I shifted my eyes to Aisling to see what she made of the story. She seemed lost in thought.

"Maybe you should try to relax," I suggested. "The memory might be closer than you think. If you push too hard, it will hide. You need to let it come naturally."

"I don't care about that." Jacob was adamant. "I care about Casey, about our baby. I don't even know if it's a boy or girl. We wanted to wait and be surprised. We knew we would only have the one shot at it."

"You'll be able to see from wherever you go," Aisling said quietly, her hand moving to the pocket where I knew she kept the scepter her father sent her. "Just because you move on, that doesn't mean you can't look back."

"Is that true?" I asked.

"Of course it's true." Aisling said the words but her tone told me she didn't really know the answer. "I have to absorb you now, Jacob, help you cross over. It will be better for everyone when you're in the place you're meant to be."

She had the scepter out and pointed it at him. Jacob balked.

"No. I'm not leaving!" He took a huge step back. "You can't make me."

"It's my job to make you," Aisling pressed. "I don't really have a choice in the matter."

"Well, I'm not letting you take me." Jacob turned on his heel and bolted, causing me to hop to my feet.

"What do we do now?" I asked. "Should we chase him?"

"I'm not chasing a soul. It's too hot."

"Why didn't you absorb him?"

"I thought we had more time. Obviously, I was wrong."

"Obviously," I echoed, watching Jacob's back until he disappeared into the trees. "So ... what now?"

"I have no idea. I can't believe I lost him. My father always warned me not to talk to souls. Suck, don't talk. I'll never hear the end of this."

"Yes, that's the most important thing," I muttered.

"Don't you start."

"I was merely making an observation."

20

TWENTY

We met Galen and Griffin for lunch at Lilac's bar. They were already seated when we entered, and Griffin jumped to his feet when he saw Aisling.

"Why are you so red and sweaty? Do you need to sit down? Do you need to go to the hospital? Do you guys even have a hospital?"

Aisling cocked an eyebrow. "I'm sweaty because we were outside." She slapped at his hands. "I'm fine."

"You're warm." He pressed his hand to her forehead by way of proof and tugged her toward a chair. "I'll get you some water. If you don't cool down in the next five minutes, we're taking you to get checked out by a doctor."

Aisling fumed as she watched him head toward the bar. "I am not going to survive this pregnancy. There's simply no way."

I clucked sympathetically as I took the seat on the other side of Galen. He lifted his chin so I could give him a kiss, but my eyes were still on Aisling. "You know, I hate to say it because you're probably going to freak out, but you are a little red. I didn't realize how much time we spent at the cemetery."

"You went to the cemetery?" Even though he'd made a point of saying Aisling drove him crazy, Galen used his menu to fan her face. "I take it the weather in Detroit isn't like this very often, huh?"

Her scowl deepened. "It gets hot in Detroit during the summer months."

"Yes, and you complain the whole time," Griffin said upon his return, handing his wife an absolutely huge glass of ice water. "I want you to drink all of that."

"And I want you to take a chill pill," she shot back. "I'm perfectly fine."

"Baby, your skin is on fire and you're sweating. I don't like it. Drink that water."

"Oh, whatever." Aisling growled and lifted the glass to her lips. Before I could think of something to say to make her feel better, she'd drained the entire thing. "I'll have some more, husband."

Griffin widened his eyes to comical proportions. "I take it you were thirsty."

"I didn't even realize how thirsty I was until I started drinking." She lowered her voice and offered him the trace of a smile. "I really am fine. We weren't exerting ourselves or anything. We were at the cemetery and we got to talking ... it's okay. I'm not having a medical crisis or anything."

"Well ... ." Griffin's expression reflected uncertainty. He didn't get a chance to push her further, though, because Lilac picked that moment to swoop by the table. She had another huge glass of water for Aisling and a bright smile for the rest of us.

"Here you go, honey. You sit tight and drink that. You'll cool down in no time."

Aisling bobbed her head and greedily reached for the water. "Thank you. I appreciate it."

"You're welcome." Lilac pressed her hand to the back of Aisling's neck without invitation. "You are warm. How would you feel about a bag of ice for the back of your neck? That will cool you down faster than anything."

"I'm sure I'm fine."

"If you wouldn't mind, we'll take the bag of ice," Griffin interjected, grimacing when Aisling scorched him with a dark look. "It's that or the hospital."

"I'm not sick!"

"You threw up this morning."

"That's because your kid thinks it's funny to make me sick."

"Oh, so now it's my kid?"

"You're the only possible father."

Griffin sighed, love practically oozing out of him when he looked at her. "You're going to take the bag of ice and sit there until I'm convinced you're really okay. We'll go from there."

"It's sad, but I miss my father," Aisling lamented. "He would've gotten me ice cream by now and I would be all better."

"Your father would make you go to the hospital. I don't know who you're trying to kid with that crap."

"Whatever." Aisling muttered something dark under her breath, but I could tell the anger she felt wasn't directed at her husband. No, that anger was aimed inward. She hadn't realized she was flagging — and neither had I — until Griffin called her on it. Now she was feeling a bit foolish and she expressed it by acting angry.

"She'll be fine," I said pointedly, catching Griffin's gaze. "It's my fault. I forgot what it was like when I first got here. I was always hot and thirsty, too. I took her to the cemetery without thinking about it."

"Yeah, speaking of that, why would you go to the cemetery in the middle of the day?" Griffin accepted the bag of ice Lilac handed him and immediately pressed it to the back of Aisling's neck. Instead of shrieking, she sighed. Apparently she liked the feeling.

"You should see the cemetery," Aisling enthused. "In fact, we have to visit after dark."

"Why would we spend our honeymoon visiting the cemetery?"

"Because they have zombies."

Griffin stilled. "Zombies? Like the ones we faced?"

"I don't think so. They have them corralled. The cemetery has a huge fence and they're locked inside."

Griffin looked to Galen for confirmation. "Is that true?"

"It's a curse." Galen launched into the story as Griffin fawned over

Aisling. Lilac brought the rest of us drinks, and by the time he was finished with the rather interesting tale Aisling's color had returned to nearly normal. "So, basically we're trying to figure out who cast the curse. If that doesn't work, we'll have to come up with another plan. It's difficult because people don't want us going in and taking them down."

"But why not?" Griffin pressed the back of his hand to Aisling's forehead and smiled. "Feeling better?"

She nodded and waited for Galen to answer.

"Think about it," he replied. "If your mother ... or sister ... or child was in there, would you want someone to stab them in the head to put them down?"

Griffin made a face. "I guess. They're not the people who passed. Their souls are gone. I've actually had the occasion to see a few zombies, if you can believe that. I don't know that I'm comfortable knowing they're allowed to get up and walk around unattended after dark."

"They're locked in," I supplied, my voice shriller than I intended. "They can't get out. Don't worry about them, because they can't hurt you. There's no reason to hurt them."

The look on Griffin's face told me couldn't understand why my voice had suddenly gone so screechy.

"Her mother is one of the zombies," Aisling explained on my behalf. "It's none of our business."

Realization dawned on Griffin's face, but he didn't back down. "Since when do you mind your own business?"

"Since now." Aisling was firm as she forced a smile for my benefit. "It's okay. He's just blowing off steam. The thing with the other zombies was difficult."

"You almost died," Griffin grumbled.

"That's hardly the only time I almost died. Besides, I was the only one who believed it was zombies at the start, if you remember correctly. You told me zombies weren't real."

"And we're done talking about that." Griffin made a face as he grabbed the menu. "What's good here?"

"Everything is good here, sugar." Lilac winked at him. "We have seared sea scallops on special if you're interested."

"That sounds good." Aisling handed her menu back to Lilac. "Can I have some stuffed mushrooms, too? Oh, and some fried pickles … and a plate of maraschino cherries as a snack."

"Coming right up, honey." Lilac left with our orders, and as soon as she was gone, Aisling decided it was time to tell the men about the rest of our afternoon.

"So, we found Jacob Dorsey," she started, causing Galen's and Griffin's heads to snap in her direction.

"Why didn't you lead with that?" Galen snapped.

"Because I was dying of heatstroke and needed to be pampered."

Galen's lips curved down. "Seriously, dude, how do you live with her?"

"She's an acquired taste." Griffin readjusted the bag of ice and grinned at his wife. "She's actually a lot of fun when she's not in a mood. Unfortunately for you, humidity always puts her in a mood."

"Definitely," Aisling agreed. "As for your buddy Jacob, he remembers being at the job site and thinking that he should be home. He saw a shadow and got spooked, but he can't remember if he ever made it home. That was the primary thought going through his head. He wanted to go home."

"I'm pretty sure Casey would've known if he made it home," Galen argued, leaning back in his chair and stretching his long legs out in front of him. "She said he didn't come home from work. She assumed he went out with the guys, but I'm guessing that never happened. Did he say anything else?"

"He was scattered," I volunteered. "He seemed ... out of it. I'm sure that's normal when one is murdered, but he seemed confused and upset. He bolted before Aisling could suck his soul. It was too hot to chase him, so we need to be on the lookout in case he pops up again."

"Oh, our little expert didn't get her man, huh?" His teeth gleamed as he smirked at Aisling. "That has to bite."

"You would think so, but you would be wrong," Aisling countered. "I've lost a number of souls. I always make the mistake of chatting instead of sucking. I'll get him eventually ... or leave it to your next reaper, if anyone ever arrives to take on the job."

"Speaking of that, have you talked to your father?" Griffin asked. "I would have thought he'd already have someone here."

"I informed him of what's going on. You were there." Aisling's frown was back. "He hasn't called."

Griffin gave her a sympathetic pat on the hand. "Baby, he'll be fine. I've been in contact with Aidan and he says your father is already ten times better than he was at the wedding."

"You mean when he threatened to cut off your hands — and other stuff — while chasing you around the church?"

Griffin smiled at the memory. "I think that was kind of fun. It was a workout. Got my blood pumping so I was breathless when it came time to exchange vows."

Aisling rolled her eyes. "You were scared spitless. You refused to come out of the back room unless he promised to keep his hands to himself."

"I'm pretty sure you're exaggerating."

"And I'm pretty sure you're purposely forgetting what really happened so Galen won't laugh at you," Aisling shot back. "I know differently."

"I don't care what Galen thinks." Griffin said the words but his surreptitious glance at Galen told me otherwise. "He doesn't care anyway."

"On the contrary. I would love to hear the story of Aisling's father threatening to cut appendages off mere moments before the wedding," Galen drawled. "It sounds like a fun tale."

"Who is getting what appendage cut off?" Lilac asked, returning to the table. The bar was relatively busy for the middle of the week, but she left her staff to handle the tables and drew a chair between Griffin and me so she could join the conversation. "I love a good appendage amputation."

Now Griffin had the red face, so I decided to swoop in and save him. He was a nice guy and he had his hands full with Aisling.

"What did you guys do this morning?"

"We headed out to talk to Barry," Galen replied, sipping his drink and making a face. "He wasn't exactly happy to see us. It didn't go well. He demanded a warrant, so I have a judge signing off on one because I don't have many options."

"You visited the cult?" Aisling leaned forward so fast her bag of ice threatened to fall off her shoulders. Griffin righted it, checked her temperature with his hand again, and then moved his fingers to her back so he could slowly massage away some of the tension.

"I don't think they appreciate being called a cult," Galen said.

"But that's what they are," Griffin argued.

"Oh, they totally are," Lilac agreed, fire sparking in her eyes. "Did I ever tell you about the time they invited me to witness one of their fertility rituals?"

My mouth dropped open. "You can't be serious."

"Oh, I'm serious." Lilac nodded. Even in the most ridiculous circumstances, she was enthusiastic and eager to spill the gossipy beans. This was no exception. "I've known Taurus for a long time."

"Barry," Galen corrected. "If you insist on calling him by that ridiculous name he'll expect others to do it, too."

"You called him by his preferred name yesterday," Aisling noted. "You only called him Barry behind his back."

"That's because I was worried there would be an incident," Galen shot back. "In case you didn't notice, they outnumbered us by a large margin."

"There were four of them."

"And just Wesley and me to fight them off."

"Um ... I believe Hadley and I were there, too," Aisling snapped. "And while I might not look big and strong, I'm ridiculously tough. Ask Griffin."

"It's true," Griffin nodded, solemn. "She's never met a tickle war she didn't win."

Aisling pinched his flank. "I'm serious."

"So am I. I'm a slave to your tickles."

"Whatever." Aisling folded her arms over her chest and glared.

Wisely, Lilac decided to ignore the pouting and return to her story.

"He stopped in for a drink one day when he was in town for supplies. This was two or three years ago, before they lost the legal battle for the parcel near the water."

"Why is that important?" Griffin asked, his fingers on Aisling's back as he rubbed.

"He was happier then," Lilac replied. "You have to understand, when they first started their cult, people assumed they were merely kooky morons who wanted to smoke pot on the beach. You know, live a bohemian lifestyle and the like."

"That sounds horrible," Aisling commented. "My father took us camping once. It was the worst experience of my life."

"The way he tells the tale, it was worse for him," Griffin said. "I believe you guys ended up in a hotel after a few hours. I don't think that counts as camping."

Aisling rolled her eyes, which was Lilac's cue to continue.

"They had a big spread on the land, and I went out of curiosity more than anything else," Lilac said. "I wasn't really interested in participating, which Taurus said was fine, but when I got out there I couldn't believe the number of people at the event.

"There were people there I had no idea had ties with him," she continued. "They did a big dance and banged some drums. They did some chants, some of the men spit fire. I have no idea where they learned that, but it was wicked cool."

"And what did the ritual entail?" Galen asked.

"I'm not a hundred percent certain," Lilac admitted. "The women all went up and laid on this wooden altar that someone had obviously carved. He put a hand on their foreheads and chanted some gobbledygook that I couldn't quite make out. Then the group started chanting and the next thing I knew all the women were up and dancing naked."

I hadn't anticipated the second part of the statement, so I choked on my rum runner. "What?" I sputtered, coughing.

Galen gave me a solid thump on the back to clear my airway as he grinned. "I've heard there're some nude hijinks up there. I've never actually seen them doing anything, but the stories are fairly prevalent. Wesley swears that they were in his cornfield once."

"Doing what?" I asked, appalled.

"I believe shucking was probably involved," Griffin quipped.

"Pretty close," Galen confirmed. "When we went up there today. Everyone was dressed. Barry was angry; said you guys were spying on him and he wouldn't have it. He warned that something terrible would happen if the town tried to move him again. He's mostly talk, if you ask me, but I don't doubt he could do some damage if he put his mind to it."

"I still don't understand how the women ended up naked," Aisling pressed. "I mean ... was it magic? Did he chant away their clothes?"

Lilac shrugged. "I have no idea what caused it. All I know is that all of sudden everyone was naked and dancing. I couldn't get out of there quick enough ... after watching a bit of the dancing, of course."

"You watched?" I was horrified, and mildly intrigued.

"Of course I watched." She wasn't the least bit embarrassed. "How often do you get to say that you saw thirty women dancing naked to help the fertility gods spread sperm to the world?"

My cheeks burned as Galen's shoulders shook with silent laughter. Griffin averted his gaze, but Aisling was officially intrigued.

"Was there sex?" She asked the obvious question. "I mean, did you see your buddy the bull mount anybody?"

"Aisling!" Griffin's voice was sharp. "I don't think we need that much information."

"Oh, like you're not curious," she scoffed. "Seriously, did you see any hanky-panky?"

Lilac shook her head. "I didn't, but I left before things got serious."

"It gets more serious than that?" Aisling was incredulous. "Everything we saw was boring. I can't help thinking we missed out."

"And you're going to keep missing out." Galen's tone was firm. "You both promised you wouldn't go back out there. I'm holding you to that promise."

"I have no intention of going back out there," Aisling said. "I'm just curious how this fertility ritual works. I mean ... they're a cult. There are obviously some men for security purposes, and to keep them happy Taurus must be letting them graze with his flock. Most of those women are there for him, though. I'm simply trying to figure out how it works."

"You leave that to me," Galen ordered. "I'm not sure they have anything to do with this. It makes sense that they might go after Jacob at the construction site because if they cause enough trouble Barry might believe that the developers will pull out. But what's the motivation for Adam Grimport?"

Aisling shrugged. "I don't know. I bet if you find that answer, though, everything will fall together pretty fast."

"So, now you're a detective?"

"I would make an awesome detective."

"Of course you would, baby." Griffin kissed her cheek. "But for now your main job is being my wife. Can't you just stick to that for a few days? For me?"

Aisling graced him with an angelic smile. "You bet, snookums."

Griffin's smile slipped. "I know you're just placating me, but I'll take it."

Galen nodded. "You're a wise man."

Griffin grinned as they fist bumped.

21

TWENTY-ONE

Once Griffin was convinced Aisling was back to her normal self — which essentially meant zinging insults and twisting her face into a sarcastic mask — he kissed her goodbye and headed out to the golf cart to wait for Galen.

Perhaps sensing my deep thoughts, Galen tugged me aside for a lingering kiss and hug before pulling back and scanning my features.

"Do you want to tell me what you're thinking?"

"Several things," I admitted, forcing a smile. "Some things Aisling said at the cemetery kind of threw me for a loop."

"What things?"

"The things about my mother. I don't know how to explain it. We talked a bit about how she was close with her mother and lost her but was suspicious the moment she returned. That didn't stop her from longing to make the woman who came back the mother she remembered."

Galen's fingers were gentle as they combed through my hair. "And you wonder if it's worse to never know your mother and pine for what could have been. I think it's a vastly different scenario. Besides that, Aisling had her father and brothers. It sounds as if they're a big tribe. You only had your father."

"Who isn't a bad man." I don't know why I kept saying those exact words to Galen. It was as if I was trying to convince both of us by repeating the mantra.

"I never said he was." Galen briefly rested his forehead against mine. "It's okay. You don't have to make excuses for him. I'll like him regardless because you love him."

"How can you be sure?"

"Look at Griffin. Aisling's father apparently threatens him with great bodily harm at the drop of a hat. I've never heard Griffin say anything other than respectful words about that man."

"I don't know that it's the same thing."

"Well, whatever it is, we'll get through it." He gave me another kiss and turned somber. "I don't know what you have planned with your buddy for the rest of the day, but you might want to keep her in the shade. She is clearly not used to the heat and humidity here, and Griffin might melt down if she looks that rough when we meet for dinner."

"I'll keep her in the shade," I promised. "We basically got side-tracked with Jacob's soul."

"Next time, if you find him, collect him and leave it at that. Jacob was a nice guy. I would hate for his soul to go crazy."

"Yeah. I think we both learned our lesson."

"I don't believe Aisling learned her lesson, but it's not my business." Another kiss and he backed away. "I'll see you later. Be good."

I waved, smiling, and was wistfully thinking of things we might do together once it was just the two of us later that evening when Aisling appeared at my side.

"Oh, wipe that goofy grin off your face," she ordered, shaking her head. "You have lust in your eyes."

"So what?" I snapped, reality smacking me across the face. "We're in that lovey-dovey portion of our relationship. Sue me."

"Yes, I remember that period with Griffin." Aisling adopted a far-off expression. "I believe it was a Tuesday ... and then my father caught us sleeping together in my old room at Grimlock Manor. Suffice to say, after that, we were more careful around my father."

Something other than her intended message occurred to me. "You named your house? I mean ... Grimlock Manor. It really does sound like a castle."

Aisling heaved out an extended sigh. "My father named it. The house is his baby ... other than us, I mean. He would trade the house for us if there was ever a ransom demand, but it's kind of like a sixth child to him. Anyway, I have an idea about where we should go."

"Oh, yeah?" I perked up. "Where?"

"The wife's house."

"You think Jacob ran to his old house to be close to Casey?" I'd thought it about it, and it did make sense. "It certainly couldn't hurt. I'll find out where she lives from Lilac."

"That's not the only reason I want to head over there," Aisling added. "There's another reason."

"What?"

"That fertility ritual."

"I don't get it."

"That ritual supposedly helps those who can't help themselves, right? Well, Casey is pregnant with a miracle baby she was never supposed to be able to carry. What if all of this is part of that ritual?"

Worry clawed through my stomach as I considered the statement. "Oh. You think Jacob is dead because Casey is pregnant."

"I think it's a possibility that we should check."

"Okay, but ... how are we going to approach her? That won't be easy to broach in a normal conversation."

"Trust me. I've got everything under control."

I hated it when she said that.

AISLING WASN'T KIDDING WHEN she said she had everything under control. Once we parked in Casey's driveway, she marched to the front door. She didn't hesitate to bang as hard as possible. That saying about being loud enough to wake the dead? I think that's what she was going for. After waiting a few minutes, she did it again. Once we were reasonably assured Casey wasn't there, she slid her eyes to me, the question obvious.

"Absolutely not," I hissed, keeping my voice low and glancing over my shoulder to make sure we weren't drawing attention. "If you break into another house Galen will melt down like you wouldn't believe. He really will lock you up."

"It would hardly be the first time I've been locked up," Aisling pointed out, covering her eyes with her hands so she could stand on her tiptoes and peer through the glass panel in the door. "I think we should go inside."

"No!" I grabbed her arm and firmly shook my head. There was no way I was going to allow this to happen a second time. "We can't. I promised Galen."

"I didn't promise Galen. You can wait here and I'll break in. That way you'll keep your promise and I'll get the important information."

"No!" I gripped her wrist so tightly my knuckles turned white. "You swore to Galen that you would behave yourself."

"Yes, but that's a sliding scale. I believe figuring out what sort of murderer you have running around your island is more important than keeping Galen's fragile ego in check."

"His ego isn't fragile."

"Please." She rolled her eyes. "He's one of those really thin but pretty wine glasses that last for one use and then die in the dishwasher. That's how fragile he is. I'm going to check inside whether you like it or not. You can't stop me. You can, however, choose to remove yourself from the situation and wait outside. It's totally up to you."

I was furious. "I don't want to break and enter."

"So, stay here." Aisling already had her lock pick out. "I'll be quick. Trust me."

IN THE END, I COULDN'T LET her go in alone. Even though I knew Galen would be furious if he found out, the idea of someone hiding in the house and perhaps attacking Aisling as she searched for information was too much to bear. I had to go with her, serve as backup and, yes, see if there was anything of interest inside the house.

What? I guess I'm a busybody, too.

My natural urge was to crouch low and press myself to the walls as we walked into the house. Thankfully, no foul smells were waiting to assail our olfactory senses when we stepped inside. The small ranch house was cool, quiet and empty.

"Where do you think we should start?" I whispered.

Aisling slid me an amused look. "I don't know. I think a home office would be best." She didn't whisper, and instead strode through the house as if she owned it. "Come on. Don't be a baby ... and stop walking like some horror movie creeper. You look ridiculous."

I straightened. "I'm new at this."

"Yeah, yeah, yeah."

I followed her through the hallway, heading into the first room on the left. Sadly, that was the guest bathroom. Aisling didn't see my sheepish expression when I walked out because she was already in the room across the hallway. I hurried to join her, my mouth dropping open when I saw the way it was decorated.

"Holy ... !" I slowly circled, dumbfounded as I took in the outrageous decorations. There had to be at least twenty tiki masks littering the walls, and that was on top of some other rather interesting art.

"Look at this." Aisling's attention lasered in on the large painting that served as the artistic centerpiece in the room. She moved closer, furrowing her brow as she took in the bright splashes of color.

I had trouble looking at the painting. That probably had something to do with the fact that it depicted a horned beast having sex with a woman in the middle of a crowd. The art itself felt deviant, but the painting was telling.

"I'm guessing this is local," Aisling muttered as she leaned closer to the slashes in the bottom right-hand corner to read the artist's signature. "Ever heard of Aries?"

"No."

"It fits in with that astrological thing they're doing out there. I'm guessing Aries is the chief artist." Aisling dragged her eyes from the painting and focused on the masks. "These look similar to the masks that were found on the bodies."

"They do," I agreed, pulling one of the masks off the wall to study it closer. "I think it's safe to say that the tribe had something to do with the deaths."

"Definitely. I … ."

I gave Aisling a moment to rediscover her train of thought as I studied the mask. When she didn't start speaking again, I looked in her direction and found her gaping at the woman standing in the open doorway.

It was Casey, her pallor white, and she looked absolutely stunned to find us in her house. I couldn't blame her.

"We need to talk," I said, holding up the mask. We were already caught. There was no sense in not asking questions before she called Galen and had us arrested. "I'm guessing you know more about Jacob's death than you're letting on."

IF CASEY WAS UPSET TO find us in her house, she didn't show it. Instead, she ushered us into the kitchen, grabbed a pitcher of lemonade from the refrigerator, and joined us in the blissfully cool dining room.

"This is the coolest room in the house," she explained, pouring three glasses of lemonade. "I prefer the chill right now."

"I'm a big fan of air conditioning myself," Aisling said. "I don't suppose you want to tell us what's going on?"

"I'm not supposed to." Casey stared at her lemonade. "If he finds out … ."

"I don't see where you have much choice," I pressed. "We need to know what happened to Jacob."

"You don't understand. It's … above you. You're blaming me, but I didn't know what was going to happen. I swear it."

"You didn't know what?"

"That he would be the sacrifice."

She wasn't making sense. "What sacrifice?"

Casey didn't immediately answer, instead gnawing on her thumbnail as she stared at that wall. I exchanged a brief glance with Aisling, who looked as baffled as I felt, and then pushed harder.

"Casey, I'm not trying to make this difficult for you. It's the last thing I want. But we have two dead men. One of them is your husband. Don't you want to see his death avenged?"

"Of course I do," Casey snapped, recovering. "It's just ... I feel so lost. I don't know what to do. I'm afraid ... so very afraid."

"We can't help unless we know the whole story," Aisling pointed out.

"There's not much to tell." Casey took another sip of her lemonade. "I'm not sure how much you know about our fertility problems."

"I've heard most of the story," I admitted. "My understanding is that you guys tried throughout your twenties to have a baby and then essentially gave up because it was taking too much out of you."

"That's mostly true," Casey agreed, nodding. "Jacob and I were at a breaking point. We loved each other beyond reason and we desperately wanted a child. Neither of us could take the visits to the specialists ... or the hormone injections … or the crushing broken hearts that occurred each time something didn't work ... so we agreed to take a step back. Jacob was keener about it than I was, but I knew our marriage would break if I didn't focus on him and let go of what couldn't be.

"I was downtown one day when I heard Marla Simpson talking, and that's what got me back on the baby track," she continued. "You probably don't know Marla. Well, let me tell you. She's a fifty-year-old woman who started following Taurus five years ago. Her husband left her because she couldn't get pregnant and he married some young woman who was pregnant before they even filed for divorce. Marla was crushed. No baby. No husband. Except ... she was pregnant that day in the store. She was fifty and pregnant.

"Of course I asked her about it," she said. "I mean ... who wouldn't ask? It was a miracle. She told me about Taurus's fertility ritual, and I had to check it out for myself. I mean ... I had to, right?" She looked to me for a nod of agreement. I wasn't sure I could give it to her, so I merely spread out my hands and shrugged.

"I went to him because I was desperate. I know that was a mistake," Casey explained. "He welcomed me to the group, spent a full three hours giving me a tour of their facilities, and then he promised he could get me pregnant ... and not in a gross way, so don't let your mind go to the gutter," she warned Aisling.

"I guess I'm curious about how you became pregnant," Aisling said, choosing her words carefully. "I mean ... I get that your barren womb is now full, but is the baby even your husband's kid?"

"Of course the baby is Jacob's." Annoyance flashed in Casey's eyes. "How can you even ask that?"

"Because we've heard about the fertility ritual before and it sounds like a bunch of naked dancing that turns into an orgy."

"Well, that's not what I went through," Casey countered. "There was some chanting ... and dancing. Taurus warned that I would have to make a sacrifice and I agreed to his terms. If I could have a baby, what sacrifice wouldn't I make to give Jacob and myself the one thing we've always wanted? I assumed it would be money. Now that we weren't paying for fertility treatments we had some put away."

My stomach twisted at her earnest expression. "You think the sacrifice was Jacob, don't you?"

"Who else? You've seen the masks. I didn't put those decorations in the office willingly. It was part of the process. They were provided by Taurus. He insisted they had to stay up until I gave birth."

"That's weird." Aisling rubbed the back of her neck as she considered Casey's conundrum. "Have you seen Taurus since Jacob died?"

"No. He's called three times wanting to pay his respects, but I've ignored the calls because I'm afraid. What am I supposed to do?"

"Why didn't you call Galen?" I asked gently. "He would've helped."

"Yes, but then I would've had to admit that I was part of it, that it was my fault my husband died. I did this. I thought I was providing him with the answer to our prayers and instead he lost his life. How am I supposed to make amends for what I've done?" She buried her face in her arms and sobbed.

Aisling's expression was as grim as mine as our eyes snagged.

"I think we're dealing with some sort of black magic," she said quietly. "I don't think Jacob was the sacrifice for Casey's baby. I think someone else was ... someone who was conveniently helped by Barry's fertility ritual. So someone else died for Casey to get pregnant and Jacob died for someone else to get pregnant. That's the only way the timeline fits. I obviously can't be sure, though."

"So, what should we do?" I asked as I rubbed Casey's back. She was a mess, her sobs coming in hiccups.

"I don't know." Aisling was thoughtful. "We can't let that crazy freak get away with this. We have to stop him ... and protect Casey. She didn't realize what was going to happen. That means Taurus is being purposely vague. There has to be a reason for that."

22

TWENTY-TWO

Casey was such a mess we suggested she pack up and move out of the house. If Taurus came after her, if his patience at being ignored wore thin, she would be safer surrounded by family. She fought the effort, argued that this was Jacob's house and she felt closer to him in it, but Aisling was adamant.

"You need your family," she stressed, refusing to back down. "Trust me. Family is important. Once this is all settled, you can come back and start over. Until then, you need backup."

Casey was weepy, but followed our instructions as she packed a suitcase. Then we loaded her into the golf cart — Aisling took the back seat with the luggage while Casey directed me toward her parents' house — and once we were assured she was safely inside we started plotting.

"I have to call Galen," I insisted after parking in the shade outside the grocery store.

Aisling, who was guzzling from a huge bottle of water, nodded. "You'd better. He will have a conniption fit if you don't."

I was nervous as I selected Galen's name from my contact list and pressed the phone to my ear. After four rings, it became apparent that he wasn't going to pick up, so I left him a voicemail insisting that he call me as soon as possible, stressing that we weren't in trouble and simply had information.

When I was done, Aisling decided to call Griffin. He could relay the information to Galen, who was potentially busy with interviews or other issues. Griffin's phone went to voicemail, too, leaving us perplexed.

"What should we do?" Aisling asked after she left a much terser message. "Should we try to find them? They didn't say what they were doing after lunch, so I don't know where to start looking. Maybe we should go to the station."

I pointed across the road to the police station. "They're not there. Galen's truck is gone. They could be anywhere ... including out in the boonies with Taurus and his merry band of misfits. Galen said he was getting a warrant. I just didn't think he would be using it today."

"We could look for them out there."

"Don't even think about it." On this I refused to back down. "We're not going out there. I promised Galen we wouldn't, and I meant it."

She pursed her lips. "Who else might be able to offer us some help? Someone who has a vehicle would be nice."

My mind immediately went to Booker. "I know someone, but he probably won't be happy."

"Well, he'll have to get over it."

AS PREDICTED, BOOKER WAS LESS than thrilled when he caught sight of us approaching him at the same tiki bar he'd been working at earlier in the week. He scowled when he saw us moving in tandem, and merely shook his head as he placed a piece of wood against the outside of a window – perhaps repairing a rotted frame – and glared.

"Whatever you two are up to, I'm not interested," he growled.

"Oh, don't be like that," I whined, adopting my best "you like me and know you want to help me" look. "We're here with our hats in hand."

Booker flicked his eyes to Aisling. "Do you have your hat in hand?"

She shook her head. "I don't look good in hats. Sometimes I wear them, but only if I wake up late and don't have time to wash my hair." She moved closer to him and grabbed the piece of wood to hold it in place. "Start hammering."

He smirked, her attitude causing him to grin. "You're full of yourself, aren't you?"

"I've been told that a time or two," Aisling agreed. "You smell different today." She leaned and sniffed. "Grilled cheese sandwich and tomato soup. Interesting."

"I think your hormones are playing havoc with your olfactory senses," Booker countered. "I smell of sweat and sun."

"I'm interested in this cupid thing," Aisling admitted. "We have other things to worry about right now, so it'll have to wait. We need your help ... and you're going to give it without argument."

"Oh, really? What makes you think that?"

"Because you're genuinely fond of Hadley," Aisling replied without hesitation. "She intrigues you. If I had to guess, it's because she doesn't react to that musk you exude. It must be exhausting to be in your position, to have women throwing themselves at you wherever you go."

"Actually, I happen to like it."

"You make a big show of liking it," she corrected. "You probably did like it when you were a teenager. That's every teenager's wet dream, after all, but you're not overly fond of it now because you're getting to an age where notions of settling down are taking over. How can you settle down when you're never sure if these women like you because of you or the fact that you smell like grilled cheese sandwiches?"

"You're the only person who has ever said I smell like a sandwich."

"I'm not a normal girl."

"Definitely not," Booker agreed, his eyes flashing with something I couldn't identify. "You're more intuitive than people give you credit for, aren't you?"

"I never get the credit I deserve."

"Yeah, well ... what do you want?" Booker was resigned as he looked to me. "I can already tell I'm going to hate this."

I related our day, leaving nothing out but sprinting through the high points. When I was done, the look on Booker's face was straight out of a horror movie.

"Wait ... Casey thinks that Jacob was a sacrifice for whatever fertility ritual Taurus used on her?"

"Pretty much." I bobbed my head. "Aisling has an interesting hunch that maybe there's some overlap — we have no idea how Adam Grimport plays into this. We need to find Galen but he's not answering his cell phone."

Booker scrubbed at the back of his head as he raised his eyes to the sky. "Why me?" He was seemingly asking it of a deity, but I had no idea about the belief system of a cupid and was instantly suspicious.

"What do you know?"

"I might — I stress *might* — have run into Galen and Griffin about two hours ago when they were leaving town," he hedged. "They were on their way out to visit the cult after securing a warrant. They mentioned something about wanting to check on the people staying out there. I'm pretty sure it was a fishing expedition, but they seemed determined."

My heart dropped. "But ... if Taurus thinks they're spying on him, trying to shut him down, he might hurt them. Griffin and Galen will be woefully outnumbered."

"I would like to point out that Galen can take care of himself ... and he's armed."

"That won't stop fifty crazy people from jumping him," Aisling hissed, her expression darkening. "Griffin is on vacation. He's not armed, and he's not a shifter like Galen. He can only do so much."

"I'm sure they're fine."

"Well, if you're sure," Aisling sneered, pressing the heel of her hand to her forehead. I could practically feel the tension rolling off her. "We have to get out there."

Even though I wasn't as opposed to the idea as I had been the first time she suggested it, I balked. "I'm not sure that's a good idea."

"Yes, well, I'm not sure I care. I'm not leaving Griffin exposed to a group of fertility-challenged cult members."

"Slow your roll," Booker ordered. "Your husband is a trained detective. He can handle himself."

"And I'm going after him." Aisling was firm as she turned on her heel. "I don't care if you go with me. I won't leave him out there."

"Wait a second." Booker dropped his hammer and strode after her, fury evident on his face. He grabbed her arm before she got too far and spun her so she faced him. "You can't go out there. You're pregnant. You could get hurt."

"I don't care. I'm going after my husband." She was defiant as she stared into Booker's eyes. "There's nothing you can do to stop me."

"There's something I can do to stop you."

I froze at the new voice, my eyes going wide when I realized we weren't alone. The man who stood about ten feet behind Booker and Aisling was tall, distinguished and wearing a very expensive suit on the beach. He looked weary, as if the weight of the world rested on his shoulders. He had black hair, and his purple eyes stared directly at Aisling.

When she turned to meet his gaze, she didn't shrink in the face of his obvious annoyance. Instead, she burst into tears and strode toward him.

The man — who I assumed was Cormack Grimlock — wrapped her in a hug and rocked her back and forth. He stroked her hair, rested his cheek against her forehead, and sighed. "Kid, you are a pain in the butt. Has anyone ever told you that?"

"Griffin is in trouble."

"So I heard. Tell me what's going on." He tipped up her chin and swiped at the free-falling tears. "Stop that. You know I can't take it when you cry."

"I can't seem to help myself," Aisling admitted, her lower lip trembling. "I don't know what's wrong with me."

"I do. You're a pain in the behind."

"I can be a pain in the behind without crying. I don't know why I can't stop. I watched a commercial last night. It had a puppy and a horse, and I cried then, too."

"It's the hormones." Cormack sounded weary as he shook his head. "Your mother was the same way the first time she got pregnant. She made me watch *Little House on the Prairie* episodes so she could have a reason to cry. She wasn't quite as ashamed of her actions as you are."

Aisling sniffled. "We have to get Griffin."

"And we will ... just as soon as you tell me what's going on." He was calm as he rubbed her back. "Introduce me to your friends and we'll go from there."

"I'm Hadley." I stepped forward and extended my hand, my eyes scanning the older man's expressive face. "Has anyone ever told you that your resemblance to your children is eerie?"

He chuckled as he accepted the handshake. "Everyone. Aisling says we look like a science experiment gone awry." He flicked his eyes to Booker. "And you are?"

"Booker." They shook hands. "Your daughter is an absolute joy, by the way. Good job raising her to never accept 'no' for an answer." He flashed a sarcastic thumbs-up. "Way to go."

"My daughter is ... a force to be reckoned with." Cormack never stopped soothing his child, making me realize there were all sorts of parent-child relationships in the world. When his wife died, he obviously took over and became the emotional rock his family needed. My father was vastly different, and it made me yearn for the sort of relationship the Grimlocks clearly enjoyed. "Now, if you don't mind, can we take this conversation inside so I can enjoy some air conditioning?"

"We have to go after Griffin," Aisling insisted, a fresh bout of tears unleashed. "We can't leave him."

"I have no intention of leaving him, Aisling. If anyone is going to kill him, it's going to be me. I need to get out of this infernal heat, though, and you need some water. Your face is extremely red."

"I don't take the humidity well."

"I'm aware. Come along. You can have some water and a snack, and then we'll go from there."

. . .

WE WENT TO LILAC'S bar because it was comfortable and we didn't have to worry about people eavesdropping in the middle of the afternoon. We settled at a table in the corner — Lilac brought drinks for everyone — and then the conversation turned serious.

"I need to know absolutely everything," Cormack stated as he watched Aisling suck down her water. "To start, how are you feeling, kid?"

Aisling knit her eyebrows. "I'm sick of people asking me that question. I'm not fragile. I'm perfectly fine."

"I didn't suggest you weren't perfectly fine. I'm simply asking how you're feeling. You are carrying my first grandchild, after all."

She exhaled heavily and wiped her hand across her forehead. "I throw up every morning and I can't take the heat. This already sucks. Is that what you want to hear?"

"No."

"Why aren't you going after Griffin?" The question came out a whine, but Aisling clearly didn't care. "He could be in trouble."

"And he could be perfectly fine. I need all the facts before I race off to get him."

"I think you're leaving him out there because you hope something will happen to him."

"And I think you're being ridiculous," Cormack shot back. "Griffin is as much my son now as the others. I love him. I want to hurt him right now — as I would want to hurt your brothers if they got a girl pregnant before marriage — but I still love Griffin."

"Then go get him." Aisling's tears were starting to dry. "He's in trouble. There's a cult out there and they're killing people. I want him back right now."

"Don't take that tone with me." Cormack extended a warning finger. "I may let you run roughshod over me because you're spoiled, but I deserve some respect. And, quite frankly, you need to pull yourself together. Griffin needs both of us. I need to know what we're up against before we run out there half-cocked."

Aisling scowled. "Oh, whatever."

Because she didn't seem willing to do it, I launched into the story from the beginning. I felt as if I'd told it so many times that the details were now second nature. When I was done, Cormack was calm as he rubbed his chin.

"And we have no idea why the reaper was targeted?" he asked.

I shook my head. "I can't think of any reason."

"I can, but I'm not sure I like the implications." Cormack's hand was steady on Aisling's back as he rubbed at the tension eating away at her. "It sounds like this was a concerted effort. Whatever ritual they're doing requires souls. Souls aren't always easy to get."

"Booker says there aren't many wraiths here," Aisling volunteered. "I think that means most souls are accounted for."

"I would guess that's true," Cormack agreed. "It's not like Detroit, where we have innumerable souls and wraiths running rampant. If this group needs souls, perhaps they went after the reaper because they wanted to keep him from transferring souls to the home office."

"How does that work?" Booker asked.

"It's a complex procedure, but my understanding is that your reaper didn't have much work. It was a cushy gig. You needed a reaper, obviously, but it was almost a retirement position of sorts for Adam."

"Did you know him?" I asked.

"I met him a time or two. I can't say he was much of a risk-taker. He did his job, stuck to the schedule. That's probably why he fit in so well on the island. Either way, he's dead. The home office is finding a replacement even as we speak. I knew Aisling was here, but I didn't want her running around absorbing souls on her honeymoon. I agreed to pinch hit for a few days."

"And here I thought you came for me," Aisling groused.

"I did come for you. Your constant calls home were getting to be a bit much ... and your brothers wouldn't stop giving me grief. Even Braden took up for you and said getting pregnant wasn't a big deal."

"It's not," Aisling agreed. "If I'd come home from the honeymoon pregnant, would you have been so upset?"

"I don't know. I still would've known what Griffin did to my baby even under those circumstances."

I had to bite my lip to keep from laughing at the aggrieved expression on Aisling's face.

"We were sleeping together in your house ... and quite often," Aisling pointed out. "You had to know it was coming eventually."

"Maybe I wanted you to have time to settle."

"And maybe we don't always get exactly what we want at the exact time we want it," Aisling countered. "It's done. I'm going to have a baby. We have to move forward."

"I know." Cormack ordered Aisling's hair. "We'll move forward."

"We have to get Griffin first. That means going out to visit the cult."

"I understand." Cormack heaved out a sigh and shifted his gaze to Booker. "I don't suppose you have any strong and magical friends you could rope into a potential fight? I would rather not risk anyone if it's not necessary."

Booker's grin was impish. "I have a few ideas. What do you have in mind?"

23

TWENTY-THREE

I had no idea how Cormack managed to secure a vehicle, something that should have been an insurmountable feat. He had two men with him, both dressed in suits — very *Men In Black,* frankly - and he loaded us in the vehicle before taking a moment to talk privately with Booker.

I had no idea what they were talking about, but the conversation looked serious. When I spared a glance for Aisling, I found she was impatiently drumming her fingers on the seat.

"He's trying to drive me insane," she hissed. "He knows I want to get out there and find Griffin but, no, he has to take his sweet-ass time playing kissy face with Booker. Because that's important."

"I don't think they're playing kissy face."

"My father is very charming. If anyone could seduce your cupid, it's my father. I swear I'm going to ... ." She mimed something vicious with her hands that I couldn't quite make out.

"Is that code for athletic origami or something?"

Her glare was vicious when it landed on me. "Do you think you're funny?"

I held up my hands. "I'm sorry. I don't think you're doing yourself any favors by getting all worked up. There's no reason to freak out."

"Oh, I'm not freaking out." Aisling stomped her foot as hard as she could on the floor to get her father's attention. "Right now!"

Cormack calmly raised a finger in silent admonishment and continued talking to Booker. When he was finished a few minutes later, he strode toward us, an air of cool sophistication wafting off him as he fastened his seatbelt. "We're heading out."

I glanced through the window, to where Booker was talking to Lilac. "What about Booker? We might need help."

"He'll be right behind us. He's gathering a few friends."

"Oh." That made me feel a little better. "Aisling and I know where we're headed. We'll lead you there and they can catch up."

"We're meeting at your grandfather's ranch," he countered, ignoring the protesting sound Aisling made. "We won't be there long. He says that's the closest place for our group to assemble. Can you sit up front with my driver and direct him?"

"I guess." I shifted my eyes to Aisling, who looked as if she was about to throw herself on her father and start kicking. "Are you sure this is the best way to go?"

"I'm sure that I don't know what we're walking into and I want to be as prepared as possible. We might only have one chance at this. I want to make sure it's a good one."

That sounded reasonable to me.

THE DRIVE TO WESLEY'S farm felt longer than normal. The driver went the speed limit, which irritated me, but I managed to bite my tongue and keep from verbally lambasting his driving skills. Aisling was another story.

"Pull over right now and let me drive," she bellowed from the back seat, where she was pinned between her father and the other man he'd brought with him.

"Ignore my daughter, David," Cormack instructed. "She's overwrought. I think she needs a nap. In fact, if she doesn't stop causing a scene, I'll make sure she doesn't leave the farm we're heading to."

"You and what army?" Aisling snapped.

"I won't let you serve as a distraction, kid." Cormack was firm. "We need to make sure Griffin is all right. Right now, we don't even know if he's in trouble. That's an assumption you've made, and I'm not sure it's correct."

"He would've called by now," she insisted, fury propelling her to grab his wrist. "You know he would have returned my call. He wouldn't torture me like this."

Cormack's expression softened. "Not on purpose, no. Maybe he doesn't get cell service out there. Have you considered that?"

One look at Aisling's expression told me she hadn't considered that. "Galen said there are only two cell towers on the island," I offered. "It's possible they aren't getting service. We didn't stop to see how many bars we had on our phones when we were spying."

"See." Cormack winced as he removed his wrist from Aisling's iron grip. "You must calm yourself. I can't remember the last time you were this worked up."

"Yes, you do." Aisling's eyes went flat as she stared out the front window. "It was when we got word that the building Mom was collecting her soul in fell ... and she wasn't out yet."

Cormack exhaled heavily. "I guess I do remember. Your reaction didn't help then, and it won't help now. Griffin needs you to be strong, not this mess of moods. I'll blame your pregnancy hormones for this little outburst — which is vastly different from your other outbursts because of the emotions attached — and ask that you calm yourself."

He sucked in a cleansing breath, never breaking eye contact with his lookalike daughter. "Now, tell me about this pregnancy. I didn't get a chance to talk to you at the wedding. Are you having a boy or girl?"

Whatever she was expecting, that wasn't it. Aisling's mouth dropped open and a strangled sound escaped. "We don't know. I've only taken a home pregnancy test. We won't go to the doctor until we get back."

"All right." Cormack nodded curtly. He reminded me of the sort of man who had a list of questions to ask and he'd just ticked one off. "Do you want a boy or a girl?"

"I don't know." Aisling leaned back against the seat, and to my surprise, rested her head against her father's shoulder. "We're probably safer with a boy, but you always said karma was going to get me, so I'm convinced it will be a girl."

"Little girls aren't so bad." He patted her knee. "They're simply a different sort of trouble. You'll be fine. You're not alone. You'll always have me ... even if your husband is a demented pervert who needs to be smacked around a bit."

"We need to get him back."

"We will. I promise you. You need to calm yourself first. You won't be of much use in a fight if you're crying. What did I always tell you when you were little about crying?"

"Only do it if I really wanted you to buy me something special."

Cormack snickered. "I don't believe I used those exact words."

"You said to only cry when it matters, when it's important."

"We don't know that anything has happened yet," he stressed. "We'll know soon. If you expect to go on this little adventure with me, you need to hold it together. Okay?"

"Okay."

"Good." He pressed a kiss to her forehead. "Everything will work out. You'll see."

WESLEY OBVIOUSLY expected us because he was waiting on the front porch when we pulled into the driveway. Cormack helped Aisling out of the vehicle before striding straight toward my grandfather and shaking his hand.

"Thank you for letting us meet here to strategize."

"No problem." Wesley's eyes moved to me. "Booker called and told me what's going on. Are you sure this is the way you want to do things? We don't even know if Galen and Griffin are in trouble. They could be fine."

"They could be," I agreed. "They might also be in real trouble. From what Casey told us, she participated in Taurus's fertility ritual because she was desperate. He told her there would be a price. He didn't mention that price would be her husband."

"He also made her put up goofy masks and a pornographic painting in her house," Aisling added. "The guy is all kinds of bonkers. I don't trust him ... and I want to make sure Griffin is safe. I don't care if we look like idiots going in as long as we find our people."

"Fair enough." Wesley held his hands up in a placating manner. "Booker is bringing a few friends. He said he would be about thirty minutes behind you. What can I do to help?"

"I don't suppose you have an aerial map of the area, do you?" Cormack asked.

"As a matter of fact, I do." Wesley led us into the house, directing us toward his first-floor study. I hadn't spent much time at the farm, so I was naturally curious as we navigated the hallways. I made a mental note to visit again when I had time for a real tour. I spent most of my time on the front porch when I visited. That should probably be rectified.

"This is good," Cormack noted when Wesley laid out the map on a table. "Where are we on this map?"

Wesley pointed. "And the cult camp is right about here." He pointed again.

"Out of curiosity, where did they used to be?"

I gestured toward the correct spot on the map. "There. Why does that matter?"

"I'm simply trying to get the lay of the land," he replied, his gaze intense. "When were they informed they would have to move?"

"Years ago," Wesley replied. "The hotel has been planned for a good seven or eight years. Barry has been running around in the wilderness for a very long time, since right after he graduated from high school. It was a slow move to Crazy Town. At first he kept his house and simply started hanging around the beach during the days.

"Then it turned to nights and weeks at a time," he continued. "For at least two years he kept coming into town and acting like nothing was different. During that time, more and more people started gravitating toward the area.

"You should understand, no one realized it was a cult right off the bat," he said. "We thought they were just hippies grouping together to party on the beach. It was all bonfires and the occasional public fornication. Nobody was getting hurt."

"Along the way it changed, though, correct?" Cormack prodded. "When did you start to notice that things were going south?"

"I guess it was sometime in year three." Wesley scratched his cheek as he accessed his memories. "Barry got a notice from the DDA because he wasn't keeping up his property."

"Why would the Downtown Development Authority care about a residential issue?" Cormack asked, puzzled.

"Apparently the DDA is big and scary here," Aisling volunteered, moving closer to her father to study the map. "It's not like the DDAs by us that are just in it for the money. These guys have actual rules and are supposedly terrifying."

"She's right," Wesley acknowledged. "Our DDA means business. After six warnings went unanswered, the DDA seized his house and demanded he show up for judgment."

"That sounds ominous." Cormack slid his arm around Aisling's back. "Was he flogged or something?"

"No. We don't flog. He brought his followers to the meeting, though, and that's when we realized things were getting out of hand. He insisted everyone call him Taurus — even though half the people at the meeting were laughing — and he spouted some nonsense about not being beholden to the government.

"The DDA members responded by saying his property would be seized and sold at auction if he didn't take care of it," he continued. "He kept spouting his nonsense, so they seized the property. They sent movers in to pack up his stuff, put the money he made from the sale in an account for him, and had the sheriff deliver everything to Barry on the beach."

"Galen?" I asked, trying to picture my boyfriend serving as a delivery boy.

"No, this was before he was elected," Wesley replied. "Barry accepted his stuff, took the bank book and then kicked the sheriff off his land. He said a divine entity — I can't remember the name he gave the god he created — had given him the land to start a commune. The sheriff told him that's not how things worked. Barry argued and all the people he had staying with him started yelling and screaming. Sensing he was outnumbered, the sheriff came back and reported what had happened."

"They were obviously allowed to live there for some time," Cormack pointed out.

"Because they technically weren't hurting anyone," Wesley explained. "The development was in the beginning stages even then, but until they were ready to break ground no one wanted to borrow trouble with Barry and his followers.

"Then the original group that wanted to build the hotel lost its financing — I think the president of the company died under mysterious circumstances or something — and it took another few years for a new group to come in," he continued. "In that time, Barry's group tripled in size from what we could tell ... and they got weirder and weirder."

"They're clearly a cult," Cormack said, his eyes on the map as he kept his hand moving over Aisling's back. It was a similar technique to the one Griffin used to calm her. I couldn't help but wonder if Cormack purposely taught it to his future son-in-law, or it was something Griffin picked up. "When they got final notification that they were being forced to move, how did it go down?"

"That was an ugly business." Wesley rested his hip against the table as he folded his arms over his chest. "The DDA sent in a variety of business owners, all able-bodied men and women, and Barry didn't have a choice in the matter. They were forcibly moved."

"To the spot where they are now?"

"No, to a spot in the ditch across the road. Barry remained behind long enough to pout and whine, claiming the developers were angering the gods, but the land was surrounded and a couple local witches put up wards to keep him out."

Hmm. That was interesting. "Obviously the wards worked," I offered. "Otherwise he would've simply moved back to the spot as soon as everyone left."

"They did, and Barry moved on," Wesley said. "When he picked a place so close to my farm, I wasn't sure how I felt about it. They've been mostly quiet. On calm nights you can hear the drums. And I guarantee there's a lot of sex happening out there. Sometimes they don't wear clothes when they're wandering around the countryside. For the most part, they mind their own business. That's what I care about."

"This here." Cormack tapped the map. "This looks to be a rather large body of water. Is it a river?"

Wesley shook his head. "No, that's an inlet, even though it doesn't look it. There's ocean access to the north. See, follow through here." He used his finger as a guide. "It's saltwater, but turns to fresh water in the basin because there's a freshwater river feeding it from this side."

"How big is the lake?"

"A few miles. They're using it as a backdrop to their camp. I'm on that lake occasionally and I see them."

"I'm assuming he picked this location because nobody can approach from that direction," Cormack supplied. "That means he only has to defend on three sides."

"And that west side is really nothing but rock and difficult to traverse," Wesley noted. "It's more like defending only two sides."

"That puts us at a distinct disadvantage," Cormack said. "I don't know that we have the brute force to take them on."

"You won't need brute force," Booker announced as he entered the room, Lilac close on his heels. "I've got reinforcements moving in through the inlet. They'll be in position in twenty minutes. Barry won't be able to fight them. They'll stay hidden unless they're necessary."

"What sort of reinforcements?" I asked, my curiosity getting the better of me.

"Aurora," Booker replied simply. "She has some friends and they're going in."

"Who is Aurora?" Aisling asked.

"She's essentially a mermaid."

"Mermaids are real?" Aisling was incredulous. "I always said I wanted to be a mermaid. Now I feel ripped off."

Cormack made a sympathetic noise with his mouth as he patted her shoulder. "It's okay, kid. You're already more than most of us can handle. If fins were added to the equation, everybody would be too exhausted to fight you."

"You say that like it's a bad thing."

My eyes drifted to Lilac, confused. "No offense, but why did you bring Lilac?"

Booker's smile was grim. "Because there's a good chance we might need her. She can bring the fire like nobody's business. She's a good person to have on our side."

I was confused. "What fire?"

"You'll see."

"I'd rather you tell me."

He was done being patient. "You'll see. Now, let's get going. The reaper wants her husband back and I'm dying to save Galen so I can hold it over his head for the foreseeable future."

That sounded about right. Things were about to take a turn. I just hoped everybody lived to complain about it.

24

TWENTY-FOUR

Lilac's presence had me questioning Booker's sanity. That, in turn, made me feel guilty. Lilac had been appropriately vague, stumbling over explanations about her true nature since we'd met, admitting to being an empath but not expanding. Now it seemed she would no longer be able to evade my questions.

"What's going to happen when you get out there?" I asked as she double checked to make sure her shoes were tied before getting into Booker's ancient van. It was the only vehicle large enough to hold everybody.

"It'll be fine," Lilac replied shortly. "Don't worry about it. We'll figure it out."

I wanted to push her, press until she had no choice but to answer. Booker's appearance forced me to abandon my pursuit of answers and focus on him.

"We don't know what to expect from inside the encampment," he said, his eyes grave. "Mr. Grimlock is in charge of the operation, so we all need to listen to what he says and follow the same plan." His eyes were heavy when they landed on Aisling. "Does everyone understand?"

"Why are you staring at me when you ask that question?" Aisling asked, pouty.

"Because I can tell you're going to be trouble."

"She'll be fine," Cormack interjected, moving to his daughter's side and handing her a gun. My mouth dropped open when she accepted the weapon, expertly checked the clip, and then slid it into her waistband. "We may only have one shot at this, so everybody pay attention. That goes double for you, Aisling."

"Yeah, yeah." She shook her head and stared at the weapon he carried. It was a huge sword and I had no idea where it came from. "Why can't I have one of those?"

"That would force you to get too close to the action, which is not something I want to encourage. You're to use that gun only as a last resort and stay behind us otherwise."

Aisling scowled. "What if I don't want to stay behind you?"

"Then you'll stay here with Wesley." Cormack's tone was no-nonsense. "I'm not risking you, kid. Don't think for a second you'll be able to wheedle your way into trouble. I won't allow it.

"And, before you start whining about Griffin, I guarantee he won't want it either," he continued. "He may be a handsy cop who needs a reckoning, but he loves you and wants to keep you safe above all else. That's one of the few things we agree on."

Aisling glowered. "We're so going to have a talk about this later."

"We definitely are," Cormack agreed. "Let's head out. We don't have much time and I don't want to waste any more of it nitpicking. Let's get going."

WE PARKED ALMOST HALF A mile from the camp, Booker selecting a spot under some trees so his van was partially covered. I realized that was only part of the benefit when he headed straight for the water access to his left upon exiting the vehicle. A crane of my neck told me he wasn't alone as a familiar figure leaned out of the water.

Aurora King was naked, her tail firmly displayed. She didn't seem self-conscious as she talked to Booker, and a quick look at Cormack told me he wasn't interested in staring at her body. Aisling, on the other hand, was infatuated with the tail she saw whipping about.

"Cool!"

"Aisling." Cormack swiped at the back of her shirt to haul her back, and missed. Aisling edged forward until she was close to Aurora's tail and then reached out to touch it. Aurora, like an angry cat, kept swishing it around, so Aisling didn't have much luck.

"They're in there," Aurora announced, her eyes flashing. "They look okay, but Galen might have the beginnings of a black eye. They're tied to trees in the center of a circle, and both of them are sweating profusely. I think the worst we have to deal with is dehydration, and maybe a bruise or two."

"You saw Griffin, too?" Aisling asked as she determinedly poked her finger toward Aurora's tail, frowning when it darted away at the last second.

"I saw another man with Galen," Aurora stressed. "I'm assuming that's the man you're looking for. Brown hair, dark eyes, very attractive."

"That's Griffin," Aisling agreed, crowing triumphantly when she finally touched Aurora's tail and then pulling back quickly. "Weird. Does it hurt when you shift into your water form?"

Aurora cast her a sidelong look. "I'm used to it. I have four friends in the water, by the way. What do you want us to do?"

"That depends," Booker answered, his expression thoughtful. "How many people does Barry have hanging around Galen and Griffin? Do you get the feeling he has something specific planned?"

"As opposed to what?" Aisling asked, her annoyance on full display. "Do you think he's trying to tame their wild spirits and adopt them as pets?"

"He's asking if it's possible that being tied to the trees is psychological warfare," Cormack explained. "If it is, it would be smarter to wait until the sun sets and go in under the cover of darkness."

"Oh."

That sounded smart. "Is that a possibility?"

"I don't know," Aurora hedged, clearly uncomfortable. "I didn't see Taurus. There are guards watching our friends. I don't think it's wise to leave them there. I don't know what's planned for them, but I doubt it's good."

"That's what I figured." Booker rubbed the back of his neck as he crouched and lowered his voice. I had to move closer to hear when he whispered to Aurora. "Stay in the water unless you have no other choice. Be prepared to deliver a distraction if you have to. It will take us a few minutes to get there. Draw their attention if you can. We'll handle the rest."

"You'd better." Aurora's expression darkened. "I'd hate to think what will happen if Taurus decides he's king of the world and tries to claim Galen as a follower."

I had to agree with her there.

Booker straightened and met Cormack's gaze. "We should go. It's time."

"Then let's go."

CORMACK KEPT AISLING CLOSE during the walk. They didn't speak much. No one wanted to draw unnecessary attention to our small group even though the odds of Taurus forgetting to post sentries seemed long. Whatever Cormack said to his daughter didn't go over well because she occasionally sounded like an annoyed cat in response, but otherwise acquiesced. He was in charge and she knew better than to argue with him under these circumstances.

"We're here," Booker announced, moving to stand close to me even as his gaze locked with Cormack's. "Do you want to do the talking or should I?"

"I think you should start. You know him. Indicate I'm a money man and willing to pay for Griffin's return."

"And Galen," I added hurriedly. "You're not just going to leave him out here, are you?"

Cormack's expression softened. "I will not leave either of them. I promise you that. I'm sorry my attention is focused more on Griffin.

He is my son-in-law and the father of my incoming grandchild. I won't leave Galen behind."

That was at least some comfort. I wiped my sweaty hands against my shorts and then frowned, something occurring to me. "Why don't I have a weapon?"

"You are a weapon," Booker replied, his tone no-nonsense. "You've already hurt them once. They'll be leery of you because of what happened on the road. We might need some magical help again, so be prepared."

"Oh, well, no pressure or anything," I drawled.

"You'll be fine," Aisling supplied. "Don't turn into a whiner. Apparently that's my job because I can't control my hormones."

"You'll learn to live with it," Cormack chided. "It's a small price to pay for a baby. By the way, if you have a boy, you should name him after me."

"If you get Griffin out of this and we have a boy, you've got a deal."

He smiled at his only daughter and briefly gripped her hand. "It will be fine. We're not leaving without Griffin. I promise."

"Then let's do this."

INSTEAD OF SPYING FROM above, this time we approached from the front. Cormack and Booker took central positions inside the group, the men Cormack brought with him sticking close to him and Aisling. I was next to Booker, and Lilac was on the other side of me. Her expression was hard to describe, but she looked altogether ready for battle ... which was a frightening thought because I'd never really considered her a soldier.

"I really am happy to have you here," I whispered, hoping my voice wouldn't carry. "But I'm confused. Why did Booker select you?"

"Because he wants to win." Lilac's response was short and to the point. "This isn't the time to discuss this. We'll talk about it later."

"Right."

Once we crested the hill that led to the camp, the first thing I saw were the two trees Aurora mentioned. Galen's big frame was tied to the closest, and I could make out limited movement on the second tree, to which I assumed Griffin was tied. I tried to focus on the cult members as we approached, but my eyes kept traveling to Galen ... and he didn't look happy when he snapped his head in our direction and scowled.

"Oh, you've got to be kidding me!"

Aurora was right. He had a black eye. The distress washing over him was evident, and even though I wanted to soothe, I wisely kept my spot in the lineup. Booker said he would do the talking. I was mildly curious what his words would entail.

"Hey, Barry," he yelled out, causing me to jolt at his tone. "We need to talk, man."

"Should you call him by his old name when he prefers being referred to as Taurus?" I whispered, legitimately worried. "Shouldn't we be playing to his delusion?"

"You don't know him," Booker snapped. "I do. I've got this."

He was clearly agitated, so I didn't press him, instead gripping my hands into fists and holding Galen's conflicted gaze as we stepped to a spot in front of the trees.

Taurus finally made himself visible as he strolled through the trees to our left. His ragged Bermuda shorts were ripped at several seams and he was shirtless. His long brown hair had a multitude of light streaks that I assumed were teased out by the sun, and he looked amused rather than worried.

"Hello, Booker," he intoned, holding out his hands as if in welcome. "I wondered if you would ever visit. If anyone was geared for living in the light with us, it's you. You're all about the love, right?" His lips curved.

"I'm about more than one thing, Barry," Booker replied evenly. "Right now, I'm here about my friends over there. I think it's time you released them."

"And why would I do that?"

"If you don't, I don't think you'll like what happens."

"I'm not beholden to your earthly rules," Taurus spat, his green eyes flashing. "I am above the laws of man."

"Barry, do you remember when we were in high school and you basically said you were above the laws of biology class and you refused to dissect a frog?" Booker challenged. "What happened then?"

Taurus's smile slipped. "I do not answer to my child name. That is not the name I go by."

"Well, I'm not calling you Taurus." Booker was matter-of-fact. I recognized he was trying to taunt Taurus, cause him to make a mistake and perhaps move within striking distance, but the way he interacted with the man was intriguing. "You need to let them go."

"They crossed the boundary," Taurus snapped. "They were not invited into Eden, and yet they stole in like thieves in the night."

"We parked on the road and walked," Galen barked, my heart rolling at the way his voice cracked. He was clearly dehydrated, and I wanted to get him out of here as soon as possible. "We weren't trying to cross your barriers. We were merely checking on the females in your group because we heard some reports. We have a warrant, which means we're here legally. There's no reason to get bent out of shape."

"You crossed our boundaries without invitation and you must be punished," Taurus hissed. "You were not invited. You're a usurper."

"Oh, geez. It's like he's picked up every ten-cent word from the dictionary to throw around to confuse people," Galen complained. "You can't get through to him, Booker. I've been trying for hours. He won't listen."

"I'm starting to figure that out." Booker folded his arms over his chest and shifted his stance. "I don't see where you have many options here, Barry. If you don't give us Galen and Griffin, things are going to get ugly."

"We outnumber you."

"Maybe, but we have more power in our arsenal and you know it," Booker shot back. "Do you see who I brought with me?" He inclined his head toward Lilac. "You know what she's capable of. You remember that rather infamous prom a few years after we left the school?"

Lilac balked. "That was not my fault. I can't believe you brought that up."

"Well, this might not be your fault either," Booker said. "She's here with us because she's willing to fight for Galen. And this man here, the one who wore a suit to an island fight, he's the other guy's father-in-law. He's a reaper, but not just any reaper. He's one of the head reapers."

Taurus narrowed his eyes as his speculative gaze fell on Cormack. "Head reaper?"

"Amongst other things," Cormack replied, his voice cold and disinterested. "I'm willing to pay for the safe return of Griffin and Galen. I will make this offer only once. If you refuse to hand them over, I'll be forced to do things my way."

"And what way is that?" Taurus spat.

"I wouldn't push him, Barry," Booker warned. "He singlehandedly took out Genevieve Toth."

I wasn't expecting Booker to take that tack, and a small exclamation of surprise escaped before I shuttered my emotions and held firm.

"Genevieve Toth?" Taurus took a step forward and focused his full attention on Cormack. "But ... that's impossible. Genevieve is forever."

"I believe she was still saying that exact same thing when I cut her head off," Cormack noted. "She shouldn't have gone after my family. When someone goes after my family — even a handsy son-in-law — I take it personally."

"You studied Genevieve for a long time, Barry," Booker volunteered. "She was something of a hero to you because she lived so long and inspired loyalty over decades. I remember the things you said about her in history class junior year. You were convinced she was a god."

"A *goddess*," Taurus corrected, his expression thoughtful. "How do I know she's really dead?"

"Because her whole network fell in the months following," Cormack replied. "You must have heard about that. They're all gone now. There's nothing left."

"What about Fontaine?"

Aisling jolted out of the corner of my eye, making me realize she recognized the name. I was lost and confused in the conversation, but apparently some of the players were coming up Grimlock ... and I had no idea what to make of that.

"I killed Duke Fontaine," Aisling volunteered, her voice cool and strong. "It was a year and a half ago. I burned him alive in a tomb."

Taurus was taken aback. "You burned him alive?"

"Yeah. I'm not sorry about it either." Aisling's lavender eyes darkened. "If you think I'll be sorry about any of this, you've got another think coming. In fact ... ." She broke from her spot in the lineup and strode closer to Taurus.

"Stop her," Griffin growled, fruitlessly fighting against his bonds. "Cormack, don't let him touch her."

Cormack was already moving before Griffin gave the order. It was too late, though. Aisling had a plan and she clearly wasn't going to deviate. She drew the gun her father supplied her with before leaving Wesley's ranch from the back of her pants, raised the barrel until it was pointed at Taurus's forehead, and uttered her warning in a cool voice that promised hellfire and brimstone if she didn't get her way.

"I'll do worse to you if you don't give me my husband right now," she threatened. "Let him go. If you don't, I'll blow your head off and make sure your soul gets a one-way ticket to hell once I collect it. You have no choice in the matter. Give me Griffin or I'll give you death. What will it be?"

25

TWENTY-FIVE

"Son of a ... !"

Griffin struggled so hard against his restraints I worried he would dislocate his shoulder. Booker managed to keep his face implacable, but I could feel the despair rolling off him in waves.

I was moved to action before I even realized what I was doing. I took a bold step forward, calling on the magic zipping through my body and screaming for release before I could give thought to what I was doing.

The fireball I conjured smacked into Taurus's face with little warning, hissing as he screeched and frantically swiped at his face to extinguish the blaze. At the same moment, the women in the water popped their heads above the surface. Instead of unleashing a tempest of magic, they began singing, causing me to furrow my brow as several of the men in Taurus's group immediately turned in their direction, abandoning the fight to stumble toward the water.

"What the ... ?" I didn't get a chance to finish my statement. Booker was already moving, his limbs pumping fast as he raced in Galen's direction.

Aisling kept the gun pointed at Taurus as Booker worked. Taurus was no longer focused on her — or even what was happening with his disciples. Instead, he was smacking at his face to extinguish the fireball, which was persistent and refused to flame out.

It was utter chaos, and before I could release another fireball, Galen was free. Booker immediately went to Griffin, who was still straining against the ropes so he could get to Aisling. Perhaps reading his mind, Cormack strode forward and grabbed his daughter around the waist.

"That was incredibly stupid," he hissed in her ear.

Aisling either wouldn't or couldn't hear him. She was lost in fury, and she had no intention of backing down. "I haven't shot him yet. Put me down!"

"Shut your mouth," Cormack barked, keeping a firm hold of her as Booker freed Griffin.

Even though they were clearly exhausted and bruised, Galen and Griffin ran to us. Griffin stopped long enough to collect his wife — although it took considerable effort from both Cormack and himself to wrest the gun from her grip.

"Knock it off," Griffin ordered, swinging Aisling into his arms. "Which way?"

Cormack pointed. "We're a half mile down the road."

"Where is your truck?" I asked Galen when he appeared at my side. He was sweating and the bruising around his eye seemed to be darkening by the second.

"We'll worry about that later." He grabbed my hand and tugged me behind him. "Come on, Hadley. We have to get out of here."

"But we haven't won the battle yet."

"And we're not going to on their property. We have to move the battle. Come on."

His tone told me that arguing was a fruitless endeavor so I fell into step with him, the sounds of Taurus's angry bellows giving chase. I didn't look back to see if anyone else followed. Instead, I gave in to my instincts and focused on Galen. He was strong despite whatever horrors he'd suffered through, and his muscles worked relentlessly as we burned the distance between the camp and Booker's van. By the time we made it to our destination, everyone was sweating and gasping, but no one had caught up to us.

"In," Galen barked, pushing me into the back seat. We had limited space, so he pulled me onto his lap so Cormack's men would have somewhere to sit. Griffin did the same with Aisling, who was still putting up a struggle, and Booker had the vehicle in gear and on the road within seconds.

"Whew!" Lilac enthused after a full minute of everyone sucking oxygen. "That was fun! You guys didn't even need me."

"The fight isn't over," Booker reminded her. "That was just round one."

"What happened with the chicks in the water?" Aisling asked as she gave up wriggling and let Griffin hug her close. "What were they doing? What's the deal with the song?"

"They're sirens," Galen explained, his hand moving over my back as he caught his breath. "They can lure unfaithful men into the water."

"Like the woman we met at the restaurant the other night?"

"Exactly."

"But ... most of the men headed in their direction. You said only unfaithful men were drawn to sirens," I pointed out.

"And the type of men who would join a cult are probably prone to being unfaithful." Galen exhaled heavily and rested his forehead against my temple. "Don't worry about Aurora and the others. They won't kill them. They can't. They're bound by rules. They'll disappear in the water and head back to the main part of the island. They'll be fine."

"Are you okay?" I asked, the terror slowly subsiding. "I was really worried about you."

"I guess that's why you amassed an army to come get me." He flashed a smile. "I'm fine. They ambushed us when we arrived. I think they were expecting us."

"What were you guys thinking coming after us?" Griffin groused. "You should've stayed at the hotel, Aisling. You would've been safer there."

"Hey, she helped by finding some friends," Galen countered, his eyes moving to Cormack. "Where did you guys come from, by the way?"

"I'm Aisling's father." Cormack introduced himself. "I came because I was worried about her."

"I guess that makes you the father-in-law who keeps threatening Griffin with great bodily harm for knocking up your daughter," Galen said.

"I still have plans on that front."

"I think you should give him a pass." Galen's voice was clear and strong. "He tried to save me. He had a chance to run, but he refused to abandon me. If you ask me, that deserves a reward ... not punishment."

Cormack twisted in his seat and met Galen's gaze head-on. "And if he knocked up your daughter before marriage?"

Galen balked. "I don't have a daughter."

"Talk to me when you do." Even though he was clearly in papa bear mode, Cormack briefly flicked his eyes to Griffin and Aisling, his expression softening. "Besides, I won't do anything that will wound him permanently. We definitely need to have a talk, though."

Griffin sighed. "You saved me. I guess you get whatever you want out of the deal."

"I didn't save you. I stupidly brought Aisling along for the ride and she almost ruined everything."

"I did not." Aisling straightened. "You weren't doing anything, so I handled the situation. And, look, everyone is safe and accounted for."

"No thanks to you." Cormack was firm. "You're lucky he didn't grab you as a hostage."

"He wouldn't have gotten the chance. I wasn't bluffing about shooting him."

"I'm starting to believe that."

"Nobody kidnaps my husband and ties him to a tree." She was vehement, causing Griffin to smile.

"How did I get so lucky?" he chortled, kissing her cheek. "My brave and foolish girl."

"I was smart. Everyone got out safely."

"You were a moron," Booker countered. "Everything worked out despite that. Thankfully you told me the Genevieve Toth story. That was actually our greatest weapon."

"Yes, I would like to hear more about that," Cormack said. "How does your friend Barry know Genevieve?"

"I'll tell you when we get back to Wesley's place. Galen and Griffin need to hydrate. We need to pick up your vehicle, and then we need to come up with another plan ... because they're going to come after us. There's no way Barry will let what happened slide."

"He can't," Galen agreed. "He'll lose face with his followers."

"Then we need to go to Wesley's house," Cormack said. "I have a feeling that is a story I want to hear."

"HERE'S MORE WATER."

Wesley delivered a third pitcher of ice water to the table, taking extra care to check on Galen and Griffin before moving to the wall and leaning against it. He was as eager to hear Booker's story as everybody else.

"I can't go into the whole history of Genevieve Toth because we don't have time," Booker started. "I'm going to give you the Cliff's Notes version, and if things work out we can delve deeper when a crazy cult isn't trying to kill us.

"Genevieve was a witch who found she could defy death by stealing souls," he continued. "She basically consumed the souls of those around her to prolong her life. She's hardly the first being who figured out souls could extend life, but she was the first — at least to my knowledge — to discover a way to do it without losing her own soul in the process."

"That's what wraiths are," Cormack volunteered. "They eat souls to prolong their lives, but it erodes who and what they are, their sense of self. It's a half-life. Genevieve found a way to circumvent that, but there was a price. Her soul wasn't exactly intact."

"And Genevieve came to Moonstone Bay?" I asked, confused.

"For ten years," Booker confirmed. "She arrived in the fifties and left in the sixties."

"No one realized what was happening when she was here," Galen volunteered. "No one understood that she was consuming souls to survive. Back then, the tourist business was barely starting and people were more trusting.

"When the town elders of the era figured out what was happening, they went after her," he continued. "They were going to burn her at the stake, but she had other plans. She'd amassed a group of about ten wraiths, and she sent them out to fight while she made her escape."

Aisling widened her eyes. "Booker mentioned before that wraiths aren't really a thing on the island. I never thought to ask why. I'm guessing that had something to do with Genevieve."

"You guess right," Galen said. "The wraiths were eradicated within days, and a local coven erected wards to keep them out. It was important to make sure what happened never happened again ... especially after someone noticed something odd about Genevieve's basement and they unearthed fifteen bodies."

I was officially horrified. "What?"

"The people she killed to prolong her life," Booker explained. "She buried them in her basement."

"That is ... ." Words failed me.

"I don't understand why your buddy Barry is so infatuated with Genevieve," Aisling pressed. "When you brought her up, he seemed to be in awe. He was actually angry that she was dead ... and how did he know Fontaine?"

"Genevieve took on mythical proportions around here," Galen explained "The witch who wouldn't die. That's how a lot of people referred to her. She'd lived for centuries by the time she landed on Moonstone Bay. And while we have some long-lived paranormals, most of the population has a normal lifespan, but I don't know anyone who doesn't want to live forever."

"Most people would change their minds when they learned the price," Aisling countered, resting her head on Griffin's shoulder as he sucked down water and continuously rubbed her back. He seemed as worried about her as she was about him. "You don't live forever without giving part of yourself up in return."

Something occurred to me. "There's always a price. Isn't that what Casey said? She wanted a baby, and in return Taurus took Jacob's life. What if he didn't care about the ritual of the death as much as the soul?

"I mean, you said he was infatuated with this Genevieve Toth because he thought she was immortal," I continued. "Maybe he wanted to follow in her footsteps, and that's why he wanted the souls."

"And he killed the reaper," Cormack mused, rubbing the back of his neck. "That actually makes sense. He wants to live forever. He's got an overinflated sense of ego. He might not have realized that word would spread to the reaper office if Grimport suddenly stopped transferring souls."

"Or maybe he thought he had time," Booker said. "Maybe he didn't need to get away with it forever, but just for a short time."

"I'm not familiar with Genevieve's method," Cormack noted. "Our only source on that matter is gone." His eyes briefly linked with Aisling's. "Wanting to live forever is a motive for madness as old as time. If your tin god cult leader really believes he's something special, I can see him trying to carry out her plan ... and taking lives is part of the process."

"I don't understand about Fontaine, though," Aisling pressed. "What does he have to do with this?"

"He showed up here looking for information on Genevieve about five years ago," Galen replied. "I wasn't sheriff yet, but I was with the department. He came swaggering in, all bravado and ridiculous posturing. He thought we were a small-town department and he could simply bulldoze us."

"That must have been before he hooked up with Genevieve and Lily," Cormack noted. "He aligned himself with both of them for a time, which was ultimately his downfall."

"Probably because he wanted to live forever, too," Aisling supplied. "I talked to him right before he passed. He tipped me off that Mom was alive. He almost acted as though, at least in that moment, he was sorry for all the wrong he did."

"I don't know about sorry, but he did us a service when he warned you," Cormack said. "I very much doubt any rogues are on this island helping. Last time I checked, they were all following Xavier Fontaine — Duke's brother — and most of them were in Michigan trying to regroup from the fallout of Lily's death."

"And Lily is your mother?" I asked Aisling, my heart rolling because it felt like a stupid question. I had to be sure.

She nodded. "Yeah."

"So ... what happens now?" Wesley asked, his eyes shrewd. "I don't mind waging the battle here if you think it's best — fewer innocent bystanders would be hurt in the process — but this place is going to be almost impossible to defend."

"That's why you're coming with us to town," Galen said. "Cut your workers loose now. Get them out of here. We have to leave this place. I doubt Barry will head out until after dark — he'll consider the darkness a weapon — but we need to give ourselves time to prepare back in town."

"Where are we going to hide?" I asked, my stomach unsettled. I pressed my hands against it and made a face. "He'll find us no matter where we go. We can't hide from him forever."

"We're not going to hide." Galen rested his hand on top of mine and met my searching gaze. "We have to fight tonight. I'm not the running type, and I'd wager most of the people here feel the same way. We need a location that's easy to defend, one where people can't sneak up on us."

"So ... where?"

Things clicked into place a second before he spoke.

"The lighthouse," he said simply. "We can see in every direction. Water covers three sides. There's only one way they can come in if they don't want to risk tangling with the sirens in the water."

"Do you really think he'll come after us?"

"He has no choice," Cormack said, standing. "He'll lose face with his followers if he does nothing. Without his followers, he won't be able to finish what he started."

"And what's that?" I asked.

"He's killing his male followers," Aisling volunteered, taking everyone by surprise. "What? I'm smarter than I look. It simply makes sense. He keeps the women, helps them get pregnant — probably by some ancient pagan spell — and then kills the husbands. He keeps a few men around because he needs the muscle, but only the true believers because they're less of a risk."

"I hate to say it — for more reasons than one — but Aisling is right," Galen said. "There should've been a lot more men out there. It was ninety percent women. He's obviously killing the men."

"And now we have to kill him," I mused. "Is that what you're saying?"

Galen hesitated before responding. "We'll try to take him alive. I don't think he'll give us many options, though. I won't hesitate to kill him to keep you safe."

"He needs to go down," Booker agreed. "We've let him run free for too long. He thinks he's omnipotent."

"We should get going," Cormack suggested. "It's only a few hours before nightfall. We have plans to put into action."

Galen slowly got to his feet, dragging me with him. "It's time for battle, honey. I hope you have more of those nifty fireballs at your disposal, because I think we're going to need them."

26

TWENTY-SIX

The ride back to the lighthouse was tense. Lilac and Cormack's men rode back with Booker, which left Galen, Griffin, Aisling and me with a blustery Cormack and Wesley. I had a feeling that lineup was on purpose.

"What were you thinking pulling that gun, Aisling?" Cormack demanded once we were on the road. He let Galen drive so he could bellow to his heart's content without worrying about traffic.

"I was thinking that I wanted my husband back," Aisling replied. She was situated next to Griffin, his hands wrapped around hers. "I'm not sorry I did it, so if you're expecting an apology ... ."

"You don't have to apologize," Griffin said, refusing to back down despite the dirty look Cormack shot him. "Give her some breathing room, Cormack. She's supposed to be on her honeymoon and almost nothing has gone right. She deserves a little leeway."

"And you guys claim I spoil her," Cormack groused. "You spoil her worse than I do."

"Yes, well ... she's carrying my baby." He flashed an adoring grin at Aisling. "Besides, she hasn't been able to do any of the things she envisioned for the honeymoon. No drinking, no boat rides."

Cormack stilled. "Why no boat rides?"

"They had a rule. No pregnant women."

"Well, that doesn't seem fair," he growled, his face flushed. "I'll fix that ... and you can have a few more days for your honeymoon when this is over. Don't worry about that."

"And you don't spoil her," Griffin snickered, shaking his head. "Not that I'm not thankful, but how did you know where to look for us?"

"Booker," I replied simply. "You told him where you were heading."

"I did it on purpose in case there was trouble," Galen admitted. "I wish I would've thought to talk to Casey again before I headed out there. I have no idea what they did with my vehicle. They'd better not destroy it. It's hell to get a replacement through the DDA."

"I'm dying to meet these DDA people," Cormack noted. "They sound like real pieces of work."

"You don't want to meet them. Trust me."

GALEN DROPPED US in front of the lighthouse and then moved Cormack's vehicle. Booker did the same. They didn't say it, but I think they wanted time to confer with one another, come up with a plan. It was obvious Cormack fancied himself in charge, and he was obviously a frequent participant in combat, but this was their home turf.

May was waiting on the other side of the door when we entered, wringing her hands as she glanced between faces. "I've been so worried. The island is buzzing that something terrible is about to happen."

"We ticked off a cult," I explained. "Apparently they're coming here to teach us a lesson."

"Barry?" May made a face as she caught Wesley's gaze, her frown deepening when he nodded. "Well, we all knew it was only a matter of time before he lost his head and did something stupid."

Cormack, his eyes busy as they glanced around the room, said, "I never considered living in a lighthouse, but it has its merits. What a lovely space."

May beamed. "Thank you."

"This is my grandmother," I said by way of introduction. "This is Aisling's father. He's here to help us."

"I definitely am," Cormack agreed, turning serious as he drew a tablet from the bag he'd carried from the vehicle. "Aisling, call your brothers. Tell them to get bodies on this island as soon as possible."

Aisling took the tablet without complaint and pressed a button to log a call. This time the face that swam into view looked nothing like Aisling.

"Bug, I've been so worried," the man snapped. "I can't believe you found trouble on your honeymoon. That could only happen to you."

"Who is that?" I whispered to Griffin, confused. "He doesn't look like a brother."

"That's Jerry," Griffin replied, smiling as he hunkered down so he was on an even level with Aisling. "He's a force to be reckoned with. Hello, Jerry."

"Oh, I'm not talking to you," Jerry sputtered, smoothing his peach polo shirt and glaring. "You got my Bug in trouble on her honeymoon. Haven't you caused enough problems?"

Griffin's smile never wavered. "You're going to love being Uncle Jerry. Don't bother denying it."

"That's neither here nor there," Jerry waved away the statement. "I had plans. A baby doesn't fit in them. I wanted us to have kids who were the same age so they could be best friends. How am I supposed to find a kid on such short notice?"

"You could try finding a woman and knocking her up," Wesley suggested. "I hear that works."

"I don't think that's a possibility," another voice interrupted. This time the face that appeared on screen looked familiar. I was certain this was a brother I'd yet to meet, which meant he was Aisling's twin. I remembered the other three faces. "Hey, Ais." He greeted his sister with a wide smile. "How did you manage to find a war on your honeymoon? Only you, I swear."

"Believe it or not, the guy we're fighting with worships Genevieve Toth ... and he knew Duke Fontaine," Aisling volunteered. "Apparently it doesn't matter how far you travel, because your past will catch up with you no matter what."

Aidan sobered. "Are you okay? I can be there in eight hours if we can get the council to sign off on letting us use the private jet."

"You have more important things to do than screw around on the private jet," Cormack barked. "You need to get the home office on the line and see what soldiers they can spare in Florida. It's imperative they get them here as soon as possible. Point them toward the lighthouse."

A momentary jolt of fear flitted through Aidan's eyes. "What's happening?"

"Your sister pulled a gun in the middle of a diplomatic negotiation."

"Oh, yeah? Who gave her the gun? I know she didn't take it on her honeymoon."

Cormack scowled. "I gave it to her as a means of self-defense. Why are you pointing the finger at me? I'm trying to take care of my family. She flew off the handle and made things worse."

"She always does." Aidan was pragmatic. "I'll call the home office and get as many men there as possible. Do you want us to come?"

"The fight will be over before you can get here," Cormack replied. "No matter how it pains all four of you, there's nothing you can do."

"Five of us," Jerry corrected, his head popping into view. "I'm part of this family, too. I'm marrying your son."

"Well, that explains the baby thing," Wesley mused.

"Jerry, you've been part of my family since Aisling brought you home from kindergarten and you declared yourself her fashion advisor," Cormack said. "There's nothing you can do in this particular instance. There is something Cillian can do, though."

Aidan nodded. "Let me guess ... research?"

"You've got it. I want Genevieve tracked during her time here. It would've been in the fifties, maybe early sixties. I don't know that it will be important, but I'd like to know for my own edification. Apparently she was feeding here and buried bodies in her basement."

"That sounds like her." Aidan made a face. "What else?"

"That's it. Get us reinforcements. We'll call as soon as it's over. Everything will be fine. Don't fret ... or freak out. Definitely don't freak out."

Aidan didn't look convinced. "Maybe you should hide Aisling. She shouldn't fight now."

"Hey!" Aisling was affronted. "I can take care of myself. I won the first fight!"

"Hadley won the first fight with her fireball, and the sirens sang to distract the others," Cormack corrected. "You made things worse."

She jutted out her lower lip. "That's not how I see it."

"Well, you're lucky to be part of the team at all. If I thought you'd stay put you'd be in the hotel even as we speak. I can't trust you to do that, though, so you're with us."

Aidan mustered a smile. "It'll be okay. Dad is there. He'll protect you."

"I'm here, too," Griffin pointed out.

"Yes, but if Dad has his way you won't have any hands by the end of the day." Aidan offered up a half-salute. "Good luck. We'll be waiting for word as soon as you can get it to us. Don't leave us hanging."

"Don't leave us hanging either," Cormack said. "Get us reinforcements."

"I'm on it. One way or another, you won't be alone. I promise you that."

ONCE THE PHONE CONVERSATION ended, we didn't have much to do besides prepare. Galen, Booker and Cormack seemed to be mired in a tug of war over who was really in charge, and for once Aisling decided to stay out of their way. I followed her lead because I had no idea what to expect, and I was still reeling from the first battle.

"You've been in fights before, right?" I asked her, keeping my voice low. "Do you think we'll win?"

She cast me a sidelong look, amusement playing over her features. "My father doesn't lose. From the looks of it, neither do Booker and

Galen. It'll be okay. Besides, you can create fire out of nothing. That means we'll definitely win."

"I think that was a fluke." I was mortified to admit it, but I didn't want them relying on me in the middle of a fight only to have my hands fail to spark. "I just reacted. I'm still not sure how it happened."

"It happened because you're powerful." Aisling was matter-of-fact. "You understood there was a need and delivered the goods. You'll do it again. Don't worry about that." She patted my hand. "My father and Griffin are good in a fight, too. I'm curious about the others, though. Galen shifts into a wolf, right?"

I nodded.

"What's that like?"

"I've only seen it once ... and then it was really dark, so I didn't see all that much. I don't know what to expect."

Aisling, interest sparking in her eyes, shifted to stare directly at me. "Are you afraid to see it?"

I balked. "Of course not."

"I would be afraid to see it," she admitted, taking me by surprise.

"You would?"

"Of course. The dude you're sleeping with turns into a hairy beast. That would totally freak me out. And I'm kind of curious, too, to be truthful. It's weird to think about. What about your cupid? Does he have any special abilities?"

"I have no idea." That was the truth. "He seems brave and eager for a fight, but this is the first battle I've ever been in. I don't know what to make of it."

"Well, I'm sure things will work out." Aisling flicked her eyes to Lilac, who stood in the corner listening to the men talk. Her face was unreadable, but she seemed intent. "And what about her?"

That was the question of the day. "I don't know," I said after a beat. "I always assumed Lilac had some paranormal abilities. Most everyone on the island has some sort of power or ability. I just assumed hers was being super personable or something."

"You never asked?"

"I did." I searched my memory for the conversation. "Now that I think about it, she kind of sidestepped and didn't answer, other than admitting to be an empath. I was flustered at the time — I swear, I was flustered twenty-four hours a day that first week I was here — and then it kind of fell by the wayside. I guess that makes me a bad friend."

Aisling chuckled. "No. Quite frankly, I'm impressed with how you're dealing with all of this. You've been on this island for less than two months. In that time, you've discovered you're a witch, started using your powers, snagged a boyfriend, made friends with a cupid and managed to coexist with your ghostly grandmother. That's pretty impressive in my book."

"Thank you." Her words, surprisingly, made me feel a bit better. "I'm still nervous about what's to come."

"You'll always be nervous. I've been in so many fights I've lost count. If you ever lose the fear, that's when you should be worried. I think you're acting appropriately."

"I don't know if that's a compliment coming from the woman who pointed a gun at a cult leader and threatened to blow his brains out."

"Hey, if I'd been thinking I would've threatened to blow his balls off. He clearly favors those over his brains. Maybe I'll have another chance."

That was a frightening thought.

I SUPPLIED EVERYONE WITH what little food I had in the house, sandwiches and iced tea, but no one complained. About thirty minutes before the sun set, we had a plan in place. The men who came up with it seemed to think it was the best we could do.

I was still nervous.

I was about to go to Galen to voice my concerns and admit I was worried my newfound powers would fail at the wrong time when there was a knock on the door. Startled, we all traded glances. When I got to my feet to answer, Galen shot out a hand.

"I think I'll get this one." He offered me a wan smile before striding to the door and looking through the peephole. When he pulled back, his face was a mixture of curiosity and concern. "I don't believe this."

He pulled open the door and immediately reached for the person on the other side, giving a not-so-gentle yank and drawing the woman through the opening. I recognized her immediately despite the hoodie she had pulled over her features — it was hard to ignore her huge stomach — and hurried to Casey's side as fast as my legs would carry me.

"What are you doing here?" I asked as she drew down the hood. "This is a really bad time. You shouldn't be here."

"Do you think I don't know that?" Casey was frazzled as she dragged a hand through her long hair. "Everyone in town is talking about what's about to go down. The locals are doing their best to keep the tourists in the bars and hotels, but everyone else is clearing out of the area. News is spreading fast that you're going to take on Taurus."

"We've technically already taken on Barry and won," Booker pointed out. "This will just be a more thorough beating."

"We hope," Wesley echoed.

"We *know*," Galen growled, his eyes dark as they wandered over Casey's flushed features. "If you know what's about to happen why did you come here in your condition?"

"He killed my husband."

"Technically we don't know that." Galen opted for practicality. "That's our best guess because of what you said, but so far all we've really got him on is taking Griffin and me hostage. I expect that he's guilty of murder, too, but I have no proof of that."

"It's the only thing that makes sense." Casey stubbornly crossed her arms over her chest. Given the size of her stomach, it was more like she was using it as a shelf, but her message was clear. "I want to be part of it. Jacob was my husband. I owe him for ... everything. This was supposed to be our miracle. I somehow managed to turn it into our nightmare, and he's the one who paid."

My heart went out to her and I instinctively grabbed her arm to lead her to the couch. "You need to sit. You shouldn't be running around in your condition."

"She looks okay to me," Aisling countered. "I think she knows the limitations of her own body."

Cormack shot his daughter a withering look. "You're only saying that because you know we're going to lock you in the house when you get that big. It won't work. In fact, shut your mouth. When I want your opinion, I'll ask for it."

"You shut your mouth," Aisling muttered under her breath, earning a small smile from Griffin as he slipped his arm around her back and began rubbing.

"I have to help." Casey refused to budge on her stance. "Jacob was my life. I don't know if you believe in soulmates, Galen, but he was mine. He was my whole heart, and now he's gone. I did this. I need to make sure that Taurus pays for what's been done."

Galen briefly glanced at me before focusing his full attention on Casey. "I do believe in soulmates. I'm sorry about Jacob. You'll never know how sorry. But I don't think this is the right place for you. We need to get you out of here."

"That's no longer an option," Booker said as he watched through the front window, a muscle working in his jaw. "Our company has arrived ... and they don't look happy."

My heart dropped. The battle was finally here, and I had no idea what my part in it would be. I was more than terrified, almost frozen in fear. Despite that, I only knew one thing with absolute certainty: I could not let my friends down.

27

TWENTY-SEVEN

I moved to Booker's side, my heart pounding. Sure enough, the front yard was filling with bodies. Taurus, a bandage on the side of his face, was front and center. The dark expressions and the way they moved as one caused a chill to run down my spine.

"Oh, my ... ." I trailed off, fear coursing through me.

"It'll be okay." Galen grabbed my arm and pulled me in for a quick hug. "I swear it'll be okay. There's no reason to get worked up."

I could think of fifty reasons, and they were all standing in my yard. "They're going to kill us, aren't they?" The question sounded odd coming out of my mouth, as if I were speaking another language.

"I won't let anyone hurt you." Galen was firm as he ran his hands up and down my arms. "You're really cold."

"Which is ridiculous because it's hotter in here than a night at a strip club when you have a wad of twenties," Aisling commented, staring out the window over Booker's shoulder. When no one immediately responded, she turned around and snickered when she found me frowning. "I guess you only get that one when you have brothers."

"Everyone gets it," Cormack snapped. "I don't think it's funny when your brothers say it either. I especially didn't think it was funny when Redmond taught it to you when you were eight."

"I didn't know what it meant when I was eight."

"And he got in big trouble."

Aisling stepped closer to her father. "I kind of wish he was here to laugh with me right now. I think it would make me feel better."

Cormack slid his daughter a sidelong look. "He's with you here." He tapped the spot above her heart. "You'll see him again. You'll see all of them again."

"I don't need to see Braden again."

"Yes, you do." Cormack ran his hand down the back of Aisling's hair. "You need to see him most of all."

"And you will," Griffin insisted, moving behind her. "You need to stay away from that window, though. I don't want you getting involved unless you absolutely have to." He was stern as he drew her away. "You don't want to hear this — I know that you don't, but I'll say it anyway — but you're pregnant. You have to protect yourself and that baby. Focus on that instead of your mouth."

Aisling scowled. "Do you think I'm not focused on that?"

"I think you're terrified." Griffin was frank. "I am, too. We'll get through this together, like everything else. It'll be okay."

Aisling didn't look convinced. "I still wish the others were here," she grumbled, scuffing her foot against the floor. "They would already have taken out everyone on the lawn."

"Next time," Griffin said brightly, pressing a kiss to her forehead. "Stay away from the windows. It's important."

"Yeah, yeah."

I turned my attention back to the movement outside and shook my head. "What are we going to do? Shouldn't we at least try to talk to them?"

"We will." Galen's hand was warm on the center of my back. "I'm heading out there right now."

"What?" I balked. That didn't sound like a good idea at all. "You can't do that. He'll kill you."

"He won't get the chance. I know what I'm doing. I promise." He flicked his eyes to Booker. "If they try to take me ... ."

"I'll handle it," Booker shot back. "I know what I'm doing. This is hardly the first fight we've been in together."

"We *both* know what we're doing," Lilac agreed, her expression unreadable. Her eyes were dark, and there was nothing fun or gregarious about her attitude. She was like a different person ... and it frightened me. Something very odd was going on with her, and this was the absolute worst time to find out what that was.

"I'm going to talk to him, warn him this is a bad idea because we're stronger than he is," Galen said. "If he's smart, he'll turn around."

"Barry was never smart," Booker pointed out.

"Which is why it's going to end here." Galen was grim. "The sirens are in the water, right?"

Booker nodded stiffly. "Along with a few marine shifters."

"Shark shifters?" Aisling asked. "I totally want to see a shark shifter."

"They're rare," I replied, almost absently. "There aren't any on the island."

Galen grinned. "See. You are learning things left and right. I told you that not long after meeting you."

"I believe I mentioned it, too," Booker pointed out. "She was obsessed with the idea of shark shifters and kept asking questions."

"Yes, well, I'm the only one who counts." Galen gave me a lingering kiss, one that promised more for later, and then released me. "I'm going out there. If they try to grab me ... ."

"We'll be here to help," Cormack insisted, mustering a wan smile. "Good luck."

"Yeah."

"Wait." Aisling lurched forward and grabbed his wrist before he could exit the lighthouse. For a moment I thought she was going to offer words of encouragement, apologize for the trouble she'd caused since arriving. I should've known better. That's simply not how Aisling rolls. "Maybe you should let me do the talking. I have a way with people."

Galen's forced smile slipped. "So now you're an expert on diplomatic negotiations?"

"You would be surprised."

"Stay here." Galen was firm. "Keep your mouth shut." He turned to Cormack. "Under absolutely no circumstances give her back that gun. She's a menace."

Cormack shrugged. "She's good in a fight. She'll surprise you."

"She's spoiled rotten," Galen shot back. "Absolutely nothing she does now surprises me."

"You shouldn't say that," Griffin said. "She'll take it as a challenge."

"Right now I want her to keep her mouth shut." Galen gave me one more kiss, this one quick, and then moved toward the door. "Do what Booker and Cormack tell you to do, Hadley. They have your best interests at heart. Trust me."

I did trust him. That was the problem. "Don't get hurt." I blinked back tears.

He smiled before slipping through the door, his gaze heavy as it locked with Booker's. "You know what to do."

"Always. It will be just like that cave troll uprising three years ago."

Galen snickered. "Let's hope it doesn't end up like that."

I WAS A BUNDLE OF NERVES as Booker killed the living room lights and moved to the nearest window to watch Galen interact with the cult members on the lawn.

"It's best if they can't see us moving around," he explained, his voice low.

I nodded as I edged closer to him, my heart pounding as I caught sight of Galen moving toward the steps that led to the yard. I would've preferred he stay as close to the lighthouse as possible, but that simply wasn't how he operated.

"You shouldn't have come here, Barry," Galen called out. "That was a mistake. I think you know that. You can turn around and go. There's still time. Don't make this worse."

The expression on Taurus's face — which was partially covered by a bandage — was positively chilling. "It's far too late for retreats, Galen."

"You can't win this," Galen argued. "I have Booker inside ... and Hadley ... and Lilac. You know what she's capable of."

I shifted my eyes to the bar owner and found her intently looking out another window. She didn't as much as glance in my direction.

"I have might and right on my side," Taurus hissed. "You invaded my home, broke our laws, tried to take my land."

"That's not your land." Galen's temper flared. "How many times do I have to tell you that? The beach spot wasn't your land — and you knew going in that you would be forcibly moved at some point. The parcel you're squatting on now isn't your land either. The DDA is simply allowing you to live there because nothing else is planned for the acreage at this time."

"It is my land. We'll get the ocean spot back, too. We're growing faster than you can imagine."

"Is that why you killed Jacob?" Galen demanded. "Did you find him on what you consider your land and decide to send a message through him?"

"Jacob was a victim of his wife's urges," Taurus replied. "She wanted a baby above all else. There's a price for creating new life."

Casey whimpered from the couch, and I heard Wesley trying to comfort her.

"Don't listen to him, Casey. You didn't know. Jacob will forgive you."

"You're running a fertility racket?" Galen pressed. "I guess I should've seen that coming. You always liked to pretend that you were some sort of divine sex deity — even when we were in high school — and some people actually believed you. I'm betting you got off on the power you wielded over those women, tried to twist it to your advantage."

"You know nothing of my power," Taurus boomed. "I am a god!"

"You're a tool," Aisling shot back, taking me by surprise. I scanned the room for her, my heart pounding, and I realized relatively quickly she was nowhere to be found.

"Where is she?" Booker hissed, his temper on full display as his eyes darted to every corner of the room.

"Upstairs," Griffin replied, sighing. He looked as exhausted as I felt. "She slipped up there when I wasn't looking. I think she's at Hadley's bedroom window."

"Well go get her!" Booker's eyes fired red in the darkness, catching me off guard. "Hadley, I don't care if you have to physically drag her out of that window. Shut her up!"

"Okay." I raced for the stairs, taking the steps two at a time until I hit my bedroom. Sure enough, Aisling was in the window, and she had what looked to be a gun in her hand. "Who gave you that?" I hissed, storming toward her.

She ignored the question and focused on the people below us. "I'm guessing you have a very small appendage in your pants, little Barry boy," Aisling offered, smirking when Taurus lifted his gaze to her. "That's why you spend all of your time over-compensating."

"Little girl, you'll see the true scope of my power very soon. You should start running."

"I'm good."

"Is that child you carry good, too?" Taurus challenged. "What will you feel if your actions cause the loss of your offspring? Will you finally be convinced that some women should be seen and not heard then?"

"Hey!" Galen roared to life a floor below us as I moved to stalk to the window to tell Taurus to blow it out of his behind. I pulled up short when I joined Aisling at the window, anger coursing through me with each beat of my heart.

"Don't talk to her that way," Galen ordered. "She's not one of your disciples. And while we're at it, don't threaten that baby. I think you're going to find the people inside don't enjoy that."

Something occurred to me. "How did you even know about the baby?" I called out, racking my memory for instances when we'd mentioned Aisling's hitchhiker in front of Taurus. I came up empty. "How can you possibly know that she's pregnant? She's on her honeymoon, just visiting. I know we didn't say anything in front of you during our previous altercation."

"I know all and see all," he intoned.

"You're full of crap," Aisling shot back. "You couldn't find your own butt with two hands and a case of the trots. Shut up for a second. I think we're all tired of listening to you." She lowered her voice and pinned me with a look. "What's bothering you?"

"Someone told him you were pregnant," I said, my brain working at a fantastic rate. "How many people knew?"

"It's not as if it's a secret," Aisling argued. "I've been complaining about it since I found out."

"You haven't interacted with very many people since you arrived," I pressed. "Booker knew. Lilac. Your father. Griffin. Galen. Wesley. May. None of those people would share that information."

"Okay." Aisling was blasé. "Who are you suggesting shared the information?"

"Who else is in this house?"

Aisling's face drained of color as she moved away from the window. "Oh, crud on a cracker. You're saying we have a pregnant Trojan horse in our midst."

"That's exactly what I'm saying."

We tore down the stairs together, Aisling close on my heels. When we returned to the living room, we both focused on Casey rather than Griffin.

"Thank you so much for opening your big mouth, Aisling," Booker growled. "Now Galen is spending all his time taking up for you instead of negotiating a way out of this mess."

"We all know negotiation won't work," Aisling said dismissively, her eyes brimming with lavender fury. "Barry the wonder idiot can't back down because he'll look weak to his followers. If he looks weak, someone might try to break ranks. His power comes from the fact that he can keep everyone in line ... no matter what the occasion. This will be a fight regardless."

"I happen to agree, but you didn't need to make things worse," Booker growled.

"Forget about that," I snapped, my eyes locking with Casey's fearful orbs. She seemed to sense that we'd figured things out, that at least part of the puzzle was about to be solved. "You've been in contact with Taurus, haven't you?"

"What? No." Casey's voice squeaked. "Why would you think that?"

"Because he knew Aisling was pregnant. She's not showing. Only a few people know. You were one of those people. It was mentioned in front of you, and you told Taurus. You've been working with him this whole time."

"That's ridiculous." Casey acted offended, but there was something about the way her eyes darted that told me I was right about what she'd done. "He killed my husband. Why would you possibly think that I would help him?"

"Because you think he's going to take the baby from you," Aisling answered simply. She didn't appear nearly as angry as I felt. "In your head, he gave you the baby and took your husband as payment. You're afraid that he'll take your reaction as insolence, assume you're not thankful for what he's given you, and take the baby. You can't lose both of them. The baby is the last piece of Jacob you have."

As if on cue, Jacob's soul walked through a nearby wall and moved closer to Casey. He didn't look angry. In fact, he looked anguished.

"Leave her alone," Jacob barked. "Don't treat her this way. She doesn't deserve it. She's frightened."

Casey didn't react to Jacob's presence, which told me she wasn't aware that his soul was still around.

"Jacob is here, Casey," I said softly, keeping my voice low. "He wants us to leave you alone."

Casey's eyes widened as she wildly looked around the room, baffled. "How can he be here? He's dead. I ... is he really here?" She looked so hopeful it almost broke my heart despite the fact that she was a traitor.

"He's here," Aisling said. "He's worried about you. He loves you." She briefly held Griffin's gaze before continuing. "We won't let Taurus take your baby. He may have threatened you with that, but he doesn't have the power. Everyone here is working together to take him down. We need your help to do it."

"You said that you were angry and upset and wanted Jacob's murder to be avenged," I reminded her. "Was all that an act?"

"No!" She swiped at the tears flowing freely down her cheeks. "I meant it. Then he found me at my mother's house a few hours ago and said if I didn't help him get to you, tell him everything I knew and act as a spy, that he would take my baby. I can't lose Jacob's baby."

She looked so desperate I wanted to hug her ... even though I was furious she had turned on us. "We won't let him take your baby."

"Definitely not," Aisling agreed, straightening. "What's going on out there?" she asked Booker. "Is Galen making any headway?"

"No." Booker shook his head. "Barry is full of himself, as always. He thinks he has the upper hand."

"Talking won't accomplish anything," I argued, my temper growing. "We have to fight. It's time. He thinks he's won simply because he outnumbers us. We have to make him aware that's not true."

"That's the plan, but let Galen make his move. Just ... don't let her escape. If she tries to get out of this lighthouse, tackle her. I think Barry is waiting for word from her before moving."

I looked to Casey. "Is that true?"

She nodded. "I'm supposed to message him information about your numbers and locations in the lighthouse. I haven't done it yet." She handed over her phone, and when our fingers touched I realized she was profusely sweating.

"Are you feeling okay?" I pressed my hand to her forehead. "You're sweating."

"I think I'm in labor," Casey admitted, squirming on the couch.

"What?" I was horrified.

"I think I'm in labor," she repeated as warm fluid gushed from the couch, from between the hems of her skirt to be exact, and covered my sandals. "Oh, my ... what was that?"

"Her water broke," Wesley replied, calm. "She's most definitely in labor."

"Oh, my ... this can't be happening," Casey wailed.
Those were my thoughts exactly.

28

TWENTY-EIGHT

"Oh, this is just ... ridiculous." Aisling was furious. "You have to hold that kid in. No one here is going to deliver it."

"We'll do what we have to do," Wesley said tersely. He seemed more worried about Casey's needs than anything else. "She doesn't need you yelling at her."

"Whatever." Aisling turned petulant. "We need to get this show on the road so she can go to the hospital. I'm not delivering a baby."

"Aisling, come over here," Cormack instructed, holding out a hand. He was standing next to the window with Booker. "Just ... come to me."

She did as instructed, making a petulant sound in the back of her throat as Cormack wrapped his arm around her back. I joined them out of curiosity, and found Galen and Taurus still embroiled in a rather deep discussion.

"You're not fooling anybody," Galen supplied. "You're not as powerful as you pretend, no matter what you've convinced your followers of. You don't have a choice here. You either turn around and leave or we will fight."

"I expect you to fight," Taurus snarled. "You're a warrior. I'm a warrior. When you've fallen I will make sure everyone on the island knows you fought bravely. Perhaps I'll even erect a statue in your honor."

I pressed my lips together at the absurd statement.

"Enough is enough," Booker muttered, pushing away from the window and heading toward the door. "It's time we end this."

I opened my mouth to ask what he planned to do, but the question never escaped my lips. I was flabbergasted when his eyes momentarily went opaque and his hands glowed red, a magical bow and arrow seeming to leap into his hands.

"What the ... ?" Aisling stumbled away from her father. "Where did that come from?"

"Don't worry about that," Booker growled. "It's time. Everyone, get away from the front door. I'm going out ... and I'm taking no prisoners." He clearly meant business as he nocked an arrow. "The goal is to take out Barry. Once he falls, the others will flee. Does everyone understand?"

I nodded dumbly, my fingers suddenly itchy. It was as if the magic wanted to take over, a small voice whispering in the back of my head as something inside prodded me to join the fight. "Be careful."

"I'm always careful." He winked at me. "Besides, you're forgetting my superpower."

"You have a power more super than creating a bow and arrow out of thin air?" Aisling challenged.

He nodded. "What do you think happens when I try to attract women? What happened to you was a byproduct of what I am. I wasn't using my powers to entice you. When I use my powers, well, let's just say that women are helpless."

Aisling cracked a smile. "And most of Barry's army is made up of women."

"You're smarter than you look." He offered her a smile. "You need to stay inside, though. What I'm about to do will impact you, too. Stick close to your husband and father. I don't want you rubbing yourself all over me. That will make things difficult."

Her smile slipped. "I don't rub myself all over people."

Griffin cleared his throat as Cormack shook his head.

"Stay inside," Booker repeated, his gaze hopping over faces until he landed on Lilac. "I'll clear the way."

She nodded, grim. "I'll be right behind you."

Booker took a deep breath and then threw open the door, his bow gripped tightly in his hands as he strolled out. He let an arrow fly before he was clear of the threshold, and the reaction from the yard was intense as voices raised in alarm.

Then the screaming started, and my heart jolted. It was officially on.

I WATCHED FROM THE WINDOW as Booker joined Galen on the porch. They didn't speak, instead utilizing a form of shorthand they'd clearly honed over the years, and Booker gave Galen a wide berth as my boyfriend extended his hands to his sides ... and started to shift.

The one previous time he shifted in front of me I hadn't been able to see anything. It was too dark and he was hidden in the foliage on the side of the road. This time I saw everything, and the sound of shifting bones and muscles – even though he was ten feet away – filled my heart with cold dread.

"Holy ... !" Aisling's mouth dropped open as she watched Galen turn from a handsome man rippling with muscles to a beautiful wolf twice as large as it should be. The beast on the porch boasted black fur, but when its eyes moved to the windows they were blue ... just like Galen's eyes.

I tried not to gape, and he didn't linger more than a second before leaping into the fray. I assumed his transformation would be enough to scare many of Taurus's followers — and if that didn't work Booker had his magic bow and arrow — but I was wrong. The people in the yard didn't flee at the sight of Galen, even when he raced toward the nearest man (who was armed with a sword) and attacked with snapping jaws and excited howls. No, the yard occupants stood their ground ... and some of them began to shift, too.

"This is unfreaking-believable," Aisling hissed, shaking her head as a woman at the front of the pack turned into what looked like a giant serpent. "Look at that! That woman turned into a giant snake."

"She's a lamia," Wesley volunteered from behind us. He'd left Casey's side long enough to take a look. The laboring woman wasn't alone. Jacob and May were close and trying to help, but she couldn't see them and was too focused on her breathing to pay attention to what was going on around us.

"I don't know what that is," I said.

"She's a giant snake."

"Oh, well ... ."

Aisling's eyes drifted to Griffin as he moved toward the front door. "Where are you going?"

"I have to help, baby." He was firm. "I know you don't like the idea, but they can't do everything themselves."

"I'm going with you." Cormack detached from Aisling, a large sword in his hand.

"Where did that come from?" I asked, confused.

"I gave it to him," Wesley volunteered. "I brought more if you want one."

"I want one," Aisling said, stepping forward. "I'm going out, too."

"No, you're not." Cormack shook his head, firm. "You're staying here. That's the one thing Griffin and I agree on right now. You have to protect my grandchild. That's your primary job."

Aisling didn't look as if she agreed. "But ... ."

"No." Griffin snapped out the word, making me realize that no matter how indulgent he was, he put his foot down on important things. "You are staying here. I'm sorry if that upsets you, but you are not going outside. Aisling, promise me."

She jutted out her lower lip, defiant. "I'm mad at both of you."

"You can punish us later." Griffin gave her a small salute. "I'll be back before you know it."

"You'd better. I ... love you." She looked pained at laying herself out there for everyone to see, but she never moved her eyes from his face.

"I love you, too."

Cormack patted her shoulder as he moved past. "I love you, too, Aisling. We'll be back. I promise."

"I'm going to punish both of you like you wouldn't believe," she gritted out.

"I have no doubt about that."

Once they were gone, it was only the women and Wesley left. His main focus was Casey, but he kept glancing at the door, as if readying himself to bolt through it.

"I should help them," he said over the strangled cries that emanated from the yard. "They're still outnumbered."

"You're needed here," Lilac said, finally pushing herself away from the wall. The determination on her face was chilling. I had so many things I wanted to ask her, but she was almost to the door. "I'll take care of them."

Wesley watched her, a mixture of worry and relief on his face. "Be careful, Lilac. You know what happens when you lose your temper."

"It's a bit late for that." Her normally blond hair started glowing red. It started at the tips, the color spreading fast, and before I realized what was happening she was completely covered in orange and red flames. Her eyes, normally so friendly and welcoming, had gone completely black.

I was too surprised to draw back. That would've been a mistake, but one I wouldn't realize until hours later. I was too stunned to do anything but gape.

"I'll be back," Lilac announced, her voice suddenly much deeper. "If you hear someone scream, don't worry. I'll try to stop myself from killing as many of them as possible."

I stared in her wake for so long I thought I'd imagined it. Inside, though, I knew I hadn't. I finally managed to scramble toward the door. Wesley caught me before I could go through it.

"Where are you going?" he demanded.

"What was that? I ...who?" There were too many questions running through my brain.

"She's half-demon," Wesley explained. "She doesn't like to talk about it. If she wants to share information with you, she will. For now, you have to let her do her thing."

It turned out, her thing was fairly spectacular. When I stepped to the front door I found Lilac already in the middle of the fight. Booker was on one side of her, magical arrows zinging in a multitude of different directions. When the arrows hit, they didn't kill. They wrapped their targets in a tangled net, and no matter how hard they struggled, they couldn't get out.

Galen, still in his wolf form, fought with one of Taurus's male followers, one of the big guys who was armed with an ax. I wanted to help him, but I recognized I'd be more of a hindrance, so I remained rooted to my spot.

Cormack and Griffin were fighting two other men, and although Cormack slashed at his opponent his intent looked to be maiming rather than killing. There were bodies scattered all over the yard, odd magical nets anchoring them to the ground. Taurus was still on his feet.

"You cannot beat me," he bellowed when Booker missed him with an arrow and Lilac's burst of dark magic glanced away from his head, leaving his hair singed. "I am the end of time. This is my island, my home. You cannot beat me!"

He was clearly losing his mind.

Slowly, as if sensing a new player had joined the fight, his eyes tracked to the door and pinned me with hatred. He ignored everyone else and started striding in my direction. As he moved, his muscles twisted and his form turned from that of a man to a charging bull ... complete with horns.

I opened my mouth to call for help, and then realized that was idiotic — and weak. I didn't have to think about using the magic this time. My fingers simply flared to life as I raised my hands to fight him off.

"Hadley!" Booker yelled my name as he swiveled, another arrow ready to take flight. Galen responded to the sound of my name and pulled away from the man he was fighting, the intent to run down Taurus evident on his wolf face.

It was too late. I didn't need them. I knew exactly what I was going to do.

I extended my fingers, a ball of fire growing. It surged out of me, hot anger and fierce determination fueling it, before the bull hit the front steps. It barreled into Taurus with such force that he was bowled over, flipped onto his back. I thought it would be enough to stop him, but he fought to regain his footing.

He was hurt badly enough that he couldn't maintain his shape and slowly resumed human form. His face reflected fury, and I knew he would come after me a second time. I was readying myself to fight even as Galen and Booker struggled to close the distance, and then a figure appeared behind me. Aisling had her gun in her hand.

"What are you doing?" I gasped, fighting to form another fireball.

"I'm sick of this." Aisling strode directly in front of me, leveled the gun at Taurus's head, and then pointed the gun about three feet down before firing.

The sound was deafening, causing everyone in the yard to cease fighting and focus on Taurus. The bullet hit exactly where Aisling aimed — his groin — and he whined like a child about to throw a tantrum, grabbing his testicles as he listed to the side.

He hit the ground hard, tears leaking from his eyes, and Aisling showed zero remorse as she looked down on him. "You had that coming and we all know it."

"I was going to take him out," I complained, finding my voice. "I had everything under control."

"Well, you weren't working fast enough." Aisling wasn't the type to apologize, and this time was no different. "By the way, that chick inside is insisting on pushing. We need to get her to the hospital ... and now."

THINGS HAPPENED IN RAPID succession after that. Wesley, Griffin, Aisling and I loaded Casey into the golf cart and headed to the hospital. I wanted to stay, to help Galen and talk to Lilac about what had happened, but we each had a job to do and I intended to hold up my end.

Casey's parents met us at the hospital, and her mother accompanied her into the delivery room ... as did Jacob's soul. He would still have to be absorbed, but Aisling seemed resigned to letting him witness the birth of his miracle baby.

"He's not hurting anybody," she said quietly.

I cast her a sidelong look. "You're not turning into a softie, are you?"

"Nope. I'm as hardcore as they come."

"I think you proved that when you ... um ... took the bull by his horns," Griffin offered, wrapping his arms around her from behind. He looked more amused than upset. "You probably shouldn't have done that, baby, but you always know how to end things with style."

"That's my superpower," she agreed, resting the back of her head against his chest.

"One of them." He kissed the top of her head. "The others will be here soon, Hadley. You don't need to fret."

He seemed to read my angst, and I was thankful for the words, but I wouldn't be able to relax until I saw my friends and family ... all of them. I didn't have long to wait. Galen and Booker strolled through the double doors of the maternity ward, grime lining their faces. They seemed happy, chatting away as if they didn't have a care in the world. That didn't stop me from throwing my arms around Galen's neck the second I got to him.

"Are you okay?"

"I'm fine." He stroked his hand down the back of my head and kissed my cheek. "Booker is fine, too."

"Everyone is fine," Booker volunteered. "In fact, things are so fine Lilac is going to throw a victory party at her bar tomorrow night. After the cleanup is complete at the lighthouse, she's going to focus on those preparations."

The statement took me by surprise. "She's not here? I wanted to talk to her, to ask why she didn't tell me what she was. I ... she was amazing."

"She was," Galen agreed. "You have to understand, demons aren't exactly welcome in most circles. Lilac tries to keep that side of her nature suppressed. She helped us today because that's who she is. That doesn't mean she's not embarrassed."

I didn't understand. Of course, I understood very little about the paranormal world. That was becoming more and more apparent. "Should I go to her?"

"I would give her a little time." Galen gave me a long kiss. "She'll be fine. This isn't the first time this has happened. She needs to calm down. It's the rage that fuels her demonic side, the hate. She needs to decompress after embracing the darkness. She's throwing a victory party tomorrow, and then everything will be fine. You'll see."

I was dubious, but he seemed to know what he was talking about. "What about Aurora and the water warriors?"

"They only saw a few people run into the water. They're all fine."

"And what about the other members of the cult? Where are they?"

"Those that haven't run have been taken into custody," Galen replied. "The rest will be easy to round up. As for Barry, he's being wheeled into surgery. It seems Aisling's bullet did quite a bit of damage."

"A lot," Booker agreed. "So much that the doctor is doubtful he'll ever be able to perform again. Barry was on drugs when he heard that, but he started screaming anyway. I can't say I blame him."

"Yeah, well, he had it coming."

"He did," Galen agreed, grinning at my worried expression. "Are you afraid that I'm going to arrest your friend? If so, you can relax. I don't want her staying on this island for one second longer than necessary."

That was a relief. "Casey is giving birth. Jacob is with her. Aisling is letting him stay until after he sees his baby."

"That's good." Galen's smile lit up his entire face. "You did good, honey. I mean ... really good. You would've taken Barry down yourself if Aisling didn't get trigger happy."

"We all took him down."

"I guess we did. You still did good."

I couldn't stop myself from smiling. "I did?"

"I'm going to reward you properly later."

"We still need to talk, Galen," Wesley barked when he realized what Galen was implying. "I haven't forgotten."

Galen rested his forehead against mine and sighed. "I guess this day isn't over quite yet."

29

TWENTY-NINE

True to form, Lilac hosted the victory party to end all victory parties the following evening. She was in a good mood when we entered the bar, holding court with several regulars as she described the fight. She offered me a wave, but didn't move to intercept me. Apparently she wanted me to make the first move.

I was fine with that.

She almost appeared relieved when I immediately crossed and gave her a long hug. Galen had to talk me out of tracking her down after we'd left the hospital the previous evening, reminding me that she needed time to decompress. Giving her that time was painful, but I finally acquiesced. Now, there was no power on this island that could pull me away from her.

"You were amazing," I offered, grinning. "I had no idea."

"Yeah, well .... " She shifted from one foot to the other, uncomfortable. "It's not something I like to talk about."

"I don't know why. What you did ... you saved everyone."

"They were holding their own before I went out there. I just helped them along. You saved everyone when you took on Taurus. You're the real hero."

I didn't feel like a hero. I felt like a woman still catching up. "You did the heavy lifting. I only showed up at the end."

"And I'm the one who took down Barry the nutless bull," Aisling announced, appearing behind me. She looked fresh and relaxed, none the worse for wear after our battle.

"Yes, you were the hero, baby." Griffin slipped his arm around her waist. "I need a drink to toast your heroics. You're not going to give me grief for drinking, are you?"

"Not even a little." She gave him a playful shove, waiting until it was just the three of us to speak again. "He's been a little clingy. I'm hoping he'll get over that by the time we get home. It's going to be difficult carrying out my regular duties if he's glued to my side."

"He loves you," Lilac noted. "You should be thankful for that. Not everyone gets to enjoy a love like the two of you share."

"I guess." Aisling watched him for a moment and then shrugged. "By the way, that demon thing you do is awesome. That would come in handy in Detroit, if you ever want to visit." She flashed Lilac an enthusiastic thumbs-up and then drifted across the bar to join her father. He seemed to be expecting her, because he flashed an indulgent smile when she approached and handed her a plate full of maraschino cherries.

"She's odd, huh?" Lilac said, breaking the silence we'd lapsed into.

"She defies categorization," I supplied, amused. "I think I'm going to miss her."

"I think I'll miss her, too." Lilac's expression was rueful. "She was fun for a few days, though, right?"

"Definitely." I bobbed my head, sliding my gaze back to Lilac. "If you ever want to talk ... ."

"Thanks. I'm not sure I will. It's not something I like to dwell on."

"But if you do, I'm here." I didn't want to push her. "We don't have to. You're still the best friend I've made on this island. I just want you to know, what you did, well ... it was spectacular."

Lilac's cheeks flooded with color. "It was nothing. Seriously, don't get all crazy. I've done it before and I'm certain I will have to do it again. You don't need to freak out or anything."

"I have no intention of freaking out."

"Good."

Silence again. This time, Lilac grew uncomfortable first and broke it. "So ... how is Casey? I know you guys went to the hospital with her last night. I'm sure I would've heard if things went poorly, but I needed some space. After the transformation ... well, I always need to cool down."

"Casey is good." I thought back to the last time I'd seen her, which was shortly after giving birth. She couldn't stop the tears and thanked me profusely for saving her. "She had a boy. Jacob. She named him after his father, who witnessed the birth."

"Is he still around? The first Jacob, I mean."

"He's not. Aisling turned weepy seeing the family together, so her father had to absorb Jacob's soul. It was sad all around, but it was happy, too. I don't know if that makes sense."

"I understand what you mean. One door closes, another opens. Jacob's legacy is intact even though he didn't get a chance to be a father to his miracle baby. Something tells me Casey will never let his memory die."

"No," I agreed. "He'll be a presence in that baby's life forever."

"What about Taurus? How is he holding up after Aisling ... changed the course of his life?"

I had to bite back a laugh. Technically, it wasn't funny. Okay, it mostly wasn't funny. There were parts of it that felt utterly hilarious.

"The doctors had to reconstruct his equipment so he'll be able to urinate properly. As for other things, that's officially off the table."

Lilac smirked. "I see. That must be hard for a headstrong bull."

"I haven't seen him, but Galen was there when he received the news, and he said Taurus didn't take it well."

"I can imagine."

"In fact, he started screaming that he was trapped in a nightmare. I guess it was sort of pathetic."

"He had it coming."

"Definitely."

"Did he say why he killed Adam Grimport?"

I nodded. "Cormack's theory was correct. He wanted access to souls. He would've stolen the scepter and computer and left Grimport alive, but the reaper was home when they broke in and didn't have a choice."

"Is there a reason we haven't seen Grimport's soul?"

"A reaper's soul apparently automatically escapes to the nearest scepter once it's activated, no matter who is wielding it. It's some trick of birth or something. Taurus's followers used it in a ritual. Aisling said that means it's gone for good. They're going to check to make sure, but she doesn't think there's anything they can do to save it."

"What about Jacob?" Lilac asked, her mind clearly busy. "Why didn't they absorb his soul?"

"They didn't realize there was a trick to the scepter. Jacob escaped even though they tried to trap his soul. Only a reaper can access the magic of the scepter correctly, so they weren't counting on that."

"So ... basically you're saying it was a mistake."

"Pretty much."

"That is depressing."

"Very depressing," I agreed.

Galen picked that moment to sidle over and join us. He looked relaxed — we'd both slept for ten hours, not climbing out of bed until Wesley woke us to say he was taking May to his ranch for the weekend. He looked embarrassed to interrupt us, but promised he and May would come up with a schedule that allowed Galen and me privacy at the lighthouse. I was so relieved that I didn't even admonish him for waking us ... even when he gave Galen a dirty look because he was in my bed.

"Hello, ladies," he drawled, slinging an arm around my shoulders as he regarded us. "Is everything okay here?"

"Everything is fine," Lilac replied hurriedly. "We were just talking. Have you managed to capture all of Taurus's followers?"

"Not yet. I believe there's still a handful missing. I'm guessing they won't put up much of a fight when we find them, though. I'm also willing to place a rather large bet that they claim he forced them to follow his teachings."

"How will you handle that?" I asked.

"I'm not sure yet. I'll have to talk to the prosecutor. I refuse to let them off without any form of punishment — they did try to kill us, after all — but I'm not exactly eager to ruin their lives. I think they've all probably paid a heavy price for their involvement with Barry."

"That's good." I rested my head against his shoulder. "So ... that's basically it. What happens now that we don't have a reaper?"

"Cormack says that they're sending one to serve on an interim basis. Apparently the post is so sought after there's a lot of in-fighting going on. It's not entirely settled yet."

"We do live in paradise."

"Yeah." His smile was flirty. "Paradise is definitely the word I would use."

"Ugh. You guys are schmaltzy and gross." Lilac made a face as she grabbed her tray. "I'm going to see about drinks. I'll catch you guys later."

I watched her go, worry briefly bubbling up. When I realized Galen was watching me, I forced a smile. "What?"

"She's fine. There's no need to be upset. In a few days, it will be like nothing happened."

That's exactly what worried me, but I kept it to myself. It was a concern for another time. "So ... it's back to being quiet again. That's exactly how I like it."

"Not exactly," he hedged. "Aisling and Griffin are still here for a few days."

"Yes, but they're gooey and in love. They'll spend most of their time together."

"She insists we take her to the cemetery tonight. She wants to see the zombies."

It had been almost two weeks since I'd taken a moment to visit them, my brief sojourn with Aisling notwithstanding. When I first found out, I visited every night. It was strange, but now the zombies seemed like old news. I didn't know how to explain it. "Well, we can take them for a brief visit."

"You don't want to stay?"

"No. That's the past, and there's nothing I can do about it. I want to look forward to the future."

"That sounds like a good idea."

I beamed as I leaned forward and pressed a kiss to the corner of his mouth. "I thought you might like that."

"Have I told you the things I see in our future?"

"No, but I bet they're dirty."

"Oh, you have no idea."

Maybe, but I was looking forward to finding out.